Sela watched the boat draw up and the fully armoured men leap down, swords drawn.

Her heart went to her throat as she saw the lead warrior, recognised his armour and his sword with its intricate marking.

Vikar Hrutson.

She screwed up her eyes tight and then looked again, hoping he would be a ghost from her memory, but he remained. She had known he would be here deep down inside her from the first moment she had heard the dragon ships. Something had told her that her idyllic life of the last few years had ended. She had to face this and win.

He towered over the men, broad-shouldered. Commanding. She had no doubt his face would be as rugged as ever. He had reached the rocky shore and stood there. Proud. Arrogant. Determined.

But why now? Why after all these years?

Dear Reader

In 1908, many wonderful things happened: the house I live in was built, my paternal grandfather was born and Mills & Boon® began publishing.

I am very pleased to be part of the Mills & Boon family of authors and to be having a book published during this, their centenary year.

Several years ago, when I was in hospital, a woman in the bed next to me went in to the day room and came joyfully back, waving a book triumphantly in the air. There must have been a questioning look on my face as she confided that, in her opinion, with a Mills & Boon, you couldn't go wrong. I totally agreed with her. It was then and there that I decided I wanted to write books for them—books that offered a ray of sunshine, and a chance to escape. Books that I have loved to read ever since I was a pre-teen. Luckily, my dream came true.

Mills & Boon takes its promise to its readers very seriously. It is why each month millions turn to its publications in pursuit of enjoyment and a good, entertaining read. It is why the name Mills & Boon has become synonymous with romance. And long may this tradition of excellence in romance publishing continue.

Hopefully you will get as much pleasure out of reading my tale of romance during the early Viking period as I did writing it.

As ever as I love getting reader feedback via snail mail to Mills & Boon, my website, www.michellestyles.co.uk or my blog http://www.michellestyles.blogspot.com/

All the best

Michelle

VIKING WARRIOR, UNWILLING WIFE

Michelle Styles

MILLS & BOON

Pure reading pleasure

First published in Great Britain 2008
Harlequin Mills & Boon Limited,
Eton House, 18-24 Paradise Road, Richmond, Surrey TW9 1SR

© Michelle Styles 2008

ISBN: 978 0 263 86264 5

Set in Times Roman 10½ on 12¾ pt.
04-0608-79371

Printed and bound in Spain
by Litografia Rosés S.A., Barcelona

Although born and raised near San Francisco, California, **Michelle Styles** currently lives a few miles south of Hadrian's Wall, with her husband, three children, two dogs, cats, assorted ducks, hens and beehives. An avid reader, she has always been interested in history, and a historical romance is her idea of the perfect way to relax. She is particularly interested in how ordinary people lived during ancient times, and in the course of her research she has learnt how to cook Roman food as well as how to use a drop spindle. When she is not writing, reading or doing research, Michelle tends her rather overgrown garden or does needlework, in particular counted cross-stitch. Michelle maintains a website and a blog and would be delighted to hear from you.

Recent novels by the same author:

THE GLADIATOR'S HONOUR
A NOBLE CAPTIVE
SOLD AND SEDUCED
THE ROMAN'S VIRGIN MISTRESS
TAKEN BY THE VIKING
A CHRISTMAS WEDDING WAGER
  (Part of *Christmas By Candlelight*)

To the e-harlequin community,
in particular to the denizens
of the Mouse and Pen,
the SWC, and the Library.
Always there. Always supportive.
Always appreciated.

Chapter One

'**P**repare shields! Raise spears! Unsheathe swords! The gables of Bose the Dark's stronghold are on the horizon,' Vikar Hrutson, jaarl of Viken, shouted to his men.

'It is a serious step you take, Vikar,' Ivar said in an undertone. 'What if you are wrong? What if Bose desires peace with Viken?'

Vikar turned from where he studied the headland with its inlets and rocky islands towards Ivar, his fellow jaarl and co-leader of the felag. His dark green eyes regarded his friend and comrade. 'The time Bose is at peace is when he sleeps. The raid on Rogaland was only the beginning. He has broken the truce and declared war.'

'But will Thorkell agree?' Ivar shifted uneasily. 'It was pure good fortune we had stopped at Rogaland. My sister and her husband could never have withstood the raid alone.'

'It was a victory for the felag, for Viken.'

'It was your sword and shield that brought down Hafdan. He could have been acting alone. He sailed under his own standard.'

'Only one man could have ordered that raid and he still breathes with his lands intact.' Vikar tightened his grip on the railing, and looked towards where the dark walls of the great hall rose from the fjord. 'Bose the Dark ordered that raid, that destruction. Hafdan would never dare draw a breath, let alone attack a Viken jaarl's main hall without his express order. I warned Thorkell that Bose would strike again. It gives me no pleasure to be right.'

Ivar banged his fist against the railing. 'Thorkell should never have spared Bose. What he nearly did to Haakon was unthinkable! He should have known that Bose would not be content in the north.'

'I am not a soothsayer. I have no great insight into the king's mind. Haakon lives and thrives. Our friend is very happy with his new wife and child.' Vikar gave a slight shrug. 'Bose twists words to suit his purpose. The only thing he understands is deeds. This time, he will lose…everything.'

'And Thorkell—what will he do when he discovers that you have led a raid on Bose's stronghold?'

'He will reward me. Bose broke the truce. This time I administer the punishment.' The breeze whipped Vikar's blond hair back from his forehead. 'The battle will be long and bloody, old friend, but Thor and Tyr will be with us. Underestimate Bose at your peril. The man is a master strategist, slipperier than Loki.'

'If you say such things, I believe them.' Ivar tapped the side of his nose. 'You were once married to his daughter.'

'Thankfully it was a short alliance.' Vikar refused to think about his former wife today. Was she there with her long blonde hair, tempting curves and pig-headed temper? Or had she married again? Someone who was more willing to be Bose's lapdog? Vikar stared at the intricately carved gables. It no longer mattered. She was the symbol of all that was wrong with women, why he would never marry again.

'Is it true Bose's daughter never appeared in Thorkell's court after the divorce? And that the hall was built on the bones of wild men who will rise up and fight any invader?'

'Men at oars tell too many tales.' Vikar pushed off from the railing and strode towards the prow of the boat. There he could catch a glimpse of how his new, red sail fared in the wind. A sail fit for one of the leading jaarls in Viken, a man who had made a fortune through one single raid last summer, a man whose exploits were lauded by the skalds in the latest poems.

A low horn sounded across the water of the fjord. Their boats had been spotted. The battle would begin when he set foot on the shore.

'Exactly what are you planning, Bose the Dark, up there in your splendid hall? I cannot help but think you expected this. You longed for it.' Vikar's jaw tightened and his hand felt for his sword's hilt. 'I have ceased being the gullible warrior who married your daughter a long time ago. We will meet, and this time, this time, Bose, there will be only one victor.'

'Sails round the headland. One dragon ship, maybe more.' Sela forced her voice to remain calm as she entered her father's bedchamber.

Unlike the hall, the bedchamber was resplendent with furs and tapestries, and, in the centre, a gigantic bed where her father, Bose the Dark, lay. She winced as her father struggled to sit up right, each movement an effort with his paralysed side.

He had been such a vigorous man a few months ago. Then the affliction had struck. Cursed, some muttered in the shadowy corners of the hall. His fabled luck gone. Sela ignored such doom-mongers. Her father had suffered enough.

'Friendly?' he croaked out of the side of his mouth.

'Impossible to say. It is far too soon to see if they will lift their shields or leave them hanging.' Sela smoothed a stray strand of honey-blonde hair from her forehead, a nervous gesture from her girlhood, one she was positive he'd know. She hid her hands in the folds of her apron-dress and concentrated on the bedstead. How much dared she reveal?

'What is the lead ship's sail pattern?' Her father's eyes suddenly focused and he plucked restlessly at the furs. 'You are keeping things from me, Daughter, but I remain the master of this hall. I deserve to know the worst.'

'The sail pattern is not one I recognise.' She paused, and watched her father's face become grave. He made a small gesture with his hand, telling her to continue. 'Maybe if Hafdan were here, he would know the answer.'

'We had to find new markets for our goods. Kaupang is closed to us now.' Her father's face reddened. 'The East offers the best hope. Thorkell must allow me to feed my people. Hafdan will return and once again our coffers will cascade with gold.'

'Did I say a word? Hafdan has departed to find new

markets.' Sela pressed her lips into a firm line. 'And you remain jaarl of Northern Viken.'

Her father gave his crooked smile and held out his good hand. 'I want your inheritance to overflow with wealth, Daughter, not be a silver arm-ring and a much-mended sword like mine was. It was right to send Hafdan. You will see in time.'

'Hafdan wants his own glory. He could do anything.' Sela crossed her arms, and glared at her father.

'Hafdan has ambition, but he will return.' Her father's eyes twinkled. 'I have seen how he looks at you. He has much to recommend him. Once I am gone, you must have a strong man...'

'I tried marriage once, thank you.' Sela snapped her mouth shut to prevent more words from tumbling out. Her former husband had been a man of ambition as well. She had no wish to relive the memories or the bitter taste they left.

'You were younger then.' Her father waved a dismissive hand. 'Vikar Hrutson was a poor choice. He did not like to listen to my counsel. I sincerely regret that I did not see my mistake until it was far too late to prevent you getting hurt.'

'It was nearly four years ago. You weren't to know.' Sela touched her father's withered cheek. When her father had discovered the situation, he had moved swiftly, rescuing her and her unborn child, rather than letting her face the humiliation of a woman scorned.

'Four years? Sela, it is time you laid your ghosts to rest. Other men...'

'I have no ghosts in my life, Father, far from it. If I remarried, who would look after you?'

'Hafdan is different.' Her father gave a crooked smile. 'He is loyal. You will see…in time.'

'We have these unexpected visitors, and few men to protect the hall.'

'We shall have to be wary—wait and see.' Her father gestured towards the iron-bound chest. 'Send someone to dress me. My mail shirt, and the sword Thorkell gave me in happier days. I am not without pride. I want to give the ships a proper welcome, one that shows Bose the Dark remains jaarl of the north. They will not find easy pickings here.'

'*Far*, you cannot fight. I forbid it,' Sela said, positioning her body between her father and the chest. 'Your legs may hold you upright, but your sword arm is useless. How long do you think you would last in a fight? You would be a danger to the men.'

'Do you think you are telling me something I don't know, Daughter?' Her father attempted to move his arm and nothing happened. He set his jaw and managed with difficulty to shift it slightly. 'I am the one who has to live with it. With the arm and the face. May Odin send curses on the witch who caused this.'

'Stay here, in this chamber.' Sela caught his hand. 'Let me greet them in the correct manner. I will hide your infirmity as best I can.'

'Daughter, you are the best daughter a man could hope for,' her father said, holding out his good hand, tears forming in his eyes.

Sela straightened her back. She understood her father's wordless plea. 'I will handle our unwelcome callers, come what may.'

'I know you will.'

'*Morfar, Morfar.*' A blond boy rushed in, holding a bird's nest. 'See what I have found. The nest had fallen down on the ground. Thorgerd says that there will have been starlings in it.'

'Kjartan, how many times must I tell you not to burst in on your grandfather like that?' Sela looked at her son and saw his shining face fall, his deep-green eyes became less bright. Instantly she regretted her harsh words, but Kjartan had to learn the proper respect. If he was eventually to be a jaarl, he had to have proper training. But with whom?

'Sela, Sela, he is only three. Time enough for ceremony later.' Her father patted the side of his bed. 'Kjartan, come here and greet your grandfather properly.'

'You were never like that with Erik or me.'

'Grandchildren are different. You will understand in time, Sela.'

'*Mor*, I want to show *Morfar* my bird's nest.' Kjartan held out a jumble of sticks and mud. He wore a serious expression on his face. 'I found it by the barns. I'm a good warrior. Someday I'll be great like *Morfar,* and like my father.'

'Your face is dirty and you have torn the knee of your trousers. Even great warriors wash their faces before they greet their jaarl,' Sela said with a smile as Kjartan immediately started to scrub his cheeks with his filthy hands. Her heart expanded. She had never thought that she could love one scrap of humanity so much.

'Thorgerd says a dragon ship is coming. My father's?'

'Kjartan, show your grandfather the nest.' Sela spoke around a sudden lump in her throat. She looked down at the blond tousled curls and the trusting dark-green eyes, eyes that reminded her every day of who Kjartan's father was and of the humiliation she had suffered at his hands. A great warrior like his father—where had that notion come from? But she refused to destroy his illusions. Life would do that soon enough.

She bit her lip. If the ships were from Thorkell, her father with his infirmity was not the only one who would have to remain hidden. Her son would have to as well. Vikar remained an integral part of the court, Asa's chief confidant if the rumours that reached this far north were true. And she had every reason to believe them.

Kjartan advanced towards his grandfather, holding out the nest and chattering away. The two took great pleasure in each other. A pleasure that could be easily destroyed. Under Viken law and custom, her son belonged to his father. She had been married when Kjartan was conceived, but she'd refused to give him up, to turn him over to someone who had little concept of the notion of love and devotion. How could she permit that to happen to her only child?

Her eyes met her father's slate grey ones. He gave a slight nod and held out his good hand.

'Come here, Kjartan, you can keep me company for a while. We can recite some of the sagas together.'

'Will you tell me about Loki and the tricks he played? I like that god.'

Sela listened to her father's gravelly voice begin to solemnly recite a story. Kjartan would be safe with her father, and she would be able to see about defending the hall.

'*Far,*' she said softly.

He raised his eyes, paused in the story.

'If there is any problem, you know what to do. Promise me, the hut in the woods…'

'I know, Sela. You have other things to think about besides me. I am not so feeble that I cannot look after one small boy. Send Una to me if you wish. Your former nurse can do something besides warm her bones by the fire for a change.'

'Yes, Thorgerd can look after the women. She is sensible. Una and her tales make the women nervous.'

He cleared his throat as Kjartan drew closer to the bed. 'Now, if you will excuse us, the gods are in a rather tight spot and Loki needs to rescue them.'

She gave one last backwards glance. Grey hair next to blond, engrossed in the tale of Loki's mischief. Then she walked away, walked toward her responsibilities.

'My lady, it was as you suspected, the men in the dragon boats are armed, armed to the teeth,' Gorm, her father's aged steward said, coming to stand beside Sela where she watched the dragon ships' final approach. 'See how the sunlight glints off their shields and swords.'

'They are not coming for a social call, Gorm.' Sela fingered the hilt of the sword. For a time at her father's encouragement, she had played at swords, enjoying the thrill of mock combat, something the dainty Asa had declared as unfeminine when Sela had arrived at court. The occasional echo of mocking laughter and barbs about the overgrown clumsy women from the north still haunted her dreams. Now, her former skill might have some use. 'Neither are they coming with a proclamation demanding my father to return to Kaupang. Those days have gone.'

'It is a sad state of affairs, my lady.'

'If we stand our ground here…' Sela gestured about her '…and do not advance towards the shore, they may not even disembark. Raiders want easy pickings, not fierce fights. My father's hall is famously impregnable. It will be a bold man who tries. My father's saga is—'

'Your father sets a great store by his saga my lady, but I was there and I find it hard to believe.'

'It is not you who needs to believe, but our unwelcome callers.'

Sela kept her eyes trained on the shore. Except for the lapping of the water against the dragon ships as they drew ever closer, there appeared a sort of hush as if even the birds and animals knew that something was about to happen.

'The men will lock shields, but do you think this the right place for you, my lady?'

'I know how to handle a sword,' Sela said through gritted teeth. 'My father demanded it. I would far rather be here than cowering with the women. I have a right to protect my home.'

'But the men will want to defend you. You will destroy their concentration.' Gorm lowered his eyebrows and looked disapproving. 'Let me stand with the men, one last time.'

'You have seen me fight before, Gorm. The men have as well. I can wield the sword equal to any man.' Sela bit her lip. 'But you respond to the challenge. It would not do for the enemy to think they have a woman fighting in their midst.'

'You said it would not come to fighting.' The white-haired man gulped. 'I would never have brought you your brother's armour or your father's sword, if I had guessed.'

'It is too late for regrets now, Gorm.' Sela readjusted her helmet so that the nose-piece was more central and stared out to the fjord. 'The first dragon ship comes ashore.'

She watched the boat draw up and the fully armoured men leap down, swords drawn. Her heart went to her throat as she saw the lead warrior, recognised his armour and his sword with its intricate marking.

Vikar Hrutson.

She screwed up her eyes tight and then looked again, hoping he would be a ghost from her memory, but he remained. She had known he would be here, deep down inside her from the first moment that she had heard of the dragon ships. Something had told her that her idyllic life of the last few years had ended. She had to face him and win.

He towered over the men, broad shouldered, commanding. She had no doubt his face would be as rugged as ever. And his hair would be that certain shade between gold and brown. He had by now reached the rocky shore, and he stood there. Proud. Arrogant. Determined. But why now? Why after all these years?

Then, with heart-stopping insight, she knew what the answer had to be.

Kjartan.

Someone had whispered. Her mouth twisted. She had thought she had been so careful, had covered her footsteps, allowed the rumour to go out that Kjartan's father was dead. She'd never shown her face again in Kaupang. And now it appeared somehow he knew.

She wanted to turn back and snatch Kjartan up, then run. Put as much as possible between her son and his father. But her legs refused to move.

'What do you wish to do, my lady? I responded to the challenge. The men await your orders.' Gorm spoke in an urgent undertone.

Sela opened her mouth and no sound came out as reality struck her. The direness of the situation nearly crippled her. The men looked to her. She was stuck out here, and could not desert. They deserved a leader for their loyalty.

She should have made Kjartan her first duty. She had to hope that her father would look after him.

No pretence to peace. These warriors would take her land, her son and her very being if she let them. She stood there frozen, unable to move, following the increasing torrent of warriors.

'Shall we surrender, my lady? The odds are not with us.'

'Surrender? Would my father surrender? Never.' She withdrew her father's sword, and held it over her head. 'We fight.'

'Your instinct was true, Vikar.' Ivar nodded towards where the group of warriors massed in front of Bose the Dark's hall. 'This is no friendly welcome. The challenge has been issued and answered.'

'It gives me no pleasure.' Vikar adjusted his helmet. 'I see Bose's standard, but not his sword. It was Gorm, not Bose, who answered. What game is he playing now?'

'It's his sword there in the centre. Has to be.' Ivar pointed into the mass of warriors. 'I'd recognise the gold hilt and silver blade anywhere. A sword of legend, that one. You must have missed it.'

'I see it now.' Vikar shielded his eyes and saw where

Ivar pointed. A slender figure held aloft the sword, a gesture of defiance. Vikar scanned the mass horde. Old men and boys mostly, hardly fit for holding a sword. 'But there are too few. Where has Bose put the rest? Where is he hiding them, his fabled army of men?'

'You will have to ask Bose.' Ivar raised his shield. 'By Thor's hammer, they are moving downhill. Whoever is leading them is very brave or incredibly reckless.'

'And we will meet them. We will win!' Vikar started forward, the cries of his men thundering in his ear. Despite the swirling of spears, swords and axes, he kept his eye trained on the leader. Once he had reached him, he would engage him and the battle would be won.

'To me, men. The day is ours!'

Chapter Two

The space between Sela's defenders and the invaders shrank to nothingness in the matter of a few heartbeats. She knew she should have held her men back, but the untried amongst them charged down the slope, eager to join the battle, rather than holding firm. And once a few had gone, the rest followed, giving up the high ground. Sela's heart sank. Even with the little experience she had, she knew it meant disaster.

Her father and brother had always maintained that battle was unique. Now out here, facing the enemy, rather than engaging in a mock combat on the practice field, she knew that they were right.

A sort of wild exhilaration, swiftly followed by sheer terror, hung in the air. She glanced upwards, half-expecting to see Valkyries, Odin's maidens who gathered the fallen from the battlefields, riding on the sea breeze.

The opposing forces met with a deafening crash. Sela's ears buzzed with the dull thump of sword meeting wooden shield, reverberating throughout her body, but she forced her sword to remain high and her shield steady. She had to give the impression of leadership or the day would be truly lost.

First, and against all her expectations, the household retainers appeared to gain the upper hand. Her fears had been unfounded. She started to mutter a prayer of thanksgiving. Suddenly like the tide, the battle turned. Imperceptibly, but then like a raging flood. Gorm went down, his sword shattering on a shield. From her position on the top of the hill, she saw the outer edges begin to collapse and fold inwards. Her men faltered and fell, held up their shields to defend themselves from the merciless onslaught, but nothing worked.

Her father's banner swayed.

She started forward, clashed swords. The reverberation went through her arm so strongly that she nearly dropped her father's sword. She planted her feet firmly and struck out again, lifting her shield. She had to make it through, to help defend. She passed one man, lunged towards another. Her foot struck a pebble and she stumbled slightly, her knee hitting the ground. She struggled to right herself, cursing at the unfamiliar weight of the armour. Arms came around and held her, checking her progress. Quickly she tried to push away, to move out of the embrace, but her captor held a sword to her throat. His other arm hauled her back, so that her body was held tightly against his firm chest.

'It is unlike you to leave your left flank unguarded,' came the low rumble that slid over her like the finest fur. Teasing her senses. A remark made as if they were in Thorkell's great hall and the dancing was about to begin. 'I thought you had learnt that particular lesson years ago, Sela, Bose the Dark's daughter.'

Sela struggled for a breath. She had not thought to hear that voice again in her lifetime. Or feel his body against hers. She opted for a solemn face as she eyed the gleaming sword.

'A mistake, Vikar Hrutson,' she said around the lump in her throat. 'Thank you for pointing it out. It will not happen again.'

She twisted her body, but the action only drew her more firmly against his solid chest. She hated the flare of warmth that went through her, hated that her body remembered the last time she had encountered his.

'You face total destruction.' His voice rumbled in her ear. 'Yield now and some of your men may yet be saved. You have no hope. Do you wish to die on the field of battle, Sela? Do you aspire to become a Valkyrie?'

Sela attempted to move her head and confront the voice, but the sword pressed more firmly against her throat, forcing her to view the scene of carnage before her. The generally quiet shore teemed with dust, men and swords. And all around, her men tumbled like flies.

Had her life really come down to this? Leading elderly men and young boys to their death? She had only meant to stand firm, not yield, a show of strength, and instead she presided over a rout. Another mistake to add to her long line of failures.

She swallowed hard, trying to get some moisture back in her throat. She refused to give in to her fear, give Vikar the satisfaction.

'I had not placed you as a killer of women.' She stretched her neck higher, away from the sharp blade, and gave a strangled laugh. 'An indiscriminate lover of women, perhaps, but never a killer.'

'Some might say your attire shows a certain contempt for your status, for your sex.' The blade relaxed slightly. 'Are you now going to plead special privileges because you are a woman? The world operates by different rules, Sela.'

'It is impossible to swing a sword in a tight-sleeved gown.' She kept her chin up, ignored the gleaming blade, forced her breath to come evenly and smooth. 'Saving my home is far more important than dressing in the latest court fashion.'

'I thought everything was more important than fashion to you.'

Sela rolled her eyes towards the skies. Fashion. She had failed at that particular competition years ago. She could not wear the type of gown favoured by Asa, gowns that accentuated the queen's own petite, gilded looks, but made Sela resemble an overgrown youth with lumps in all the wrong places. She had sought other ways to shine, ways Vikar had disapproved of. And being young and naïve, she had taken a perverse enjoyment in provoking him.

It seemed unreal to be speaking of fashion and court matters with the sounds of battle raging around her, but it kept her from giving in to her natural inclinations and sinking to her knees in despair.

'Tell me,' she said through gritted teeth, 'how long does Asa decree the train length to be this year? We hear very little of such things out here in the wilds.'

'As much as I would like to discuss the state of your wardrobe, my business is with your father.' The blade lowered, but his arm tightened about her waist. 'Where he is and why does he send a woman out to do a man's job?'

With her father?

The air rushed out of her lungs, making her feel giddy. She struggled to control the sudden racing of her heart as hope filled her. She had expected him to say his business was with her, to demand to see his son.

Did he even know? Silently she offered up a prayer to Sif, Freyja and all the other goddesses of Aesir for a miracle.

'I volunteered.'

'The Bose the Dark I knew would have rejected the idea before the last syllable had fallen from your lips.' Vikar's grip forced her around, compelled her to look into his face. She realised with a start that his eyes were a far darker shade of green than she had remembered. 'Does he live?'

'My father is very much alive, but he saw the sense in my leading the men. He is indisposed and has little control over what I do.'

'It makes a change.' The sarcasm dripped from his mouth. 'I had understood he always gave the orders.'

Sela, feeling the sword give way, swung around and faced her former husband. Despite her height, he towered over her. His helmet shadowed his face, but she had no doubt that when he removed it, the arrangement of his even features would remain the same. One of the most sought-after warriors in all of Thorkell's court. Time had not altered him as much as she had hoped. 'I am a grown woman, Vikar Hrutson. I take responsibility for what I do.'

'And you take responsibility for this?' His eyes offered no comfort, no glimmer of understanding. 'For this *carnage*? Why did your men rush down the slope? That was a fatal mistake.'

'My men were over-eager and rushed forward.' She forced her head to remain high. 'I should have anticipated that. The result lies on the green slope. My failure, not theirs.'

'Save your men.' His lips were a thin, white line. 'How many more must die for your vanity?'

Sela stared at her former husband in dismay as her stomach lurched. She had wanted to save her home, her son. She had not started this battle. She had wanted to avoid bloodshed.

Vanity? Was that what he thought? She forced her head high, schooled her features, grateful that the nosepiece on the helmet would keep her face in shadow.

'I call it something else.'

'It does not matter what you call it.' Vikar gestured around the battlefield with his sword. 'Men are dying. You have lost the battle. How much more do you wish to lose? Yield now, and I may be disposed to give you favourable terms.'

Sela flinched. She could hear the cries of the wounded and the dying. One young man lifted his head, and reminded her of Kjartan. Vikar was right. She had things to live for, secrets to keep—for ever, if possible.

'As you wish.' She bowed her head and accepted the inevitable. She took off her glove and put her hand on the outstretched hilt of the sword. Her fingers grazed the ring embedded on the top, a little gesture, but one fraught with meaning. Surrender. She bowed her head, swallowed hard. 'The battle ends.'

She stepped backwards. All perfectly correct. She knew the form. She had seen others bow down to her father, but she never thought she would have to make the gesture herself. She had believed in her father's boast that no one could ever take this hall.

She opened her mouth to speak the final damning words, but her voice refused to work. She glanced up into the unyielding planes of Vikar's face, pleading silently that it was enough; she had done all she could. She wished she hadn't given in to the impulse as his lips turned further downwards. 'The words escape me.'

'No, you tell your men. It must come from you. You hold your father's sword. You say the words of surrender.' Vikar's green eyes were colder than a frost giant's. 'I know Bose the Dark's tricks. He matches Loki in resourcefulness.'

Sela glanced towards the hall, half-expecting her father to appear, half-fearing he would. The doorway remained vacant, a gaping black hole.

Removing her helmet, Sela raised her hand showing her surrender. She waited. Nothing happened. She glanced at Vikar, who gestured for her to repeat the movement. She tried again. Nothing.

Vikar nodded towards the standard. She went over to it, took it from her man's hand and waved that, then lowered it with one sweeping motion. 'The battle belongs to you…my lord.'

Bose's standard with its dark sun against a golden background fell, hitting the ground with a solid thump. And with it, her hopes and dreams.

All around her the noise subsided until the very stillness appeared to be unnatural. The men turned towards her. She saw Vikar nod imperceptibly towards his men, and they lowered their swords.

The fighting was over; the carnage littered the gentle slope.

Sela started towards the nearest fallen warrior. She wanted to use her skills as a healer to help with the wounded, but Vikar's arm clamped around her wrist, preventing her.

'Let me go.' Sela moved her arm sharply downwards, but Vikar's hand remained. Strong and determined. 'I have done as you asked. You are the victor here. The battle is over. I have surrendered. You are the master. You may take what you wish from the hall but my men need my aid. I possess some small skill that might be of service.'

'War leader, now healer. What other talents do you possess, Sela?' Vikar's hard, cynical eyes and tight mouth mocked her.

I had no talent for being a wife. The thought pierced her with its suddenness, drawing the breath from her lungs.

Gorm's broken sword caught her eye and she swallowed hard. And it would appear she possessed little skill as a war leader either. This hall was supposed to impenetrable, but it had fallen in less time than it took a shadow to cross the courtyard. Her failure at Vikar's hands was absolute. Her knees threatened to give way. She straightened her back, and drew her dignity around her like a cloak.

'What can I say? I am my father's daughter.'

'Bose the Dark absent from this battlefield? What mischief is this?' Vikar said through clenched teeth. 'The truth, Sela. How did he breathe his last?'

'My father lives.' The breeze blew strands of hair across her face. She tried not to wonder where her father was. Or if he knew that she had lost, that their world had irrevocably changed. 'He might not be able to lead his men in battle, but his mind remains clear.'

'It is only you who have surrendered, not the hall, not the jaarl of the northern lands. My men remain in danger.'

'You bandy words. We have no more men.' Sela held up her hands. 'Look around you. You have defeated us. The hall is yours, to do with what you will.'

'Your father's hall boasts of many more retainers. He keeps an army as great as Thorkell's.' Vikar gestured to where the men stood or sat with their heads in their hands. 'These are the old, the young, the infirm. Where are your father's warriors?'

'If I had had the warriors, I would have used them.'

'Are you leading me into a trap, Sela? Seeking to lull my men with the promise of victory only to have it snatched from their hands.' He gave a short, bitter laugh. 'I know about women and their honeyed promises. I learnt my lesson well, Sela.'

Sela kept her head raised, and met Vikar's eyes. 'The bulk of my father's force departed weeks ago...to find new markets...in Permia.'

'But your father remains. His standard fluttered in the breeze when we first arrived. It was his standard, not yours that you lowered.'

'He is here. My entire family is here,' Sela replied carefully. Every fibre of her being tensed as she waited to hear him reveal his true reason for making war—the command to see his son.

'Take me to Bose.' Vikar's face was hard and uncompromising underneath his helmet. 'I desire to speak with him.'

Speak with Bose. Demand that he swear allegiance if he was lucky or meet a swift death if he was not. Sela had no illusions about what Vikar intended. The rules were harsh. And there would be no recourse to Thorkell. He had allowed her father enough men to defend himself. It was not Thorkell's fault that they had chosen adventure with Hafdan, instead of their duty. For their sakes, she hoped that they had gone to Permia and had not decided to raid Viken as one of the women whispered they might.

Sela forced her mind to concentrate.

There had to be a way to stall Vikar and to allow her father a chance to escape with Kjartan. If he held out, if Hafdan and his men returned quickly enough, the hall might yet be restored. Kjartan might inherit more than a broken sword and an arm-ring. She had to find that way. She had to give her father and Kjartan a chance.

'What about my people? The wounded must be seen to.' Sela nodded towards the battlefield where the wounded lay, moaning and crying out. 'The hall will have to be secured, but neither my father nor I would desert our people. I have a responsibility to bind wounds.

'They are no longer your concern.'

'But they are,' Sela protested. 'They depend on me.'

Vikar's eyes hardened and became chips of green stone. 'You lost that right.'

The hall was very different from the last time Vikar had entered its walls. Then it had been hung with expensive tapestries, furs had lined every bench and the air had been scented with sweet perfume. No expense spared for his only daughter's wedding. Vikar pressed his lips together to form a tight line.

All of that was long gone, including the marriage. The rafters with their carved men and strange beasts stared down on a stone floor and cold hearth. Even stripped bare, Bose the Dark's hall remained an impressive site. Large, echoing.

The benches were pushed to one side. The tables stacked, ready for the last defence. A defence that had never come. Why had Bose left his hall so unguarded? Had his pride reached such a state that he thought none dare attack him? Even when he attacked others?

'Your father fails to come forward with open arms and a horn of mead to greet his former son-in-law,' Vikar said as he looked at the slim woman before him. 'Why does this fail to surprise me?'

'You expected him to be?' Her full bottom lip curled slightly and her eyes became daggers. 'My father has never been foolish.'

'It was foolish to try to hold this hall with such a force.'

'One has to do something when raiders come calling.'

'I will grant you that.' Vikar looked at his former wife with narrowed eyes. Most women would have been wailing and tearing their hair. but Sela looked as if she wanted to run him through. Her beauty had grown and matured in the intervening years since they had last seen each other. Tall, proud and defiant in her borrowed chain mail and trousers, yet somehow absurdly feminine. Vikar refused to feel pity. This situation was entirely of her making. 'Your father should be ashamed sending you out to do his job.'

'Thorkell forced it on him. My father and I had to

make the best of what little remains. And we have done so.' Her eyes flicked around the large bare room as if searching for something.

'That is open to interpretation,' he said through gritted teeth. 'My business is with your father, and as my men have paid the price in blood, I expect to speak with him, and to offer him my protection.'

'You mean his surrender.'

'If you want to call it that—yes. It is over, Sela. How many more must die?'

'You wouldn't. I surrendered. The battle is over.'

'Not until I see Bose the Dark. Take me to him.' He stared at her, and she was the first to flinch. Her head was bowed and her body hunched. Defeated.

'He was in his chambers when we last spoke. Now allow me to retire.'

'There, it was not difficult. And where is he now? He will surrender to me, Sela.'

'Thorkell will have something to say…' Now she was just trying to stall him, to give her father more time to get away with Kjartan.

'Thorkell will approve of my action and I know your penchant for disappearing.' Vikar shook his head, re-membering how easily she had vanished before. One day there and the next, gone with a scribbled rune and Bose's messenger, Hafdan delivering the news his marriage had ended. Vikar had derived a certain pleasure at Hafdan's expression when he realised who had ensured his place at Odin's table. 'Did you think I had forgotten?'

She gave a half-shrug that could mean anything. Her face turned mutinous, her lower lip sticking out slightly in a way that he had once found charming. 'I have never known what you remembered. Sometimes, I was certain you had forgotten our marriage and my existence.'

'No, I only wished I had.'

'You have fared well since we last met,' she said in a calm measured tone and Vikar allowed her to change the subject.

'You heard of the raid on the Northumbrian monastery.' Vikar wondered briefly what she had thought when she had heard the news. Did it give her pause for thought? Did she regret divorcing him, dismissing him as worthless?

'All Viken did.' Sela inclined her head and a tiny smile touched her lips. 'You and your fellow jaarls are famous. The saga of the voyage has rapidly become a favourite in this hall. You and the other jaarls of Lindisfarne will be remembered long after the Valkyries have called you to Odin's banqueting hall.'

'Sagas are meant to entertain. Much has been twisted and exaggerated in that particular tale. Haakon caused it to be written, and you know what he is like.' Vikar gave a brief shrug.

'I am hardly that naïve. The sagas about my father rarely hold any truth. Do you know one actually claims he stole an egg from the nest of the great aurorc who sits on the top of the tallest pine tree in the forest?' She shifted her weight and gave a little laugh. 'Can you imagine? My father hates heights.'

'And you are sure your father remains in the hall? You are not trying to stall me while he slips away, like a rat out of one of his fabled secret passageways?'

'Secret passageways?' Her defiant chin was in the air,

but her eyes held a wary look as her hand plucked at the bottom of her mail shirt. 'Such things are far more suited to sagas than real life. You really must stop believing everything you hear, Vikar. Truly, I say this as someone who once cared about your welfare.'

'You lie.' Vikar wrapped his fingers tightly about the hilt of his sword and regained control. 'Your father showed me one, years ago when we were first married.'

'You have a good memory, then.' Her voice was chipped ice. 'I had forgotten it. All I know is where I left him—in bed. Weak. He has not moved since the day after Hafdan and his men departed.'

'Shall we put an end to our speculation?'

'If you must, but I was enjoying our pleasant chat, Vikar Hrutson.'

'You never could lie very well, Sela, but I will humour you.' Vikar strode through the main hall, barely glancing to his left or right. It bothered him that Bose had decided to send his one remaining child out into battle while he stayed safely hidden. That Sela chose to fight did not surprise him. His former wife had never lacked courage. He had often thought she would be a better jaarl than her older brother. 'One, two, three. Are you there, Bose the Dark?'

He pushed aside the curtains that concealed the jaarl's chambers from the rest of the hall.

Empty. Still. Lifeless.

Sela released a breath and fought to keep her body upright.

Kjartan's bird's nest lay discarded to one side of the bed. She reached out and gently touched the delicate thing. Kjartan had been so proud of it. A lump rose in her throat. When would she see him again? When would she see her child again?

'Where has your father gone?' Vikar's face was ice cold as he viewed her father's empty chamber. 'You knew they had gone when you told me to come here. I am through with your games.'

'I am not my father's keeper.'

Sela fought the urge to sink down on the floor and offer her thanksgiving up to Frejya, Sif or any of the gods and goddesses of Aesir who might be listening. Her father had escaped, as had Kjartan. They had not been with the women. They were away from this place and not under Vikar's rule.

'Tell me where you think he is.'

'I was busy with other things, and I failed to see him depart.' Sela struggled to keep the laughter from her voice. Her father and Kjartan had escaped and nothing else mattered. She looked at Vikar, meeting his hard, green gaze. She had forgotten how handsome she once thought him with his rugged blond features. Once they had made her pulse race, and then she had learnt the sort of heart they concealed.

'You are too loyal. He left you to defend the hall and fled. He deserted you, Sela. Left you to die.'

Sela sobered and glared at him. 'Did you expect him to stay?'

'Coward was never a word I would have applied to Bose the Dark.'

'He had his reasons.'

Sela forced her face to remain a bland mask. She was certain her father had escaped to save Kjartan, once he knew who was leading the raiding party. She had to protect Kjartan. She could not risk him meeting Vikar. Then there would be no doubting who the father was. With every movement Vikar made, she could see echoes of their son.

A child belonged to the father, after weaning age, according to Viken law. She curled her hand. She would never give her son up. Vikar had not wanted her, and he would not want her child. She refused to have her son grow up unwanted, and uncared for. She had seen how such children ran wild, and had vowed it would never happen to her child.

'Is there anything else you wish to say, Sela?'

'If you will permit me, Vikar, to retire to my chamber and change into my ordinary clothes, perhaps we can discuss this sensibly.' Sela turned on her heel. Once she had changed, she would regain her balance, her control. She needed time to think and to plot her escape. 'There I will ponder your request, and perhaps, given time, I might be able to remember where my father might have gone.'

'No.'

Sela blinked at the unexpectedness of the sound, and swung around to face him. White-hot anger coursed through her. She clenched her fists, tried to control it. 'What do you mean—no? You complained my attire was inappropriate. I am attempting to follow your wishes and please you.'

'Please me? That is the last thing on your mind.' Vikar crossed his arms and lounged against the doorframe, blocking her way. 'You have no intention of doing such a thing. Your chief delight and pastime during our marriage was going against my wishes. Behaving how it best suited you, Sela. I know you far too well.'

Sela forced her lips to curve into a smile. 'We are strangers, you and I, Vikar. We only thought we knew each other.'

'You disappeared all too eagerly, Sela—ready to run from any unpleasantness.' A muscle in Vikar's jaw jumped. 'In Kaupang four years ago, you left without a word. I came back to our chambers—emptied of all life. The next thing I discover is that you have divorced me.'

Breath hissed through Sela's lips. She struggled to maintain a grip on her temper. Left without a word, indeed! She had waited and waited, wanting to believe in his innocence, and then his betrayal had been clear. He had given her no choice and so she had acted. 'That is not my memory of the situation at all.'

Vikar made an irritated noise in the back of his throat, reminding her forcibly of Kjartan and why this man represented danger. 'Enough of this foolishness. I do not give you leave to retire, to pretend as if nothing has happened. Your father broke his truce. He sent his men to raid Viken territory.'

Sela's heartbeat resounded in her ears. An unprovoked raid?

'Vikar, you have made a grave error of judgement. My father has not raided in years. Why should he? He earns enough from the trade of skins, soapstone and amber. Let us speak no more of his raiding, but instead of yours.'

'Mine?'

She drew a breath and began listing the points on her fingers. 'You did not come in peace. Dressed in chain mail and bearing shields, you and your warriors rushed towards us with drawn swords without issuing a proper challenge. We had the right to defend ourselves. Thorkell will be informed of this. We have that right.'

She watched with grim satisfaction as Vikar struggled for words.

'Hafdan led a raid. He was stopped. I intend to have no more raiding parties threaten Viken. Thorkell will support me. I am the new jaarl of the north.'

Sela closed her eyes. Hafdan. She should have guessed. Vikar was correct. Thorkell would not support her father, would not send his men to avenge the raid. 'And what happened to Hafdan?'

'He perished as all vermin do.' A muscle in Vikar's jaw jumped. 'He would never have gone anywhere without your father's orders.'

'They quarrelled. Hafdan left. Hafdan sailed under his own standard.' She pressed her hands together. 'My father and I knew nothing of the raid. He had no intention of bringing war to Viken. Do you mean to sack the hall?'

'Bose's lands are among the most profitable in Viken. This hall is fit for a king, let alone a jaarl. Why should I wish to destroy that?'

'And my people? What will happen to them?'

'Provided they show their loyalty to their new master, life will continue on as before.'

Sela dropped her head to her chest and felt a lump form in her throat. She would not have to watch her home burn, see the crops ploughed under and then have Vikar and his men leave. Her people would be spared that.

'And what will become of me?' she asked in a small voice, unable to stop herself

'You are a problem I had not anticipated. Your father should have taken better care of you. He should have ensured your protection, rather than have you take charge of a rabble such as the one my men and I faced.'

'It was my choice. My father did not have any say in the matter.'

'Then is your husband amongst the fallen?' Vikar lifted his eyebrow. 'You should have said earlier. I send my condolences. Or perhaps it is why Hafdan left?'

'Having experienced marriage once, and found it not to my liking, I had no great desire to return to the state, particularly not to someone like Hafdan. He was my father's favourite, not mine.' Sela kept her head high.

'Interesting.' Vikar stroked his chin and his eyes gleamed. 'It saves me having to put a sword through an innocent man.'

'Why would you want to do that?'

'No man should live if he forces his woman to fight.' A muscle in Vikar's cheek jumped. 'You should never have been out there, Sela. Women are made for other pleasures.'

'Perhaps I have giantess blood like Skathi in the legends. She put on her father's armour to avenge his death and marched all the way to Aesgard to challenge the gods.'

'But your father lives.' He lifted his eyebrows and had the bad grace to appear amused, as if he had caught her playing in her brother's armour, instead of trying to defend her hall.

'Things had to be done. A defence had to be made.'

'But not by you, Sela. Your father was the jaarl. It is to his banner the men flocked.'

'My father…' Sela hated the way her voice faltered. She would have to confess the truth about her father's affliction. 'My father is ill. He cannot lift his sword. I had no other choice.'

'If you father is that ill, that afflicted, why did he allow Hafdan to sail away?'

'Hafdan wanted more—more power, more everything. My father felt that letting him go to Permia would give him the prestige he craved.'

'Your tales grow more fantastic by the breath.'

Sela fought the urge to bury her face in her hands. He did not believe her. She had told the truth and he did not believe her. 'It is the truth, even you must see that.'

'Hafdan left, knowing you were unmarried and your father about to breathe his last?' He slapped his hand against his thigh. 'Hafdan always sailed under your father's orders. He left to war against the Viken. He is now dead and your father's plot is in ruins. Everything your father valued belongs to me…including you.'

'What are you planning to do with me?'

'You are unmarried.' Vikar took a step towards her. A lazy smile appeared on his face. 'You need a protector.'

Sela put her hand to her throat as she stepped backwards and felt the chest digging into her legs. 'What sort of protector?'

His eyes raked her form, lingered on her breasts. 'You would make an admirable concubine.'

Chapter Three

'To you?' Sela's mouth went dry as the word echoed in her brain. The walls of her father's chamber appeared to have shrunk, pushing her towards him, towards his hard unyielding body.

Unbidden, a memory of the last time they had joined assaulted her senses, the way his hands had stroked her body, playing it as expertly as he played the lyre, how his mouth had drawn the cry from her throat as the two reached their peak at the same time. She pushed it away, back in a place where she never ventured. She refused to remember what it was like before his betrayal, before she had learnt the truth. She forced her lip to curl.

'I will pass, thank you very much.'

'A challenge? You know I am never one to resist a challenge.' A hint of laughter echoed in his voice. Sela remembered when that particular sound had sent shivers of delight down her spine. Such things had vanished years ago, along with her girlish illusions. She had grown in the four years since she had last seen him, become a different person. And the person she had become would not be attracted to him and his easy charm.

'A refusal.' She crossed her arms over her breasts, stared into his eyes and forced her lips to smile. 'Surely by now, you must know the difference.'

A muscle in Vikar's cheek jumped and his body grew still. Sela swallowed hard. Had she gone too far? A tiny shiver passed over her. She took a step backwards and tried to look somewhere other than at the green flame flickering in the depths of his eyes.

Vikar's hands closed around her upper arms. He hauled her towards him until their bodies collided. The softness of her curves met the unyielding strength of his muscle.

'Are you saying we were not good together? I seem to recall differently.'

He lowered his lips, captured hers, plundered them with expertise. His mouth drew the breath from her body, replaced it with a growing heat. Her body began to melt. A soft sigh escaped from her throat. His arms came around her, cradled her firmly against his body as her lips gave way under the onslaught.

Practised. Planned. Cynical.

Sela pushed against his chest with her last ounce of resolution, controlled her breathing and his arms fell away. Cool air encircled her as she sought to regain control of her breathing. Even in that brief span of time, her lips ached, longed for the warmth of his touch again, but she forced her body to remember how he had trampled her heart in the dust. She hoped he had missed her response.

'My point proved.' He inclined his head and a dimple flashed in the corner of his mouth. 'We were good together. You and I.'

'There is more to marriage than sexual attraction.'

'Agreed, but it does help.' He ran a finger down her cheek, and another pulse of warmth went unbidden through her. 'It makes everything easier, less complicated.'

'Our marriage died a long time ago.' Sela jerked her head away. 'It cannot be remade.'

'I don't believe I offered marriage. I simply stated the obvious.' His eyes hardened. 'You need a protector.'

Sela crossed her arms over her aching breasts. She gave a short laugh. Brittle and too high pitched. She swallowed hard and tried again.

'I agree—I need protecting…from you and men like you. Men who use and discard women.' A small sense of satisfaction filled her as Vikar's jaw tightened. The barb had hit home. Good. She waited another heart-beat, then continued, making sure her voice dripped honey. 'And you? What does your new wife think of your adventures? Is she more accommodating? How many concubines do you keep?'

Sela sought to keep control of her emotions. She was over him. She had to remember what he was like. She had seen the evidence, seen them with their heads together, laughing over some quip, her hand touching his cheek. It had been a knife in her heart.

His lips twisted into a sardonic smile.

'I have yet to remarry.' He gave a slight bow. 'Like you, my first experience left a bitter taste, but Thorkell keeps trying to convince me that marriage is a worthy state. Apparently I need children tumbling about my hall, like young puppies. Haakon agrees. He says it will change my life. The touch of my own flesh and blood clutching my finger.'

Sela's heart constricted and she shifted uneasily. How could she explain, if he did not know? How could she tell him about his son? How could she have Kjartan torn from her? She dug her fingernails into the palms of her hand.

'And Asa? What does she say on the subject?' The words slipped out before she could stop them— anything to keep away from the potentially disastrous subject of children. It was only when they echoed through the chamber that Sela realised how mean spirited they must sound.

'Asa understands my reasoning.' The green in his eyes grew cold. 'It was a deep regret of hers that you two never became friends.'

Sela tightened her lips. Asa had had no intention of ever being friends with Sela all those years ago. She had taken great delight in humiliating her, pointing out her every mistake, laughing at her dress sense, shaking her head in mock despair at Sela's unsophisticated ways. It was only when Sela discovered Asa's love token beside her bed that she had known the truth. But that was in the past. And the past was finished. There was no return. There was only the future.

'I do not want to make a rash decision. Can I have some time to think about your generous offer?' Sela nodded towards the hall as the shouts of the men grew louder. 'Your men will need your expert direction about what to steal.'

Vikar looked at her for a long time. Suddenly his green eyes blazed. 'There can only be one answer, Sela.'

'There is always more than one answer in life, Vikar. Haven't you learnt that by now?'

'I have bandied words with you for long enough.'

His hand closed around her arm, and he led her to the little room where her father did his accounts.

'Why have you taken me here?'

'It is a place for you to be alone. A place where I know there are no secret passages—only one entrance and exit.' He gave a small nod of satisfaction. 'And the lock is complex. You need to turn the key three times.'

Sela gritted her teeth. Vikar had neatly trapped her. There would be no escape from here. 'My father gave you too many confidences. How will I get released from here? What must I do?'

'It will be your choice, Sela. Just as it was your choice to end our marriage. But you have a protector.'

'And if my father is found?'

'You will become his responsibility, not mine.'

With that, he swung the door and Sela heard the lock click into place. She sank to the floor and put her head on her knees.

How long until Vikar discovered that she was hiding more than her father?

'Bose the Dark escaped into the woods,' Ivar reported when Vikar returned to the dragon ships. 'It has been confirmed by three of our men.'

The shoreline remained littered with fallen bodies and armour. Vikar shook his head. So much waste. All for what? Sela had to have known that she stood no chance with her host of ill-prepared and badly equipped men.

Why had she fought? Why had her father let her fight while he had escaped? The image of Sela standing there, proud yet vulnerable in her borrowed armour, was one that would haunt him for ever. He should have seen, should have realised earlier. Thankfully, Odin had allowed him to reach her before she had been injured.

'Who has gone in the search party? How many men did you send?' Vikar glanced towards the dark forest. He knew the answer from Ivar's slightly shifting stance.

'By the time I had received word, he and his party were long gone.' Ivar fingered the jagged scar that ran down the right side of his face, but did not meet Vikar's eyes. 'Our men would not have stood a chance in those trees. It is the realm of the wild men. I know the tales of how Bose the Dark subdued them, but they still lurk out there.'

'Bose the Dark has spread many tales. Remember, this hall was supposed to be impossible to conquer.' Vikar gave a satisfied smile. 'I stopped believing in such things about the time I discovered a woman's chest makes a soft pillow on which to lay my head.'

'And I am sure many women would willingly provide that pillow.'

'Not all.' Vikar pressed his lips together and glanced towards where Sela was imprisoned. 'I have no illusions, old friend.'

'But you have proved luckier than most. Your bed is always warm. Whereas a man like me…'

'Some might say that.' Vikar stared over his friend's shoulder.

There was little point in shattering Ivar's illusions. Vikar's bed had been cold for weeks, months. He wanted something more than the physical release, something indefinable. The succession of bedfellows, amiable as they were, did nothing for him, except increase his sense of dissatisfaction, his sense that there was a huge gaping hole in his life. He felt more in that brief kiss with Sela than he had done with any of his recent bed-companions.

Vikar turned his thoughts away from the memory of Sela's lips trembling under his. Now was not the time for such things. He had an elusive jaarl to find, one who would employ every trick he could to stay one step ahead. One who would retake the hall and bring devastation to Viken if he could. A wounded animal was often the most dangerous. An old saying, but a true one.

'How many men have you sent after Bose the Dark?'

'None.' Ivar banged his fists together. 'I have no wish to send men on a fool's errand. The pathways in that forest are many. He could be anywhere.'

'Find a guide.'

'None of his men will go. I tried threatening them. Offering gold. They are a poor lot, no spirit in them.' Ivar hooked his thumbs around his sword belt. 'And I would not trust them either. There is some mischief here that I don't understand.'

Vikar gave a nod. Ivar was right. They needed someone they could trust to send them in the right direction, someone who would lead them directly to Bose. He would discover the truth of what was happening on Thorkell's northern border and he would ensure peace. Bose the Dark had to see that his time of mischief-making was over. 'Bose is obviously making for a sanctuary, a place where he can regroup or call in favours from other jaarls.'

'But why would he leave his daughter?' Ivar said. 'Surely he must know her value as a hostage, if he should try to regain any of his land.'

'It is the one piece of the puzzle I don't understand,' Vikar admitted. 'Bose the Dark's devotion to his family is legendary. Why did he deliberately put her in danger?'

'Perhaps he grew tired of her and her demands. His daughter is reputed to be quite strong-willed and unmanageable.'

Strong-willed was an understatement. Stubborn beyond any sense was a better description. Her earlier refusal rankled. He had felt her lips move against his, her body begin to arch towards him. She was not as indifferent as she pretended. He had not mistaken the passion they had once shared. They would share it again, and he would be the one to do the leaving.

'It is a possibility.' Vikar rubbed his hand against the back of his neck. 'But what I am more worried about is the remainder of Bose's men. We are vulnerable to attack should he succeed in contacting one of his allies.'

'Our situation?' Ivar ran his hand through his hair. 'Only two of our number made it to Valhalla. The other injuries are not life threatening. Surely it is a cause for celebration.'

'Our victory was too easy.' Vikar shook his head. 'It was almost as if he wanted us to win. How quickly could he raise support?'

'Would that all our fights were that easy! The gods were with us, but we did fight, Vikar.'

Vikar stared out towards the fjord. The water lapped at the ships. Had he inadvertently led his men into another one of Bose the Dark's traps? Would he be the one defeated? He who had so proudly proclaimed that Bose could no longer manipulate him. Unthinkable, and yet the prickling sensation at the back of his neck refused to go. He had to find a way to discover Bose and force his surrender. While he was out there in the blackness, his men remained in danger. Bose had to formally surrender and accept him as the master of this hall. 'It is not over yet.'

'How so? We fought, they died. We won. It is the end.' Ivar clapped his hand against Vikar's back. 'Stop seeing shadows where there are none. Our men deserve a victory feast.'

'That army was commanded by a woman and the warriors were either past their best or untried. Someone wanted us to win here today. Someone knew we were coming.' Vikar's hand went instinctively to the hilt of his dagger.

Ivar's face showed his utter dismay. He glanced backwards as if he expected to see another host rising from the forest. He let out a soft sigh as the dark pines and birches remained devoid of life.

'What do you intend to do?'

'Find Bose. He is the key to unlocking this problem.'

'Find him?' Ivar's eyes opened and his beard quivered. 'He is in the forest, I tell you—he and two others—a woman and a child.'

'So there were others. You should have told me to begin with. There will be a reason for that child.'

'It is why they were let through,' Ivar explained. 'The old man looked harmless, leaning on his stick, and his face half-covered with a cloak. It was only after he was gone that someone noticed the resemblance. It had to be him—we have searched everywhere else.'

'It will have been him.' A faint breeze ruffled Vikar's hair. The currents in this hall ran deep. He knew that nothing was ever straightforward. Sela knew far more than she was letting on. She would go to her father, if she could. She had always run to him after their fights.

'Why would he have a child with him?'

It was not a question Vikar cared to answer or even speculate on.

What was the child to Bose the Dark? A shield and ruse or something more? The answers could only come from one source.

'Bose has always been known for his personal bravery. If he can walk, he can fight. He remains a danger. Everything he does is for one purpose only—his personal gain and glory.'

'But how are you going to find him?' Ivar tapped a finger against his mouth. 'No one knows where he has gone.'

'Sela does.' Vikar nodded back towards the hall, towards where she was imprisoned. 'And she is going to try to reach him, if I allow her.'

'How can you be sure of that?' Ivar's eyes widened. 'Women are unreliable creatures.'

'Sela reveres her father. She will go.' Vikar permitted a smile to cross his face as he remembered Sela's reaction to his suggestion. Concubine to a jaarl. Most women would have taken a pragmatic approach. But Sela made it seem as if he threatened to send her to the frost giants. 'I have given her every incentive to go. I know the woman well. She will escape and I will be with her, dogging her footsteps.'

'And how will you make certain you don't lose her? I heard that when she divorced you, she vanished into thin air.'

Vikar gazed up at the sky—a hazy blue, signalling it was late in the day. The sun would not properly set this far north. He preferred not to think about that day when he had gone back to their lodging and discovered Sela gone. Later Hafdan had taunted him, beaten him. Vikar fingered his long healed jaw. He had learnt a lot since that day. It was then that he had lost his illusions, and had begun to grow up.

'She escaped me once, but she will not again.' The muscles in his neck tightened. 'We must work out how many will guard the hall and what needs to be done to repair its defences. Bose has become lax in recent years.'

'The men deserve a feast. They will want to sample the spoils. You seek to deny them their right.'

'We feast tonight, and tomorrow you begin the work. This hall will not fall so easily again. I will find Bose. I promise you that.'

'Very good, Vikar.' Ivar adjusted his sword belt. 'Can I help you with your problem? Is there anything more you need?'

'Allow me to handle my former wife, my own way.' Vikar put his hand on the hilt of his sword. 'I have planted the seed. Let us see how she reacts to a bit more subtle *persuasion*.'

Concubine? To Vikar? After what had passed between them? He was determined to humiliate her. Determined to show the world his total mastery of her and her world.

Sela shook her head in amazement. Even now, some time after Vikar had locked her in the blackness of her father's room, her lips ached slightly, giving lie to her declaration that she felt nothing for him. His final words circled around her brain, making it impossible for her to think of anything else.

Join with him? Willingly? Again?

Surely he had not been serious? He was trying to worry her, to make her act without thinking. He would offer some other man and then expect her to fall on her knees in gratitude. It would be entirely like him.

The man was insupportable. And there was no way of escape from this particular room except through the door.

Sela stamped her foot and felt a floorboard give way slightly. She sank down on the hard ground and her fingers searched for a bit of purchase. She tugged and pulled. The board gave way without warning, and she flew backwards, landing on her bottom. Gingerly Sela reached into the cavity, felt around the narrow space. Her fingertips touched the hilt of a dagger.

Hurriedly, Sela withdrew it and stuffed it into the waistband of her trousers. She felt better now that she was armed. She shrugged out of the chain mail and let that fall to the floor with a thump. Immediately her shoulders and back became lighter. Whatever happened, she had no intention of wearing that cumbersome piece of clothing again.

She bit her lip, trying to come up with some semblance of an escape plan. Vikar knew the ways of the hall as well as her father.

In those happy days when they were first married, she had taken great delight in showing him some of the secrets. Not all—thankfully there had not been time to show him where the safe houses were. It was always something she was going to do some day, but then their marriage had fallen apart.

She stretched her limbs.

Had it ever really begun?

Vikar had been a skilful lover and she, young and untried. Her body had responded to his skilled touch, but he had not cared for her. She had been naïve, overwhelmed that such a great warrior would want her. They had barely known each other. It had been a political match and it had been unfortunate that she had imagined otherwise.

The only part of the marriage she did not regret was Kjartan.

The door creaked, and Sela lifted her head, every nerve on alert. Her hand reached for the dagger, but she resisted the temptation. She'd wait, and only attack if provoked.

'Who goes there?'

'Vikar sent me.'

An unfamiliar giant of a man put a plate of dry bread, a mug of ale and a small rush light down on the floor near her, but not so near that she was tempted to rush him, and then backed away.

'Why have you brought me these?'

'Vikar says you are to eat. He will not have you starving.' The guard leered before throwing a fur at her feet. 'And he does not want you to be cold. You should sleep; soon you will not get much rest.'

'How very generous of him.'

She examined the guard from where she sat. The man resembled an over-fed ox. Vikar had chosen well. She would have to trust Loki that another less obvious way to escape would appear.

The guard made another bow and slammed the door shut. Sela waited for the sound of the lock clicking into place. But there was only one click. Then the sound of heavy footsteps retreating, going out of the room.

There was only one click. Had Vikar forgotten to tell the guard?

She pressed her hand against her head and tried to think of how to open the door. Her heart pounded in her ears. Loki had heard her prayer, and given her a sign. Freedom beckoned, if she was careful.

It was easy, her father had often boasted. She simply had to… And her mind went blank.

Sela went over to the door, and attempted to turn the handle. It didn't budge. She tried the other way. Nothing. Sela held up the little rush light, trying to find the secret way, but the wood looked smooth. It had no wish to deliver up its secrets. She beat against the handle with her fists, but it remained stubbornly shut.

'Father! You created a trap for your own daughter!'

She kicked the bottom of the door and it swung open. Sela gave a strangled laugh. The answer so easy that it was in front of her. She wiped her hands against her trousers and peered out into the darkened chamber.

No guard stood there, waiting. Her brow wrinkled. Vikar must be losing his touch. Or perhaps he thought her incapable of escape. Whatever it was, it did not matter. The only thing that mattered was breaking out of the hall, rejoining Kjartan and getting as far away from Vikar as possible.

Vikar, arrogant in his superiority, had miscalculated. His own man had failed him.

She would be free. They would not soon recapture her.

She started towards the entrance to the chamber as the sounds of feasting swirled around her, then stopped.

Her escape would only work if it was not quickly discovered. She retraced her steps and arranged the armour and fur to look as though she slept. She then held up the sputtering remains of the rush light. Not perfect, but it was the best she could do. If the guard checked tonight, it would be late, probably after the feasting.

Voices rumbled outside her father's chambers and Sela quickly doused the light, pulling the door to her former prison shut. She flattened her body against the wall, ready to run, if they entered the room.

Her heart pounded so loudly in her ears that she thought they must hear. Just when she thought she could no longer bear it and would have to act, the footsteps moved on and the voices receded. Sela relaxed against the wall. Waited. Risked a breath.

Staying here was asking to be recaptured. She might as well try to march through the centre of the feast and announce her plan to the entire hall. She had to move. She had to find a way. Kjartan was counting on her.

She eased the door back and looked out. The passage was silent. Beyond it, she could see the flickering light of the hall's fire and hear the laughter as a skald started his tale. Sela clenched her fists. Vikar had wasted no time in making himself at home. These men were making free with the stores she had worked so hard to build up.

Cautiously she made her way along the passage, keeping to the shadows. She peeped out into the great hall. Vikar sat at the high table, with his back towards her. Over-confident in his finery and hearty laugh, but breathtakingly handsome. She stood watching the way his long fingers held the goblet.

A sudden burst of laughter at a poor joke about her

father by the skald brought her to her senses. She should have expected it, but it still bothered her.

She fingered the knife and took a step forward. He deserved to suffer.

Her toe hit something—a little wooden horse. Rapidly she bent down and picked it up. Kjartan's favourite, the one he took everywhere with him.

Tears pricked her eyes and she used the back of her sleeve to wipe them away. Kjartan would be lost without his horse. He must have cried when her father led him to safety. Sela straightened. There were more important things than exacting her revenge. And this horse would be her talisman.

She had loathed that tunnel ever since her brother had lured her there as a child. Her nurse had rescued her, shaken and dishevelled, after what seemed like hours in the company of bats and spiders' webs. But there was no hope for it. She did not dare risk the kitchens or going through the main hall.

She would have to brave it and hope the bats had gone. Even the thought of the creatures in her hair turned her stomach. After the tunnels, the woods and then the long way around to the hut. It was safer and was bound to be the route her father had taken with Kjartan. She might even reach them before the fording place, if she hurried.

A sudden burst of applause as the skald reached the high point in his recitation of the saga about the Lindisfarne raid forcibly reminded her that she could not simply stay here, pressed up against a wall for ever. Her muscles tensed as she prepared to run to the next group of shadows. Vikar called something out to the skald and the place erupted in laughter. Coarse rough laughter from men who had filled their bellies with meat and ale. At the sound, she darted. Made it.

She kept to the shadows and reached the tunnel's entrance without being challenged. The outlines of the trapdoor were clear for anyone who knew where to look. She would make it through. The way was clear. There were not hidden twists or turns. She simply had to keep going until the end.

'Concubine?' she whispered before raising Kjartan's horse over her head in triumphant. 'I choose another path.'

The trap door creaked slightly as she lifted it. She descended a few steps, pulled it firmly shut and allowed the blackness to envelop her.

'Vikar,' Ivar said in an undertone as the skald began another song. 'The food has been delivered to your prisoner.'

Vikar drained his horn of ale, wiped his hand across his face and lifted his gaze to the shadows. 'I know.'

'But how can you know? The guard has just returned. He was waylaid in the kitchens. There is a lusty serving maid who caught his eye.'

The shadows shimmered and parted as a figure moved stealthily along the wall. Vikar permitted a smile to cross his face. He knew his former wife well, even after all these years. It pleased him that she had been so accommodating, so willing to take the opportunity and so foolish not to see that the way had been made clear for her. And she would be his, on his terms in the end. 'The mouse has taken the bait, as I predicted she would.'

'You are taking an awful risk, Vikar.'

Vikar raised an eyebrow. 'It is a risk, yes, but it is the fastest way of discovering where our host for this feast is hidden.'

'Someone else should go.'

'No.' Vikar banged his fist on the table and the skald stopped speaking, looking at him in amazement.

Vikar winced, remembering Bose the Dark's reputation. The skald probably thought the tale had invoked his displeasure. He gestured for the man to continue with his saga.

Once the skald's words flowed again, Vikar continued. 'We have been over this, Ivar. This is my quest, my duty. You are to remain here and direct any defence that is needed. I know what my former father-in-law is like. I and I alone will bring him back for the surrender. Then, none in the Sorting will whisper and plot.'

'I will do as you ask.'

Vikar knocked his horn with Ivar, before he drained the remainder. 'Take care of the men until I return.'

'May Odin and Thor speed your journey.'

The grey light, which a few steps ago had seemed only a cruel twist of the tunnel, grew brighter. Sela heaved a sigh of relief. She was nearly through the tunnel without incident. Her earlier fears seemed foolish now, but still she would be pleased when she made it through to the woods, when she no longer had to worry.

She reached the exit and gulped the fresh pine-scented air, a welcome relief after the close stale air of the passageway. She had lost count of the number of spiders' webs she'd had to brush through, a sure sign that her father and Kjartan had gone a different way.

But they would be in the hut. They had to be. Sela clenched her fists, refused to give way to panic. They had agreed.

She dashed across the few open yards and made it to the screen of trees. There she waited to see if the alarm would be raised, but, except for the lone bark of one of the elkhounds, the yard was silent. She thought she saw the shadow of a man, but it vanished so quickly that she decided it was a trick of the light.

Her knees gave and she sank into the soft moss under the silver birch. A jay scolded her slightly and then flew off lazily into the hazy sky.

She listened to the sound of her heart beating and fingered Kjartan's wooden horse.

Safety of a sort. After her breath had returned, she'd be away. And would not return except to free her people from Vikar. First her son, then her people. Somehow. Some way. She would prevail.

'This is not the end, Vikar. This is only the beginning. I will regain everything. Everything!'

Sela raised her fist in the air and shook it towards the hall. Useless bravado she knew, but the little gesture of defiance made her feel better.

Her hair fell forward and she pushed it back behind her ears, pressed her fingertips into her eyes, concentrated on remembering the landmarks and their correct order.

In many ways, escaping from the hall was the easy part. Now she had to find her son. The thing she wanted most in the world was to scoop up Kjartan, hold him tight and never let him go.

She took a deep breath and plunged into the wood, picking her way along the faint track and keeping her eyes peeled for the faint signs her father had left to show the way—a cut in the bark here, a pile of stones there. To keep her spirits up, she hummed one of Kjartan's favourite songs, a great rollicking one about a brave warrior.

Twice she lost her way and the track vanished into a pond or off a cliff, and she had to retrace her steps, going ever deeper into the woods. She kept one hand clasped around the dagger at all times.

A noise caused the hairs on the back of Sela's neck to prickle. She stiffened and tightened her grasp of the hilt.

An animal? Bear? Wolf, or worse—one of the berserkers who had lost their minds and become more bear than human?

She half-turned, caught a flash of dark blue cloth. The energy drained from her body. So close and yet she had achieved nothing. She could throw herself down on the soft moss and weep.

'You have had your amusement,' she said, carefully enunciating her words so there could be no mistaking them. She put her hands on her hips and stared at the place she was certain he had concealed himself. 'I wonder that you let me get this far. When did you plan to let me know that my attempt was pitiful?'

'Your escape showed faint glimmers of ingenuity, Sela, I will give you that, but they have faded. Will you never learn about concealment?'

Chapter Four

'Only a glimmer of ingenuity, Vikar? You wound me.' A huge wave of disappointment washed over Sela, crushing her to the ground with its intensity. The birch and pine that had provided shelter a heartbeat before closed around her, imprisoned her. She had thought herself to be free, but it had been the merest illusion of freedom. 'I considered my escape magnificent. A complete triumph.'

'Did you think you could escape that easily? How little you know me, Sela. Details and planning. I learnt your father's lessons well.'

Vikar came out from behind a tall birch, a little way from where she had thought he might be. The sunlight streamed from behind him, making his frame appear larger and casting his features into shadow. He stood there with his hands on his hips, much as a god might survey the earth.

Sela judged the distance between them—no more than fifty strides lay between them. Her leg muscles tightened, tensed in preparation for flight. There was a small opening between two larches.

But could she make it?

Sela hesitated and glanced again at where he stood, glowering. Vikar was one of the fastest runners at court. Whenever they held competitions at the court in Kaupang, he won. He could easily cover those lengths before she made it to the trees.

With a sigh, she rejected the idea, released the air from her lungs, and forced her muscles to relax. A dark misery swamped her senses. He had timed his entrance well. She already had experienced enough humiliation for one day, for a lifetime. He had anticipated her every movement, appeared to guess her secrets. Not every secret. That one she hid. And she would keep it hidden for ever, if the gods allowed her to.

Sela pressed her hand to her mouth, holding back a sob. Her head collapsed on to her chest, but at the sound of his derisive snort, she raised her eyes and glared at him, daring him to make the first move, to reveal what he intended to do next.

'It would appear that I misjudged the situation,' she said carefully. 'I thought no one had noticed my departure.'

'Once away from the hall, you failed to remember the need for stealth and concealment,' he said, leaning against the trunk of a birch with a deceptive casualness. 'Did you disregard my advice from long ago or were you simply seeking attention?'

The hint of amusement in his voice was clear, a noise calculated to get under her skin. He had toyed with her! Allowed her the appearance of escaping, when all along he had been tracking her, intending to recapture her.

'I did nothing of the sort!'

'You sounded like a wild boar rummaging in the

undergrowth,' he continued remorselessly, the amusement growing in his voice. 'I would have thought Bose the Dark's daughter would have been more cautious in how she walked through the woods, particularly when those woods have such a sinister reputation in her father's saga.'

'I should have been.' Sela tilted her head upward and met his green gaze. Two could play at this game. She was no longer the naïve woman who had been his bride; she had matured. He no longer had any power over her. 'What is one shadow when you are fleeing for your life?'

Vikar crossed his arms and gave a small shrug. The material tightened across his shoulders, revealing their breadth. 'All I had to do was give you the opportunity and a slight push in the right direction. You can be very predictable, Sela.'

Predictable. Dull. Unexciting.

The words thudded in her brain. She knew what Vikar must think of her. What he had thought of her in those brief months they had had together. She had not been a person to him, but a glass counter in his quest for glory, something to be used and discarded.

Only she had done the discarding first.

'You wanted me to escape.'

'It is the reason I am here.'

Sela looked up into the network of green leaves and branches rising over her head. She had no wish to show Vikar how much his casual statement cut into her soul.

She had been arrogant, so proud of her ability that she had never once questioned why the room might be easy to leave. Her desire to reach Kjartan and her father had dimmed her common sense. She had made it easy for Vikar to play his little game. Easy!

'I could have walked through the main hall and out the front door,' she said, once she regained control of her emotions.

'But it wouldn't have been as much fun, would it?' The dimple showed in Vikar's cheek as he casually swung one of his legs.

'Fun? Getting spiders' webs in my hair? Having bats scream in my face?' Sela longed for a sharp missile to throw at his head. But it would probably only provoke greater mirth. She contented herself with clenching her fists. 'You have some strange ideas of amusement.'

'I had forgotten that you did not care for bats.' His stance relaxed slightly. The corners of his mouth began to twitch as his eyes gleamed. 'This is an added treat.'

His laughter echoed off the trees, sending several ravens flapping into the air. Sela gritted her teeth.

'It is not funny. My mouth, nose and hands were covered in dirt and the sticky tendrils of a thousand spiders' webs. The tunnel is far from an easy experience. This was not done for your entertainment!'

Vikar sobered, stood up and came near her. His eyes simmered with barely suppressed fury. Sela took a step backwards, her hand reaching for the hilt of her dagger.

'No, but one way and another you have put me to a great deal of bother and you deserved some discomfort.'

'Discomfort? Was this all about teaching me some long overdue lesson?' Sela regarded his hands, strong but with long fingers. Hands that had once cradled her when she was in pain. 'Particularly as you say I am predictable. Why seek to punish me in this way? Surely I have suffered enough.'

She waited for his response, every fibre of her being alert and poised. Even the breath of wind had stopped, waiting. He shifted his weight, making a twig crack.

'Allowing you to escape served my needs.'

'You are standing in a pool of sunlight. Perhaps it is you who ought to take lessons on concealment.' She gave a strangled attempt at a carefree laugh. 'I discovered you before you revealed yourself, before your plan had finished.'

Vikar lifted an eyebrow. 'I will have to make an adjustment to my plans. It is one of my more endearing features—I learn and make adjustments.'

'Endearing features? Do you have more than one?' Sela asked through gritted teeth.

'Others think so.'

'Perhaps it is because they are unacquainted with the real you.'

'And you are?' He lifted an eyebrow.

'Let me know the full horror of your plan. Exactly how was I to provide your amusement…this time?'

'You were to unwittingly lead me to your father's bolt-hole. The scheme had its merits, you will have to admit.'

Sela cast her eyes heavenwards. She had very nearly done that. Depending on the way she went, the hut could easily be reached by early morning. The shadows were lengthening, but there would only be a short time while it was truly dark and she had to rest. She had intended on pressing on, forcing her body to move, but now there was little point. Vikar was here, with her.

She refused to betray her father like that.

Her insides trembled, but she forced her body to be as straight as a newly forged sword.

'Your scheme has failed. I won't lead you anywhere.' Her hand brushed the hilt of the dagger. If he did advance, she would have no hesitation. He was her enemy.

'You will, Sela. You will lead me directly to your father.' His voice dropped to a purr and lapped at the edges of her mind. The same silken sound he had used to coax her back after one of their quarrels. 'You will obey me. You will lead me to him.'

'Never.' Sela spat the word and regained control of her mind.

'Shall I make you?'

Vikar took several steps towards her. Her hand tightened around the hilt. Her entire arm ached—from her hand to her elbow to her shoulder. She drew a breath, felt her legs tense.

'If you come any closer…'

'The time for using that weapon has gone.'

'Then stop tempting me.' She forced her fingers to relax. At the slight movement, he halted. 'If you keep your distance, I won't use it. But I do know how to.'

'Temptation. Let's speak of temptation to do harm and see who has the greater right.' A grim smile crossed his features. 'You owe me. You left Kaupang without an explanation and you attempted to leave the hall without my permission.'

'I was not aware I needed your permission.'

'Twice is two times too many.'

The breath rushed out of her. This was all about his hurt pride. She had damaged his overwhelming sense of self-importance.

'You know why I left—or you would have if you had spared me some time from the oh-so-lovely Asa's side.' Anger filled her. Her fingers itched to draw the dagger from its sheath. 'You did not care whether I lived or died…until I was gone.'

'Maybe you should have fought for me. Maybe you used it as an excuse to get away from something you feared.' Vikar's eyes were ice-cold green as they regarded her hand, but he made no further movement towards her.

'How does one fight a queen?' Sela kicked a pebble, remembering those dreadful days in Kaupang when she had waited for him to come to her at her father's house. He had never responded to her ultimatum except to order her back. She had finished taking orders from him and had left. 'I refused to compete, and feed your vanity.'

'Was it about my vanity or yours?' Vikar's eyes became inscrutable as he took a step closer. The warmth of his breath fanned her cheek. She could see the lines in the corners of his eyes and the hollow of his throat where she used to press her lips.

'My vanity?' The words came out as a squeak.

'Yes, yours.'

Vikar came closer, so close, that if she breathed deeply their bodies would touch. Her fingers trembled. To her horror, she realised that she wanted to touch him, to feel his skin slide under her palms, to once again experience that swirl of emotion. Her body remembered the times they had spent together. Remembered it and wanted it again even as her mind willed the memory to subside back into that locked place in her mind.

'And my refusal to dance to your tune bothered you.' His voice had become a silken purr, one that flowed over her and ensnared her in its coils. 'You wanted me there, by your side. You hungered for me and my touch.'

Yes. The word resounded in her brain. For a heartbeat, Sela wondered if she had uttered the single syllable out loud. She blinked, but Vikar continue to look at her with the same smug expression. She drew a breath and regained control of her tongue, her body.

'No, you meant nothing to me.' She forced her voice to be a honeyed sweet lie. 'It was a political alliance and it outlived its usefulness. I had no desire for you. I have no desire.'

'I think there was more to it than that.'

Vikar pulled her against his body, moulding her curves to his hard planes. And she was not prepared for the white heat that coursed through her body. Was he going to kiss her again? Her mouth ached as if he had. His hand skimmed her arm and then pulled the dagger from her waistband. He balanced it on the palm of his hand before placing it in his waistband. She fancied his breath came a little faster.

'A dangerous plaything for a woman,' he said at last. 'I think I shall put it under my protection.'

Sela fought her instincts and forced her head to remain high. 'I refuse to go back to the hall, Vikar, to become an unknown man's concubine. I am not some thrall to be sold to the highest bidder.'

'I never intended *selling* you. What an intriguing suggestion.' His smile widened and his eyes danced. 'We will discuss your proposition in greater detail after you take me to your father.'

To her father. Her father, who was even now concealing Kjartan.

Sela caught her lip between her teeth, tried to think
clearly and not to simply react. Her life was nothing if
she could not hold Kjartan once more in her arms, tell
him once more that she loved him and listen to his sweet
voice asking a thousand different questions. This time,
this time, she would answer without wondering if the
corn had been ground or the fire properly lit. But
without a weapon, she could not make it through the
woods. She would never see him again.

Vikar was her only hope of reaching Kjartan alive.

She had no choice. She would have to take the risk
and pray for a miracle.

'And what will I achieve with that?' She forced her
head high, and placed one hand on her hip. 'There must
be something for me. I refuse to betray him simply
because you ask me to.'

Sela held her breath and waited for his response. He
had to accept her father deserved her loyalty. He had to
be willing to bargain. He could not guess her decision
had already been made.

'That is admirable of you.' Vikar tilted his head to one
side, and his eyes travelled slowly down her form. 'What
has Bose the Dark done to deserve such loyalty? Left you
with a few unworthy warriors while he scuttled out the
back entrance to freedom? Left you to a certain doom?
To rot? To be sold? What did you do to deserve that?'

'He is my father.' Sela planted both feet firmly and
stared back at him. She knew why her father had acted
that way and she did not have to explain it to anyone,
least of all Vikar. Her father had protected Kjartan, and

kept her secret. She knew the effort he must have made. 'That is the only reason I need. What are yours?'

'Peace for your people. A chance to end bloodshed before it was begun.' Vikar put his hands on either side of her neck and his face close to hers. 'I have conquered the hall and it will remain mine—with or without further bloodshed.'

'You raided. You will get what you deserve.' Sela took a step backwards away from him, away from his lips.

'You will be saving your people. You need to think of more than just your own needs, Sela.'

'My needs? You only think of your own.' Sela wet her fear-dried lips. A small beacon of hope grew within her. It was possible that he did not know about Kjartan and that, somehow, she would find a way to keep Kjartan's true parentage a secret. 'And after that? Will you follow through with your threat? Will you force me to be your concubine?'

'I have never had to force a woman.' His eyes became a deep green, lit with a fire from within. 'I never forced you.'

'That is no answer. I want a bargain, Vikar.'

Vikar gave a weary shake of his head. 'What is your price, Sela?'

'My mother left me some land—to the north. After I have delivered you to my father and you have spoken with him, I want to take my family there, to live in peace. After my father has placed his hand on your sword and recognised you as the jaarl, allow us to end our days in peace.'

Sela risked a glance into Vikar's face, but found it was devoid of emotion.

'You ask a high price, Sela.'

'I ask nothing more than my due,' she said and waited as the silence grew.

'After everything that needs to be done is done, we will speak of it,' Vikar said when her nerves began to scream. 'And I will not force you to return to the hall, if you take me to your father. I swear that on my sword.'

Sela rubbed her hand over her mouth. Not the exact answer she wanted, but it was better than nothing. Vikar had a reputation for being honest in his business dealings. She would have to be content with that.

'We have a bargain.'

'And how shall we seal this bargain?' His eyes were on her mouth. A warm pulse coursed through her. 'I have no wish to use force.'

Sela held out a hand. 'As equals.'

His warm fingers curled around hers as she looked up into his eyes, deep-green pools that instantly became hooded.

'As equals…if that is your true desire.'

He let go of her hand and stepped away. A small stab of disappointment shot through her middle. Why had she wanted more? How could she desire more? Why did all the memory of her humiliation flee at the thought of kissing him again?

'My dagger, if you please.' Sela held out her hand again, forced it to remain steady. 'We are friends once again. There is no need for you to keep it.'

'Are we friends, Sela? I need more than pretty words from your lips.' Vikar made a mocking bow. 'I shall keep the dagger…for right now.'

'But I—'

'I know what alliances mean to Bose the Dark's daughter. My previous experience was not—shall we say, without complication. Forgive me if I remain cautious as to your true intent.'

'As you wish.' Sela lowered her eyes and examined the forest floor with its carpet of dead leaves, branches and pine needles. The portents were only death and destruction except for a single green seedling pushing its way through. 'The truce will hold until I reach my father—whoever has possession of my dagger. I remain true to my promises.'

'Do you?' His lip curled. 'How is it that the past holds such different memories for us?'

Sela shivered and wished she had made a better bargain 'We need to go. And, Vikar, only force will ever induce me to return to that hall.'

'But we go on my terms, not yours, Sela, Bose the Dark's daughter. Remember who holds the weapons.' Vikar blocked her way. 'My patience wears thin and I am well versed in your tricks.'

An ice-cold shiver ran down Sela's spine. Her gaze travelled from his firmly planted feet to his broad chest and finally met his unyielding eyes.

'What a pity you made that remark, Vikar.' Sela jammed her thumbs into the waistband of her trousers and struck what she hoped was an unconcerned pose. 'Because I remember how you behaved as well.'

'Do you know where you are going?' Vikar called as Sela lead him around the same grove of birch for the second time. 'Or are you just pretending to know, hoping against hope that I won't discover the truth? The time that you pretended to Asa that you were an expert on the lyre springs to mind. Remember how I had to play the tune for you?'

'I never said that I was an expert! And I had hurt my hand.'

'Hurt your hand deliberately.'

'No, that was your fault. You should not have chased me around the bed and I wouldn't have fallen.'

'You were the one to issue the challenge.' Vikar pushed away the memory of them falling into bed together, her lips giving way under his, her arms pulling him down. 'The fact remains you were incapable of playing to a crowd.'

'I never ever said I could. Asa twisted my words. She made me.'

'You don't like to take the blame for anything.'

'Only for those things I actually do.' Sela stamped away, her backside slightly swaying as the trousers tightened across them. His body reacted instantly to the sight. Vikar frowned. Why should his former wife have this effect on him?

'It can be a bit tricky at this stage, but I have rediscovered the proper way.' She glanced backwards over her shoulder and gave a bright smile, transforming her face. 'I had to be certain.'

'Indeed.'

She had grown into her beauty. Four years ago, she had shown promise, but now there had been a full flowering, an enriching and deepening. Idly he wondered what had caused it, and why she did not use it to try to entice him into making an error. He would have to guard against it, for he had little doubt Sela would escape and leave him stranded in the middle of this forest if she could.

'Sela…I am warning you.'

'It is.' Her lower lip stuck out slightly. Then she laughed, running her hand through her long hair, and Vikar caught a glimpse of the carefree woman who had been his wife, so briefly, the one who sometimes populated his dreams with her musical laugh and quick-fire wit. He had never known what she would do next, from what scrape she would need rescuing, what misdemeanour would have to be explained away. 'I am starting to sound like Kjartan now.'

'Kjartan?' A cold prickling down went his back. Her entire being changed when she said the name.

Her face changed and became guarded. 'A…child I know. He often sounds like that when he is told to do something.'

'How do you know this child?'

'He is just a child around the hall.'

Vikar looked at his former wife as she tugged at her neckline and her eyes refused to settle on anything. A child had escaped with Bose. Whatever this child was to her—she did not want to tell him. But she would. He intended on discovering all her secrets.

'He is how old?'

'A few years at most.' She gave a light laugh and a seemingly unconcerned shrug, but her mouth had become pinched. 'I forget exactly. Sometimes it seems like he was been here forever, and at others no time.'

Vikar regarded her. Was this Kjartan her child? From some unknown lover? A quick stab of jealousy coursed through him. Or was it her brother's? It had to be. Bose would never allow an illegitimate child of his daughter's to live under his roof. He breathed again and wished he

had paid more attention to the news that Sela's brother
and his wife had died. But they had not been close. And
the thought of appearing to want information about his
former wife or her family had pained him.

'Where does your father rest his bones, Sela?'

'There is a hut in the centre of the woods, beside an
outcropping of rocks. My father and I agreed where we
would meet in the event of trouble.'

'But is this the most direct route? I can remember a
trail of flowers you left once, purporting to lead directly
to a bower, but instead the ladies stumbled on Thorkell
and his men in council.'

Her eyes slid away from him as she plucked at the
leg of her ill-fitting trousers. Slowly, imperceptibly, she
shook her head.

'There is a more direct route.' Her voice was nearly in-
audible. 'It is much more dangerous. My nurse told me of
another way, years ago, but I have never dared follow it.'

'Follow it now. I command you.'

'I take no orders from you!'

Vikar caught Sela's arm and then at her sharp in-
halation of breath forced his fingers to let go—one by
one. She stepped away from him and hugged her arms
about her waist. Her blonde hair fell around her face,
and she wore a mulish expression.

'You said—no force. I suppose it was one of your
more easily forgotten promises.'

'The lives of many depend on it,' he said in a quieter
tone. He reached out and touched her arm and this time
she did not move away. 'I need your help, Sela. I am
asking you to forget whatever happened between us in
the past and take me to your father.'

They stared at each other and Vikar willed her to put aside their differences. She had to understand what the consequences were.

'The path divides at the forked rock.' She gave a sort of half-shrug and ran the toe of her boot in the dirt. 'But the most direct route is fraught with danger.'

'Everything you do, Sela, is fraught with danger.' Vikar forced his gaze from the way her breasts moved under her tunic. 'I have never known life with you to be free from peril.'

Sela made an irritated noise. 'Is there any point in having me as a guide if you don't listen to my counsel?''

'What precisely is the danger—wild boar, wolves, bears?'

She hesitated and then whispered, 'Men, men who know no fear. Men who are like no other. Men who fear no death.'

Vikar stopped and instinctively felt for his sword, forced his hand to relax as the trees yielded no sound. 'Then your father's saga holds some substance.'

Sela tilted her head. 'Sagas are for amusement and entertainment, rather than for truth. Surely you know that by now.'

'There is a tale that tells how your father subdued the wild men before he built this hall. He convinced them to work for him, then murdered them. It is their bones that made the foundation that rendered the hall invincible.'

'As you proved earlier, the hall was not invincible.' A nervous smile flitted across Sela's face. 'It is not a tale my father is overly fond of. The skalds have changed it out of all reckoning.'

'Which men worry you if not the wild men from your father's first saga?'

'There were berserkers who worked for my father.' Sela rubbed a hand across her eyes, and her body slumped. 'Eventually the berserkers became more beasts than men. At my mother's request, my father turned them out into the forest. I encountered one in the forest as a girl. My nurse rescued me from him. I suspect that is where the skald got the idea for his tale.'

'Do you know if they still exist?' Vikar regarded Sela. He could not rid himself of the feeling that something else drove her, something she wanted to keep hidden from him. He would discover it in time and then he would exact his retribution for her falsehoods. 'Your mother died before we married. The berserker madness does not last long. Berserkers die once the madness deserts them. Has your father turned anyone out recently?'

Sela shook her head. Her white teeth caught her upper lip and the thought appeared to cheer her.

'You will be right, of course. I had not thought of it in that way. They must be gone, long gone.'

'Then there is no reason not to go the quickest route.' Vikar said. 'Take me the shortest way. Trust my arm to defend you. You trusted me once.'

'To my cost.'

'My arm will not fail you. I promise you that. I will defend you to my last breath.'

Sela nodded and rubbed a hand along the back of her neck, tiredness washing over her. Trust Vikar? How could she when he held the power to destroy her all over again?

His fighting skill was legendary, particularly after the successful raid on Lindisfarne. She knew how he had carved a name for himself out of nothing after his father had lost everything. It was one of the reasons her father had thought that he'd make an admirable son-in-law, that Vikar was like him in many ways. But he had been wrong. Vikar followed his own path. But now it appeared that the only way she would see Kjartan again was to trust Vikar. They would go his way. 'We turn left at the rock and go deeper into the forest.'

Sela turned to her left. Within a few hundred steps, the woods became denser and the bird song vanished. They trudged along in silence as the air turned colder and blacker. Sela matched her footsteps to Vikar's, instinctively seeking the protection his arm might afford.

The gigantic pines and birch blocked out what little light there was.

Here, it did not matter that the sun never set in the sky. Here it was always twilight.

Sela glanced about her. First right and then left, trying to peer through the gloom. The shadows appeared to form into fantastical beasts, only to vanish as she came close. She half-wished that Vikar would make some sarcastic or irreverent remark, so she could concentrate on hating him instead of on the shifting shadows. But the forest appeared to have caught him in its grip as well.

She gasped, and hastily stepped backwards, bumping into Vikar's hard chest. She turned her face into the cloth and allowed his reassuringly masculine scent to surround her. Instantly his arms came around her, held her so close that she heard his heartbeat thumping in her ear. She hated that she felt safe in his arms, that she had no desire to leave. She forced her body to move away from him. Safety was an illusion that she could ill afford.

'What is it, Sela?'

'There!' she said and shuddered. 'I nearly stepped on a skull. A human skull.'

She pointed to where the thing lay. As she turned away, she spied a scrap of cloth—green with a distinctive weave. She winced. The pattern reminded her of a serving maid that she had dismissed two years ago for nearly dropping Kjartan in the fire. Her father had assured her that the maid had gone safely home. Hafdan had seen to it.

'Whoever it was feels no pain now.' Vikar gave a slight nod. 'We can do nothing for them. If they died fighting, no doubt the Valkyries came down and took them up to Valhalla. Otherwise, they are in the ice-cold halls of Hel.'

'But…but…'

'We need to go on, Sela.'

Sela swallowed hard and allowed Vikar to lead her away from the skeleton. After a few steps, he dropped her hand and she followed him, resisting the urge to glance back.

'I simply hope it was not someone connected with the hall.' She searched Vikar's face. 'I am not a cruel person.'

'Nobody ever said you were.' Vikar's stride increased and Sela had to hurry to keep up with him. 'It is impossible to tell where that body is from.'

'I thought I recognised the cloth.' Sela wrapped her arms about her waist. 'You see, I sent one of the serving maids away. My father—'

Vikar held up his hand, stopped suddenly. He turned to face her. 'Sela, you don't know what happened. Who that unfortunate person was. Or when they died. The bones are far too scattered.'

'If you say so...' Sela looked behind her once more but the bones had disappeared. 'I have never liked this forest. My brother used to beg our nurse for tales about *tottr* men and the other fantastical creatures who inhabited the shadowed spaces.'

'Did you believe them?'

'When I was young, I believed many things, but I grew up and learnt the ways of the world.'

'And you are sure they are tales.'

'Yes, I am sure,' Sela said with more conviction than she felt. The tales of the forest had to be that. Simply tales told to frighten children and keep them from wandering too far. Had to be. She had grown beyond the stories told around the fire when the men had had too much ale and mead.

The day she'd discovered she was pregnant, she had put such childish things behind her. She'd decided the baby growing inside her deserved better. Her child would never face the humiliation that she had. Her child would be loved without reservation.

'A truth can be hidden somewhere in the rumour, if one cares to look hard enough.'

'I discovered that as well.' Sela pressed her lips together. She had not wanted to believe the tales about Vikar either, until she had found the evidence, clear, hard evidence that caused all her dreams to vanish. Even then, she had tried to give him a chance, a chance he had declined to take.

She had to remember what he was and what he was capable of. He was not here to keep her safe. He had destroyed her world once, and was about to do so again.

'People, though, will often prefer the tale,' he continued on as if she hadn't spoken.

'Sometimes, it is easier, but I prefer the truth.'

Vikar eyed her speculatively. His green eyes turned cold. 'Do you, Sela? I have often wondered about that.'

Chapter Five

'Are you speaking of four years ago?' Sela asked Vikar, a coldness creeping into her voice. She should have expected him to bring that up.

'You left me because of rumours. There was no proof to your accusations.'

'Your excuses wore thin, as my father never tired of pointing out.'

'The rumours came from one place—your father.'

Sela averted her eyes from Vikar's penetrating green gaze. Was he saying that she *chose* to believe rumours four years ago? Impossible.

There had been no fantastic tale then. She had seen the evidence with her own eyes. She had seen the looks exchanged between Asa and her husband, and had heard the soft laughter behind a locked door, laughter she had recognised. The meetings he had to go to, the dances he had to share. People talked. They laughed at her.

'My father wanted what was best for me. He wanted me to keep my pride.'

'Did he? Or did he want power?'

'He is devoted to the welfare of his family. Always!'

When she had discovered the love token in their bed, her father had understood, offering to spirit her away on the next ship leaving Kaupang. Even then she had tarried, hoping Vikar would come after her, would respond, but he had not. Finally, she had listened to her father. Her child deserved a glittering future. Nothing had happened to change her belief. She wanted Kjartan to become a warrior she could be take pride in.

'What secret are you trying to keep hidden from me? I know that look. You did believe a rumour when you should have known better.'

'No secrets.' Sela forced her mind back to the present, back to the man who stood dangerously close to her, his breath intermingling with hers. 'Our truce holds, Vikar, as we agreed. Believe me. I wish this journey to be over as quickly as possible.'

She glanced up and saw Kjartan, instead of Vikar. Or rather the two merged into one. She quickly focused on the trail as she went over the landmarks in her mind. An outcropping of rock shaped like a sword, a tree hit by Thor's lightning with its dead fingers reaching into the sky. As they passed each one, her breath became easier and her step lighter. She would find the hut this way. She did remember the way.

She had recited the landmarks since she was a child. Her mother had insisted that she and her brother know the way, in case something happened. Una, her nurse, had worked it into a wondrous tale, one that Erik had never grown tired of.

It was an exercise she had repeated with Kjartan at her father's insistence in recent months. There had never been any reason to actually take Kjartan on this route. It was enough that he knew the path through the wild places. She had wondered why her father had wanted to make sure, and had thought it was his illness, making him fretful and fearful. But had he sensed that something might happen as his own strength faded?

Ever since Hafdan had left, she had noticed a marked decline, a slowing. There had been days recently where he had not risen from his bed.

Would he have the strength to make the journey?

Fear clawed at her stomach as the images of a tear-streaked face, and a small body lying under a tree somewhere in the forest, wavered in front of her.

Her hand brushed Kjartan's toy horse and instantly she felt reassured, could breathe again. Kjartan would be there at the hut, waiting for her in the doorway. His little face would light and...

'Just a little way up here,' Sela said, pointing towards the mountain that loomed over them. 'We need to find a stone cairn near the top, and then it is straight on to the hut.'

She abruptly halted as a deep gorge appeared before her. A pebble bounced to the bottom. Her feet skidded forward, half over the cliff face, and she felt herself begin to fall. A half-scream, half-sob emerged from her throat as her arms thrashed about, desperately searching for something to cling on to.

Vikar's hand clamped around her, hauled her body away from the edge. Her curves met his reassuring chest. Another few pebbles fell down the steep embankment.

'Thank you,' she breathed and moved several steps away from the gorge, away from the insidious warmth of his body.

'You should pay closer attention.'

'I had no idea that was there.'

Her heart pounded in her ears and she struggled to take a proper breath. What had nearly happened did not bear thinking about.

'If I didn't know better, I would swear you were trying to get rid of me.' Vikar gave a crooked smile and the dimple in his cheek flashed.

'I certainly can't accuse you of trying to be rid of me this time.' Sela's hand tingled from where his fingers had held her. 'This little mishap was my own.'

'I have never tried to be rid of you.' His eyes narrowed. 'You were the one who left.'

'After you had made it intolerable for me, after you ensured that I could not stay.' The words hung in the air.

'Was I that unkind to you?' Vikar asked softly. 'Did I truly deserve what you did to me?'

Sela hugged her arms about her waist, and found her throat would not work. Her heart pounded in her ears. She knew she should give some witty answer, but none would come. Every particle of her body was aware of him—the way he stood, the breadth of his shoulders, the stubble on his chin making his face more rugged than ever. She had thought when she left him that she'd never be attracted to this man again, but now she knew she had been wrong. The attraction was there, coiled around her insides like a snake, waiting to strike.

'It was a long time ago,' she said into the void. 'Far away from here.'

'And what happens next? Where do we go from here, Sela?'

He made no move to touch her but she was aware of

his hands. Her body craved the comfort of his touch, but the gulf between them was deeper and wider than the chasm before her. She forced her gaze back towards the rocks and white swirling water below. She would never lose her heart again, not in the way she had before. She refused to let him hurt her in that fashion again.

'We will have to go back.' Sela pointed to the other side of the valley. Her heart sank at the thought. Go back through those dead woods, go back. Each footstep taking her further from Kjartan. 'We need to get over there. And this gorge appears to run on for ever in both directions. There is no hope for it. We shall have to return to my original route…if we can find it.'

Vikar made an irritated noise in the back of his throat. 'One of your tricks, Sela? A delaying measure?'

She stared across the gorge for another long moment. Then she deliberately turned her back on the ravine and started back towards the dark woods. The sun still hung in the sky. If they hurried and walked through the grey light that passed for night at this time of the year, they might make her father's hiding place by mid-day. She should never have let Vikar divert her from her chosen path. She should have remembered the consequences. 'We need to return to the route I had originally planned to take.'

'Did you know this was here?' His hand tightened on her arm, forced her to look again at the narrow gorge. 'Why didn't you say? Or did you hope I would go over?'

'I would never seek to injure you,' Sela gasped out and then remembered how she had nearly used the dagger on him earlier. A tide of heat washed through her.

'Wouldn't you?'

'I was the one who nearly broke her neck.' She lifted

Vikar's fingers from her arm—one by one. 'Do you think I would have done that deliberately?'

'If it served your purpose, I would expect you to try. I trust you about as far as I can throw you. You like taking risks, Sela. Just like your father.'

They stood there, glaring at each other. From far below her feet, Sela could hear the distant roar of a river.

'I told you I always take the long way around,' she said holding her palms upwards. A shiver ran down her spine. He had to believe her. In the mood he was in, he was quite capable of leaving her here alone with no weapons. Her brow wrinkled as she tried to concentrate.

'Una would always say that there was a bridge where one had to be sure and pay the *tottr* man who lived under it. My father would laugh and nod. He seemed to think it a great joke. I have never wanted to meet a *tottr* man.'

'A bridge?' Vikar stroked his chin. 'What sort of bridge did this *tottr*…this tiny man live under.'

'There are no such things as little men, Vikar. It is an added detail to make the story more exciting.' She gestured towards the ravine. 'Look around you. Do you see a bridge? We would be better going back. It will take some time, but this little detour was your idea. We had to go the most direct route.'

'And if we could go across the ravine?'

'But we can't.' Sela spread her hands out. She had to make Vikar see reason. If they delayed here, it would take longer to get to Kjartan, longer before her fears could be laid to rest. She fought to keep the panic from her voice. 'There is no bridge and I am fresh out of flying horses—another inhabitant of this forest, according to my nurse. Perhaps there was a bridge once, but it has washed away.'

'Your father rarely does anything without an ulterior motive.' An ironic smile crossed Vikar's face. 'Like you, I learnt my lessons well. The *tottr* men may have served his amusement, but the bridge will be here…if we can find it.'

'What are you saying—that there is a way across this ravine?' Sela peered over the edge at the jagged rocks and swirling white water far below. 'It is possible there was a way once, but I can't see it.'

'It only looks tricky,' Vikar said, swinging himself over the cliff.

'What do you mean? What are you doing, Vikar? Vikar, come back. Don't leave me stranded here.'

Sela got down on her knees and watched as Vikar reached a low ledge where a dead pine stood. He tested it.

'This pine tree reaches to the other side.' Vikar wiped his hands on his trousers. 'Very clever of your father. He has lost none of his skill and cunning. Your bridge awaits, my lady.'

Sela gingerly climbed down to where Vikar stood and looked at the tree. He had to be right. She must have mistaken her nurse's tale.

'And the *tottr* man? I can't believe there are creatures with long noses who guard such a place.'

'Added to keep the unwelcome out,' Vikar said. 'As you can see, he appears to be missing. There is no one here but us.'

'Yes, you must be right.' Sela tried to rid herself of the uneasy feeling that had been creeping up on her. The further they went down this path, the more substance the tales seemed to acquire. But they had to be fantasy. She forced her lips to smile. 'It sounds like my father. He might not believe in such creatures, but there are a good many who do.'

'I know I am right. The little men and other inhabitants of the night will be long gone. We have the wolves and bears to worry about, but not fantastical creatures.' He made a flourishing gesture, more worthy of Asa's court entertainments than the wild woods. 'Ladies first.'

Sela put a foot on the slender trunk and felt it wobble beneath her. The steep drop appeared to grow. A wave of dizziness passed over her. She dropped to her knees and crawled back.

'You go. I'll follow.' She forced a shaky laugh from her throat. 'I would not like to be accused of leaving you on the wrong side.'

'If you insist.' He swung himself out over the branch and quickly went across, hand over hand, rather than walking across as Sela had intended. 'It is simple if you do it this way. There is nothing to fear, Sela.'

'I am not afraid!' she shouted back, aware that her insides trembled. 'I can do anything you can.'

'Prove it. Come across.' Vikar held out his hand. 'Unless you want me to carry you.'

'Never!'

Sela spat on her hands, grabbed the tree trunk and swung her herself out. The rough bark dug into the palms of her hands. The first few feet were easy, then she glanced down.

White foam swirled several hundred yards below her, unforgiving, deadly.

'I am not sure I can do this.'

'Keep going, Sela, you are nearly there.'

Sela felt her fingers begin to slip. She moved her hand, searching for another grip when a piece of bark fell off.

Her body dangled in mid-air. She forgot how to breathe. Kjartan's horse began to slip. Without thinking her hand went to her belt, tucked it more securely. She let out a loud expanse of air, then drew one in. She reached up again, ignoring the sweat that poured down her face. She would do this—for Kjartan.

'Hang on, Sela.' Vikar crouched down and put his hands on the branch, trying to hold the tree steady. 'Keep going forward. Don't think. Act. Refuse to give me the pleasure of getting rid of you, if nothing else.'

'That is what I was planning to do.' She tried for a laugh, but it came out strangled. 'I didn't want to give you the satisfaction.'

'Swing your legs up.'

With her last reserve of strength, she forced her legs upwards and clung on to the trunk with them. Slowly, slowly she made her way across, one hand, one leg, never looking down.

The trunk began to shift under her weight, creaking ominously. Sela froze, screwed her eyes up, prayed some god was listening.

'Vikar!'

Strong fingers gripped her wrist, pulled her the last few feet to safety. Pulled her on top of him as they toppled backwards. Sela heard the steady thump of Vikar's heart under her ear, and felt warm heat rise from his body as his muscles shifted under her. Her whole being was aware of him, wanted to rest there in his arms. She stiffened, rolled off him and on to the cold stone. She tried to regain control of her racing heart and quickened breath.

'You made it.' The note of relief was evident in his voice. His hand touched her face. 'We have crossed it, Sela.'

'I thought…'

The tree gave a slight shudder and fell into the ravine with a resounding crash that blotted out her answer. Sela closed her eyes as her body began to shiver. He draped an arm about her, his body giving her shelter, warmth.

How close had she come?

She forced her body to move away from him. For a long time she sat there, hugging her knees and looking at the mountain that loomed in front of them.

'Don't think. Don't look back. You are here.' Vikar gestured towards the sunlit hill. His face was as eager as Kjartan's when he discovered a bird's nest. 'We made it across. Safe.'

'I am here, and we are going forward. You are right about that. We will get to my father soon.' She gave a trembling smile. 'Thank you, Vikar.'

'My pleasure.'

Sela brought her knees up closer to her chest and rested her cheek against them, watching the shadows on Vikar's face. The sunlight felt warm against her back. She was on the other side and alive. Vikar had saved her. A brambling trilled out its song, bringing her back to the present.

'Una kept the rest of the tale straightforward.' Sela stood up and brushed the twigs and dirt from her trousers. Her fingers instinctively checked that Kjartan's horse was there. It was secure. She heaved a sigh of relief. 'Shall we go? We have spent far too long here, admiring the view.'

'And it is a fine view from where I am sitting.' Vikar said. Sela glanced back and saw that his gaze was firmly fixed on her bottom. He gave a slow, insolent smile. 'Some things need to be appreciated.'

'There are other views I want to see.' Sela turned her flaming face towards the mountain and began to climb, picking her way around the rocks and scrub.

The afternoon sunlight warmed her face. In the distance white mist rose off a pond. The birds began to sing slightly. A peaceful scene of absolute, still beauty.

'You were right—the *tottr* men will be long gone now.' Sela paused and pushed her hair back from her face. 'It was mostly a tale my father told. He delights in scaring people. I used to sit there, listening to him or the skald with big eyes, and then I would find it hard to sleep, my mind was so full of fantastical creatures that live in the woods.'

'You see, your fears were groundless.' Vikar caught up with her. His shoulder brushed hers and sent a wave of awareness through her body. Sela missed a step, and his hands were there to keep her from falling. She jerked her elbow away as if she had been burnt. 'There is no one here. Your father twists words to suit his purposes. He always has.'

'He never did that to me. And he recently insisted K…I should never go into this part of the woods.' Sela gave a small shrug. She had no wish to discuss the merits of her father. She knew what he was like and how much he cared. She did not need to explain it to Vikar, the man who had destroyed everything. 'It was why I was going the long way around. You were right. It is easier to go this way. Silly, childish fears.'

'Why would he do that?' Vikar stopped and stared at her. 'Why would Bose the Dark say something like that? There is more to today than you have told me, Sela. Trust me. I do want to help.'

Trust him. It would be very easy to trust him. That was the problem. She could trust him to defend her and risk his life to save hers. Trust him with everything except the reason why she had to travel quickly. Once she had allowed him to trample her heart into the dust. Never again would she let him do that. She wanted to rebuild her world, but mostly she wanted to see her son.

'We were discussing things…' Sela paused and considered the best way to say it. She had to be careful. She had come too close earlier to revealing Kjartan's existence. Vikar was intelligent. Too many little clues and he would not even need to see Kjartan to know what she had done. How she had cheated. 'It is no crime to discuss such things with my father, surely. I have always discussed everything with him. He gives good counsel. Even Thorkell thought so.'

Vikar's face darkened and became remote. He could never see that her father had good intentions. He had never made the attempt. It was as if they were locked into repeating the mistakes of past, no matter how much she wished it might be different.

She started walking quickly, not caring where she put her feet. The sticks crackled around her and she deliberately stepped on them, making as loud a sound as possible. Childish, but somehow satisfying.

'Hush, Sela.' Vikar put his hand on her shoulder, firmly, drawing her back against his body.

Sela shrugged, trying to get him to let go, but his hand tightened on her shoulder. Every fibre of her being reacted to his touch, longed for it. 'There is no need for me to be quiet.'

'Do as I ask for once, Sela,' he said urgently in her ear. 'We are far from being alone here. Listen to the noises around us.'

Sela froze and ice cascaded down her backbone. Her mouth opened, but Vikar held up his hand, silencing her. A twig crackled only a little way from them. Steady regular sounds. She clamped her lips together. Waiting. Unmoving.

Vikar released her, bent down, examining the ground. Suddenly, he relaxed and the air came out of his lungs with a great whoosh.

'Whatever it was, it has passed us by.'

'An animal? Or maybe a raven?' Sela tilted her head to one side as the knots in her stomach grew. 'The woods are full of wild boar. They can make funny sounds. Two mornings ago, I and…that is, I saw a family of them— three little black-and-yellow striped piglets with their mother down near the fjord.'

Sela allowed her voice trail, knew she was babbling and hoping the words would calm her.

'I hope, but the movements were not random.' Vikar stayed where he was, his hand brushing the dirt. 'Perhaps whatever it was decided to find an easier prey.'

'That is not a comforting thought.' Sela resisted the urge to clasp his hand like a young child, frightened of being left alone.

'It was not meant to be.'

Sela swallowed hard as all of her father's tales crowded around her. Surely they had been tales told to amuse. The berserkers had to have died years ago. And there was no such thing as *tottr* men or trolls. Never had been. Her father had assured her of that once, when she had wakened, crying inconsolably from a dream. But something was here in these woods. She could feel it. Did her father know it was there, just as he seemed to know everything in the hall? Did he seek to give her easy reassurance, rather than the truth? She wrinkled her nose, hating the disloyal thought.

'What do you want me to do?' she whispered, crouching down next to Vikar. His tunic had gaped open at the neck and revealed the strong column of his throat. Everything about Vikar exuded strength and capability. He would get her out of here alive…if he could.

'Nothing.' Vikar stood up and started off. 'Come on. Let us find that cairn of stones. We shall know soon enough if they intend to intercept us or merely keep watch.'

'They?' Sela put her hand to her throat as her insides began to quiver. 'There is more than one?'

'Yes, and they are on the move.'

Vikar stiffened again. This time, there was a hiss as he withdrew his sword and held it in front of them. The brightness of the blade gleamed silver in the pale light.

'I don't hear anything.'

'Listen carefully, and you will hear two distinct footfalls. Maybe more. They are coming towards us again.'

Sela cocked her head, and the very slight rustling sounded again, moving off to their right, only to be answered by another rustling from the left. 'How long have we been tracked?'

'Not long.' Vikar put an arm about her. Where a few hours ago she would have resented it, now she welcomed the security it offered. She leant in, listened to the sound of his breathing rather than to the sound of the forest. 'Which way do we need to go?'

Sela pointed towards the peak just beyond the clearing. 'We go up the mountain. Find the stone cairn. The hut is by a stream and clearly visible from the cairn.'

'We go now. Side by side. Keep on your guard. Be ready at my signal to move swiftly, but do not run.' Vikar's brows went together to form a straight line. His shoulders appeared to grow and he started forward with a determined step.

Sela gave one more glance behind her, but the wood was silent. 'Are you sure?'

'Keep pace with me, slowly and steadily.' Vikar put an arm about Sela's shoulders, and, rather than shrug it off, she moved closer. 'We have to see what they do. They may let us pass.'

'Do you know what they are?' she whispered.

'Yes,' came the grim reply. 'They are men…of a sort.'

'How can you tell?'

'See in the bush to your right. Do you believe in your nurse's tales now?'

Sela turned her head, stifled a scream. A man's blue eyes peered out at her. Or a face that could have belonged to a man once. The matted hair and scraggily beard made him resemble a bear more than anything. One of the *tottr* men.

Not a legend then.

But the sort of creature who belonged to the night time. Something from her most unpleasant dreams.

The man creature emerged from the undergrowth with a roar, waving a staff. Two more joined him. There was a lean and hungry look about them. They moved with a shambling sort of gait, more bear-like than man. But their features were odd, twisted, making their noses appear long. And their shape was different. The skins they wore made it appear as if they might have tails.

Vikar lowered his sword and started back cautiously away from them. 'We mean you no harm.'

'Vikar, what is happening?' Sela glanced from him to the men. Vikar's hand tugged at her, pulling her back into the circle of his arm. 'Are these berserkers?'

'These are no berserkers. Nor are they creatures of myth. They are a different tribe of man. See their long noses and short stature. I have seen a similar sort in the far north where they tend their reindeer. They have little to do with the men of Viken. But they are men.'

'My father did have to fight for this land. I know that. It is possible that he did not manage to subdue everyone.'

'More than possible.'

She hesitated as the wild man tilted his head and stared at them with a quizzical expression on his face. No illusion or campfire vision, but a real breathing being. She screwed up her eyes and tried to remember her father's tales of how they could be tamed. 'But I thought *tottr* men were one of Una's tales.'

'Not trolls, but men, men who refused to be subdued.'

'My father used to laugh and ask what nonsense my nurse had frightened my brother and me with that evening.'

'Your father likes to twist the truth to suit his purposes. Always has.'

The *tottr* man gave a loud grunt that echoed in the clearing.

'There has to be a way around them.' Sela glanced back towards where they had been. The trees appeared to closed in around them. 'We will not be able to cross over that ravine again.'

'We are travelling through. We wish to go that way.' Each word was said clearly and without hesitation. Vikar gestured towards where they needed to go.

Sela forced air through her lungs as the men stared back at them. She had to do something. She had no weapons, no way to fight back if they charged. Equally she refused to stand here and be slaughtered because Vikar mismanaged the situation.

'Over there, we want to go over there.' Sela pointed towards the mountain. 'Give us leave to pass. My father is Bose the Dark.'

The men gave a guttural shout at her father's name and raised their staffs. The other two appeared to become more agitated. Sela put her hand to her throat, and hid her face in Vikar's shoulders as the roaring filled her senses.

'I do the talking, Sela,' Vikar rumbled in her ear. 'Keep quiet and we may get out of here alive.'

'Thank you,' she breathed.

'We mean you no harm—my woman and I. We go. We leave you in peace.'

The lead man gave a nod, turned to his companions. They drew together and stood with their staffs raised. Vikar took a step backwards.

'You're retreating?' Sela asked, keeping step with Vikar.

'Three against one are poor odds even for me, Sela,' Vikar said out of the side of his mouth. 'Go backwards. Keep your face towards them. Never look away. And we may reach your father in one piece.'

'What are you going to do? Your plan isn't working.' Sela half-stumbled over a rock. 'They are starting to advance.'

'They are not trying to attack us.' Vikar nodded to where the naked swords gleamed in their belts. 'They want us to leave.'

The three wildmen shook their staffs a final time. The stench of them filled her nostrils, making her choke.

'But they are coming closer.' Sela put her hand to her throat.

'If they had wanted to attack, they would have done so before now.' Vikar's mouth was a thin, white line. 'I have to choose our ground, make sure we have a chance of defending it if need be.'

'You are right. Shall we run?'

'No, they will see us as prey then. We want to go slowly and hope the wind doesn't change.'

'The wind?'

'They have not caught our scent. They are uncertain what we are.'

'And if they catch our scent?' Sela found it nearly impossible to speak around the lump that was forming in her throat.

Her father had assured her that these men were legends to keep out intruders, that they were not real. She had sent Kjartan in to the forest many times with Una, allowed him to play with the minimum of protection because she had been sure. The ground beneath her feet appeared to tilt sideways.

Her father had been less than truthful. He had lied. And if he had lied about this little thing, what else?

She tightened her hand around Kjartan's horse and attempted to concentrate on Vikar and the *tottr* men. He put his finger to his lips.

'Vikar? What happens now?' Her voice was high and thin and entirely unlike her own. 'What do you think they will do?'

Vikar's face became grim, frozen. He fingered the hilt of his sword and stared back at the unmoving trio of wild men.

'You do not want to know.'

'Gift.' The guttural sound came from the lead wild man as he held out his hand.

The word hung in the air. Sela stared at the wild man and then at Vikar.

Gift? She knew gifts were traditionally exchanged between Viken and other men of the north when they met, but between Viken and wild men?

How much had her father kept from her? What else had he lied to her about?

She dismissed it as a disloyal thought, but it was there lurking at the back of her mind.

'He wants something,' she whispered. 'We have to give him something.'

'He is not getting the weapons.' Vikar's lips were a firm white line. 'If it comes to it, I will fight.'

'I make no comment.'

'I will not have us defenceless.'

'And I refuse to stand here and give them a reason to

slaughter us. My nurse always said that *tottr* men want payment. If we went into the forest, we always had to take something to pay them. A game of hers. One that I outgrew. Maybe she was remembering something my father had said to my mother.' Sela looked down at her bare hands. Trying to think, she could not wrestle the dagger from Vikar. And he was right—they could not surrender their weapons. 'I have nothing to give. All my rings are back at the hall. I took them off before I went into battle.'

Vikar raised his eyebrow. 'You would.'

'Gift.' The other wild men took up the chant.

'They will attack us.' Sela fought to keep the rising panic from her voice.

'I am prepared for that.' Vikar's hand went to his sword and his eyes became determined. 'There is a chance you might survive, Sela. They will attack me first.'

Chapter Six

Sela cast her eyes towards the blue sky. They were going to die. The little men, the men whose fathers and grandfathers must have fought her father would see to that. They had nothing to give. She would never see Kjartan, never be able to give him the wooden horse. The wooden horse. Two nights ago, Kjartan had said that he no longer feared the *tottr* men because he could always give them…

'I do have something.' Sela pulled the horse from her belt with trembling fingers and stared at the small figure in her palm. She tried to speak, felt her voice break, swallowed hard and tried again. 'It belongs to Kjartan. He dropped it and I wanted to return it. He loves his wooden horses. I am sure he would want to give it to the wild men. It is a trinket, but it might be enough to let us pass.'

Vikar turned the little, carved horse over in his palm. His fingers curled around it. Her vision blurred. Vikar was holding the small horse gently between his fingers, never knowing it belonged to his son.

She looked away, surprised at the surge of feeling

washing over her. She blinked rapidly, and regained control.

'They might accept this sort of gift.' Vikar turned the horse over. 'A totem can have powerful magic for some.'

'It has to work.' She gave the horse one last lingering touch.

'Stay behind me, Sela. Be ready to move quickly, but steadily after I place the gift down.'

Sela pressed her lips together holding her instinctive protest that she should be the one doing the giving. But she knew the logic. The wild men would expect Vikar to be in charge. If they accepted the gift from him, they might release them.

'Kjartan will be thrilled when I tell him. He always likes it when his ideas work. His eyes shine like…' She clamped her mouth shut as a shiver passed over her.

'It is an interesting gift, a worthy gift.' Vikar took another look at the horse before tucking it into his belt. 'But this will be better.'

Sela caught her lip between her teeth as Vikar advanced and slowly put his cloak down on the ground, then backed away. The wild men crowded around the cloak, ignoring them. One picked it up. Another shoved him.

'We go now.' Vikar gripped her elbow with his fingers. 'Quietly and without fuss.'

Sela nodded. Keeping her eyes on where the *tottr* men argued over the cloak, she slowly backed out of the clearing.

Once they were away, Vikar quickened the pace to a jog. Twice Sela thought they were being followed, but then it was silent.

They came to a sheer drop. Sela fought the temptation to tear her hair. Mountainous country had its cliffs, but the *tottr* men were behind them, waiting.

'No bridge here.' She took a deep breath. 'We are trapped, Vikar. They are waiting for us back there.'

'If we go up there a little ways, it looks wide enough to leap across.'

'Are you touched in the head?' Sela stared at him. 'I can't jump that far. My legs are too tired.'

'You never know until you try.' Vikar walked briskly up to the spot. 'You see, Sela. It isn't far.'

Sela measured the distance with her hands. She did not want to think about her near fall from the tree earlier. Vikar was right. It was quite narrow. It only looked big. She might be able to do it.

She took several steps forward, brought her arms up, stopped. Her mouth went dry as the crags rose up. It was too wide. She'd never make it. It was all too easy to imagine her broken body at the bottom. She looked back at the woods and thought she saw shapes moving. There was no possibility of going back that way.

'Trust me, Sela.' Vikar held up his hand. A wicked smile flashed across his face. 'I could always toss you. My aim is true.'

'I am perfectly capable of making it on my own.' She did not want to think about Vikar's hands on her waist, holding her.

Sela filled her lungs with air, ran and leapt. Her ankles hurt as she landed on hard, brown dirt. Boulders of granite rose around her, making it seem like there was a passage up the mountain.

'Nothing to it!' she called across to Vikar.

'That's my girl! I told you that you could do it.'

He took one backward glance, then leapt, landing beside her. He put his hands out to steady himself, held on to her. She reached up and wiped a smudge of dirt from his nose. He gave a half-smile and his eyes held a flame of warmth.

'Just in time,' she said, smiling up at him. Her tongue flicked over her lips as she waited for him to lower his mouth.

'I do like to make an entrance.' Vikar's hands fell away and the air rushed around them. 'You can't say that you are lacking in courage.'

She regarded the baked earth beneath her feet, hating the sense of disappointment that swamped her. He had ignored Sela's invitation, as he used to do. Stupid, stupid her for wanting him to kiss her. 'I shall consider that as a compliment.'

'It was meant as one.' Vikar gestured towards the hills. 'We need to go before they figure out how easy that ravine is to jump.'

'Do you think they can?' Sela bit her lip to keep from screaming, looked up into to Vikar's face and hoped to find comfort. There was none.

'I don't want to find out.'

There was a sound of crashing behind them and the wild men emerged from the forest. They raised their staffs, threw back their heads and howled. Then started to move forward.

'Come on, Sela, think. Is there anything the *tottr* men don't like? Anywhere they don't go?'

'They don't like heights, according to Una. You always need to keep to the high passages, beyond the tree line.'

'I have no wish to discover if this is another embroidery or the truth, but I will take your nurse's advice. We go up.'

She paid no attention to where they went. Vikar doubled back and around, finally leading them up a steep slope to a small ridge. Below her feet, the wooded valley spread out, the blue ribbon of the river just visible in the middle. At last, Vikar stopped, beside a small outcropping of rock.

'I don't think the wild men have pursued us. We can rest here.'

Sela wiped a hand across her brow and caught her breath. Her limbs started trembling and then her legs gave way. She sank to the ground and put her head in her hands. She refused to think about what might have happened to her, if Vikar had not been there. They were lucky to be alive and breathing. She had to concentrate on that, not on what could have been.

'Why didn't they attack us back there?'

'We gave them a gift. As you said, your nurse might have overheard your father speaking about the wild men. Who knows, but I thank Odin and Thor, it worked.' Vikar held out the wooden horse. 'You may have this back.'

Sela felt the sudden prick of tears behind her eyes as she tried not to snatch it from him. Vikar was much easier to hate when he was not being kind. She gathered the horse to her chest and then hastily tucked into her belt, and felt the strength of Vikar's gaze on the back of her neck. She knew he must have guessed something.

'It was…nothing. Only a plaything. Kjartan will have soon forgotten it.' Sela hesitated. How could she explain what that horse meant to her without telling him its true significance? She was tempted. He had saved her life, but to tell him the truth would mean losing a part of her. She was not ready to do that. Not now. Not ever. 'You need not have given your cloak for it.'

'I thought the men would argue over that more. That horse might mean something to you. I know what it is like to be a small boy who has lost his playthings, who has had them ripped away.'

'Was that boy you?' Sela whispered.

'It was a long time ago. I recovered.' Vikar gave a slight shrug and the look on his face indicated that further questions would go unanswered. He shielded his eyes with his hand and looked upwards. 'Besides, it is high summer. I will get another cloak before winter.'

'I thought we were dead, that I would never see… never see my father. I owe you my life.'

She ran her hands through her hair and refused to give way to tears. She had survived. She would find Kjartan. The gods would be kind.

'I told you that I would protect you.' Vikar frowned and leant forward. His fingers touched her cheek. 'And I will do everything in my power to keep you safe. I will keep my side of the bargain. Believe that, if nothing else about me.'

'And what if your ploy had failed…I had no weapon, no way of defending myself, of *aiding* you. I need something. Surely you must see the sense in that.' She eyed her dagger that was stuck in Vikar's belt. She no longer wanted to use it on him, but she did want to be able to use it in a fight. She waited with her hand out for Vikar to hand it over.

'It did not come down to that.' Vikar gave a sudden smile, ignoring the hint.

'And what do we do next?' Sela forced her fingers to curl and brought her hand to her side. He asked her to trust him, but he had shown how little he trusted her.

'Neither of us was injured, and neither of us tried to run. We behaved properly.' Vikar stuck his thumbs in his sword belt, and looked back down the slope. 'They do not seem to have followed. We are safe here for now. We rest and then we go on. It has been a far more eventful day than I thought it would be.'

'Rest and tomorrow will be different, as my mother used to say,' Sela whispered. Her body began to shake and her teeth chattered despite the heat of the early evening. Suddenly all the terror, everything she had experienced that day, swirled around her. She stared at the rock ahead of her and knew her body could not go much farther.

'These tales your nurse told are simply that—tales. She used half-heard truths to create fantasies. That does not mean everything is true.' Vikar settled himself down beside her. 'Sometimes, the stories say when berserkers drink a certain potion, they become invincible. But the tales are wrong. They can be killed like any other man, if the warrior has enough skill.'

'Wasn't there a berserker who went to Lindisfarne?' she asked to take her mind away from what could have been. 'Is that why you know about their ways and the ways of the wild men?'

'Yes.' Vikar turned away from her. 'But many years before that, when I was a small boy, one killed my father. I have been wary of them ever since. I have taken care to learn all I can about them. I believe in knowing my enemies, finding out about their weaknesses.'

'And what have you found out?'

'They are fearless and will attack anyone when the blood madness is upon them. It is only the very lucky and skilful who survive. My father never learnt that lesson.'

Sela held her body still and concentrated on not breathing as she silently willed Vikar to say more.

This was the first time Vikar had spoken of his family. She knew his father had died before they married, but he had never told her about the exact circumstances. He had always changed the subject. There was no saga to his father that she knew of, no way for her to quietly learn about the family. Nothing but a great wall of silence. She had heard rumours, but had waited for him to tell her.

He never had, until now. Had something changed between them? Sela felt a trembling inside her. She wanted to find out, but she also did not want to destroy this fragile thing between them.

'I had no idea about your father's death.' Her finger touched the mane of the wooden horse. Kjartan hungered for stories of his warrior father, stories she had invented, choosing to make his father the best of Viken warriors. 'I know very little about your family.'

Vikar lifted his eyebrow. 'I thought you knew. The berserker took everything. I swore vengeance and eventually I settled the account. It is partly why your father considered me a worthy son-in-law despite my lack of lands.'

'And does your father have a saga? Is it one I would have heard?'

'It was always something I was going to do, but it seemed more important to put food on the table, and to regain the lands my father lost, than to pay second-rate skalds to sing. Some day…when I have children.' He put his hands behind his head and leant back. His long legs stretched out in front of him. 'It shall have to be at the start of my saga. That would be the way to do it. My children will want to hear of their grandfather and his exploits. I shall make sure they do.'

Sela wrapped her hands about her knees as guilt washed over her. Had she misjudged him all those years ago? She had to distract Vikar. The subject was far too dangerous. 'We can't go the way I had planned. It is too unpredictable. We shall have to find the cairn another way.'

'There is always another way.'

Sela looked out at the mist-filled scene. The half-light of the northern night was setting in. Although it would not get completely dark, it would be grey for a few hours. 'I think when the sun comes out again, we should try to find the landmarks. Go forwards, rather than trying to go back to the hall.'

'Did I suggest that?' Vikar asked quietly.

'I thought you might want that.'

'I want to find your father, Sela. He must surrender. It will be done properly.'

'And you will not force me to return.'

'I have kept this bargain so far.' Vikar's eyes deepened to dark-green pools. 'No force will be used, Sela.'

'We agreed to meet at the hut.' Sela shielded her eyes. 'I would say even with the detour we have had to make that it will take no more than a half-day, provided I can find the landmarks.'

'We rest here until the sun rises.'

'But my father…' Sela allowed her voice to trail off.

'Your father will wait for you. Any parent would.' Vikar squeezed her hand.

'How did you guess that I was worried about that?'

'You made no mention of stopping and you did not sleep when you were in his counting room, despite me providing you with a fur.'

'You wanted me to sleep?'

'I thought you might wait until the hall was quiet, but I was wrong.'

'I had to go. I had to escape.' Sela spoke to her knees. 'You need to understand that I want to reach him as quickly as you do. He has not been well…'

Sela found it impossible to voice her fear.

'He will wait, Sela. And he will have made it to the hut. He and the rest of the group he was with—the nurse and the child… Kjartan.'

'I hope you are right.' A lump formed in her throat and she found it difficult to speak. It was easy to hate Vikar when he was being autocratic, but when he was like this, he reminded her of the happy times when they were first married, when they used to play *tafl* together, or Vikar would play the lyre and she'd sing. He had started to teach her. She had been so proud of the tune he had composed for her. The memories she had carefully locked away were now threatening to spill out. 'By Frejya's necklace, I do hope you are right.'

'Your father is a survivor and he is used to the ways of the forest. Unlike you, he knew that the *tottr* men existed and that they have reason to despise every breath he takes.'

Sela closed her eyes as relief flooded over her. She wished she could confide her fears, but there was far too much between them. She pressed her fingertips into her eyes and tried to concentrate. 'Thank you.'

'You are exhausted.' His hand lifted a strand of hair

from her forehead, a little touch, but one that sent shivers down her spine. 'We go no further without sleep.'

'I will be fine.' Sela forced her eyes open, tried to focus in the growing gloom. 'We should go. We both have reasons for wanting to get this journey finished. The cairn should be easy to spot.'

'No, we stay here and rest. It is safe. Now is not the time to be walking half-asleep. We both need our wits about us.' Vikar shielded his eyes. 'How long have you been awake, Sela?'

'Does it matter?' Sela gave a careful shrug.

The narrow bed piled high with furs and pillows in her private room seemed a distant dream. How long had it been since Kjartan had awakened her by leaping on her and demanding a cuddle?

Had she known how long today would have been, she would have stayed longer, enjoyed his embrace, rather than insisting that they get up and start the day. Of the thousand jobs that had appeared so important when her eyes last opened, she found it difficult to think of a single one that had been of use to her.

She gave her mind a shake, forced her legs to stand. They refused and she sank back down as a further wave of tiredness washed over her.

'I have been awake too long.' Sela rested her cheek on her knees, longed to close her eyes. 'We can sit here a little while longer and then go. There is no need to sleep.'

'You are a danger to yourself. Everyone needs to sleep.'

'I can keep going. You have not had any sleep either.'

'This is not an endurance test. Trained warriors are different from exhausted women.' Vikar settled himself next to her, pulled her head against his body. Sela sat bolt upright. 'You need not worry. I have no desire to take advantage of you.'

Sela examined her trouser leg. She must look dreadful. 'You know how to make a woman feel special.'

He gave a sudden smile and a stretch, one where his arm went over her shoulders and pulled her close. 'I do my best.'

'And after we rest?' Sela's eyes were fluttering. She had difficulty concentrating on anything but the great enveloping darkness.

'We find Kjartan, the child you are desperate to see. The child whose toy you carry.'

'How did you know about Kjartan?' Sela tried desperately to hold the tiredness back. It seemed every nerve in her body demanded sleep.

'It is who you want to see, isn't it?' Vikar's voice was soft, lulling, almost crooning. His breath fanned her temple. 'You were willing to brave the tunnel for him and now the realm of the wild men without any respite. I think you would not do that simply for your father's sake.'

'I want to find them both,' Sela mumbled, regarding her hands. 'My father and Kjartan.'

'And the woman. Who was the woman?'

Sela swallowed hard. The tiredness swept over her, making it difficult to concentrate. She had to be very careful or she would get it wrong, but her body wanted to sleep.

'Una,' she mumbled at last. 'My old nurse, the one who told me the tales about the *tottr* men. I needed Thorgerd to watch over the women and the children. My father insisted on Una staying with him.'

'I had wondered.' Vikar leant back against the rock. His eyelids half-closed. 'I had wondered.'

Sela knew she should question him, demand how he knew a woman had escaped with her father, but the tiredness opened its embrace and held her.

'Time to move, Sela,' Vikar said, looking down at the sleeping woman as the faint streaks of rose touched the eastern sky.

Her long lashes made smudges on her cheeks. Some time in the night she had nestled closer to him, and her head had come to rest in the hollow of his shoulder. It felt right there, somehow. He watched the steady rise and fall of her breasts, then wrenched his gaze away.

He tried to tell himself that she was a woman like any other, but he knew that for a lie.

'You need to wake Sela.'

She waved a hand, a bit like a cat's paw, mumbling something about Kjartan and moving towards the hollow he had just vacated. Her lips curved into a secret smile.

'A little more time, Kjartan, and then we play.'

Vikar found it impossible to rid himself of the feeling that Kjartan was her child.

Her nose twitched as she sleepily pushed a strand of hair from her face and her lips curved into a secret smile as she murmured something indistinct.

Had she found happiness with some other man?

If that was true, the child should be with his father. It was possible the father was dead, or of low birth, but Vikar knew how well Bose guarded his daughter. A muscle jumped in his cheek—how well he had guarded his daughter? He certainly had not attempted to protect her yesterday morning.

Was this the reason he had not protected her? Was he ashamed of the liaison—but then why take the child with him?

He did not believe that the child belonged to Bose. Sela would have said 'my brother', rather than having her eyes slide away from him every time he mentioned the subject.

The child could belong to her elder brother. It would explain many things. And was the most probable explanation. But he could not rid his mind of the feeling that the bond between Kjartan and Sela was deep.

A mystery to be solved, but he had learnt patience in their time apart.

'I will discover your secrets, Sela. One by one. You can depend on that, but I would rather you told them to me willingly.'

Sela wrinkled her nose and mumbled in her sleep. Reached towards him, smiled a smile of such loveliness that he forgot how to breath, forgot that he disliked this woman. Then he remembered.

He shook her. This time more roughly. Her eyes flew open.

'It's you.' She drew her eyebrows together. 'I had hoped that yesterday was a bad dream.'

'No dream. No vanishing in the morning light. We need to find your father today.' Vikar stood with his back towards her and looked out over the mist rising in the valley. 'My men deserve answers.'

She locked her hands about her knees and her gaze went out over the mist-cloaked hills and valleys below them. Her voice when she spoke was small and thin, vulnerable. 'I am not entirely sure where we are. We need to find the cairn on the mountain, but which mountain? There are a dozen peaks I can see from here.'

'You know your father's lands. You must know the way.'

'I do, and I will find the mountain…eventually. It may take some time. It has a hook-nose shape on its peak.' She glanced up at him from under her eyelashes. 'You must understand that I have always kept away from this place. My father protected me.'

Vikar clenched his fist as he regarded the peaks that stretched out before them. 'Your father should have protected you yesterday. It was his duty to protect his daughter.'

'I've told you before, that was my choice.' Sela stood up and brushed bracken from her clothes. 'Why do men prefer trousers?'

Vikar regarded Sela's profile. The early morning sun had turned her hair a deep-honey colour and her lips were strawberry, but her eyes were turned resolutely from him.

The change of subject was a deliberate ploy, one she had used often when they were married, when she wanted to hide something from him. Why didn't she want him to know the true reason? What was she ashamed about?

When they were married, Sela had always defended her father. It had been part of their problem. She had always wanted to believe her father and his followers over Vikar. For now, he'd allow her to change the subject, but he fully intended to discover the truth and to make her see what her father had done was wrong.

But such things were for later. Maybe for never.

First, he had to gain Sela's trust, discover the solution to the mystery before it destroyed them both. Destroyed his men.

'Why have you developed a sudden dislike of trousers?' He allowed his gaze to roam over her curves, noticed how they made her look utterly feminine, utterly desirable. He shifted slightly, and tried not to think about how long it had been since he had sported with a woman. But he knew it was more than that. Sela was not just another warm body. She was temptation personified. He ran his finger around the neckline of his shirt. 'I would have thought them easier to move in.'

Their gazes met and held. He was surprised at how blue her eyes looked this morning. He had forgotten what she looked like after sleep, her blonde hair spilling over the pillow, wrapping around them both. He looked away.

'Well, are they? Easier to move in?'

'Perhaps, but when I wear my apron-dress, I have a belt with all my necessities—combs, keys and the like.' She ran a hand through her hair and took a step backwards from him, breaking the spell. 'It will be a rat's nest by the time I get near one again.'

Vikar reached into the pouch that hung from his belt. A simple request, but one that would keep him from remembering her long limbs. 'A comb and some bread. As my lady requires and requests.'

Sela delicately took the bread and comb from him, being careful not to touch his hand.

His lady? She was anything but… And yet, the thought failed to be as repugnant as she would have sworn it should be. She forced herself to remember how

many other ladies there must have been since she'd left.
How many there would be. He had trampled on her
heart once.

'Thank you.'

'For a woman who slept in my arms last night, you
seem remarkably shy.'

A faint heat rose on her cheeks. All too clearly she
remembered the other times she had slept in his arms.
How he had woken her with a kiss on the morning after
their wedding, and it had turned to all-encompassing
passion. How she had once wanted to spend her whole
life in those arms. How she had sought his kiss, and
woken to find a cold pillow and Vikar looking out of the
window. How it had been the start of the end when he
had declined to answer her question.

'I trust you were not uncomfortable with an exhausted woman lying against you.' She managed a
smile, confident that she had put such things back in the
past where they belonged.

'I managed.' Vikar gave a shrug. 'The rock provided
support.'

Sela forced the comb through her hair. She hated the
way her locks always seemed to be tangled in the
morning and wished she had taken the time to plait it
before she'd gone to sleep.

'If we keep to this ridge, we should be able to spot
the stone cairn you are looking for. It should be visible
from a long way away.' Vikar pointed towards the river.
'The hut is in the east.'

'Yes...' Sela replied cautiously. The way Vikar said
it made it seem as though everything would be easy. She
wanted to believe that she would be reunited with

Kjartan today or she would give way to despair, sink down to the ground and never get up.

'We ran towards the south. If we go north-east for a while, we should be able to find this hut of yours.'

'As long as we are away from the valley of the wild men, we should be safe.' Sela concentrated on teasing out a knot from her hair. 'After Una had thoroughly scared me once, my mother came in the night, held me and told me that the *tottr* men never left their valley, that my father had seen to it.'

'I sincerely hope your mother was correct. She sounds like a formidable woman. I am sorry she died before we could meet.'

Sela finished smoothing her hair. She loosely tied her hair back. Thankfully out here there was no need for the elaborate hairstyles of the Viken court. Somehow using Vikar's comb seemed very intimate. 'I have finished with it now.'

'It was my pleasure.'

He ran his hand through his own hair. His shirt gaped slightly open and Sela caught a glimpse of his naked flesh, realised she was staring, watching his chest rise and fall with every breath he took. In the night, she had lain there, and it was as if she had come home. Safe and secure.

'We ought to go.' Sela forced her gaze away, aware that her cheeks were burning.

'I agree.' Vikar continued to stand there, watching her with a deep-green flame flickering again in his eyes.

Sela began to climb the rocky ridge away from the hollow where they had slept, away from his body. 'I am sure we will find the landmarks before the day is out.'

'It will not be too difficult. The view from here is magnificent. The contours are intriguing.'

Sela glanced back and saw his gaze was pointedly not on the valley with its meandering river, but on her backside. She gave her head a shake. She had to remember what Vikar was like, and how he liked all women. Charm came as naturally to him as breathing. She had seen the way the women at court fawned over him. He had laughed at her for taking notice.

Unlike yesterday, the silences were more companionable. It was as if they were more comfortable with each other.

'Are those the marks of the wild men?' Sela asked, pointing to a few gashes in a pine tree. 'Have we strayed back into their territory?'

Vikar went forward and examined the gashes. 'No, they are too irregular. They will have been made by a bear.'

'I see.' Sela shifted uneasily. Bears at this time of the year should not pose any danger unless they thought their cubs were threatened. It was only in the spring when they first woke from their long slumber that they were in a terrible temper. They were safe. Vikar would protect her. He had promised. She believed him. Now.

'Here.' Vikar withdrew the dagger he had taken from her earlier. 'Take this.'

'Why are you giving me this?' Sela stared at the blade.

'I hardly think you are going to put it in my back, after what we have suffered.' A half-smile crossed his face. 'It could come in handy. Never refuse a gift, Sela. You don't know when it might be offered again.'

'You did not trust me before.'

'That was yesterday.'

Sela took the blade and tucked it into her belt next to the horse. First the toy, and now the dagger. Little things, but important. A hard lump formed in her throat. Unless she was cautious, she'd be in danger of forgetting why she hated Vikar so much. She had hated him for so long that it was like something she constantly carried with her, something that was always in the background, forcing her to keep going. But now when she tried to find the hatred again, it had disappeared.

But what replaced it?

Sela bit her lip. She had no desire to return to the lovesick woman she had been in Kaupang. Then, she'd thought the world revolved around his smile. And he'd betrayed her with a kiss.

'Sela?'

The sound of his voice brought her back to now— the sun shining on her face, the birds circling in the air, the mountain with its boulders. Real things.

'Yes, it was yesterday, Vikar. Today is a new day.'

She smoothed her hair behind her ears and tried to ignore the questions in his eyes. He had trusted her with this small gesture, but she was not ready to trust him with her secret. To do so would be to ruin her life. There was a small chance that she could keep Kjartan with her. She was not ready to give him up yet.

'We need to move. I suspect it will be a long walk before we are through.'

'I expect you are right.' She answered his smile with one of her own. 'But we will find my father, and I will make him listen to you. It is the least I can do after you saved me from the *tottr* men.'

His shoulders relaxed. It was as if some crisis had passed.

'And, Sela, we were friends once. I would like to think we could be again.'

Friends. Yes, they had been friends in a way.

If she had been content with friendship, perhaps everything would have been all right in their marriage, but she had wanted more. She had wanted him to have the same desire for her as she'd had for him. She had forgotten the rules.

This time, she would not make the same mistake.

'We are far from being enemies, Vikar.'

Chapter Seven

The shadows had lengthened and the sky had turned a hazy blue by the time the hut came into view. Small and wooden, it was nestled in the shadow of the mountain, a sight she had almost given up hope of ever seeing. A lump rose in her throat. Kjartan. Her father. Safety.

She began to run, covering the ground between her and the hut as quickly as she could. It no longer mattered that Vikar was close by her, that he might guess Kjartan's parentage. The only thing she wanted to do was to hold Kjartan in her arms. Tight. Never let him go.

An arm's length before she reached the door, Sela halted her headlong race, uncertain.

It was too quiet. Too still.

She glanced towards where Vikar stood, glowering, hand on his sword, then back to the door. Her brow wrinkled and that well of hope within her was replaced by a great gnawing fear. She shook her head, tried to clear the buzzing from it, attempted to take a steadying breath. Kjartan would be here.

'Sela, wait!' Vikar thundered.

'I have to see my father and Kjartan.'

Sela pushed away the fear, reached the door, began to knock. Quietly at first, but then with greater ferocity.

There was no answering sound from within. Nothing but silence.

Her hand fell to her side. She had half-expected the door to be flung wide open and Kjartan to run out at the first sound of her voice. And yet he hadn't. She tried to keep her mind focused. There could be all sorts of reasons, but her head kept whispering the awful ones, the ones she did not even want to think about. She willed Kjartan to open the door, to be there.

The door remained firmly shut with a bar across the entrance to discourage bears. She craned her neck and looked up into the sky. No welcoming curls of smoke drifted in the air. No sound, but a terrible stillness.

She looked beseechingly at Vikar's hard face, hoping that some easy answer would spring from his lips. But the frown on his face grew sterner with each passing heartbeat.

'What are you expecting to find in this deserted hut?'

'My father.' Sela blinked up at him. Surely he had to know. Had to understand the despair welling up within her. Her father. Una. Kjartan. They should be here. 'We agreed.'

'Are you positive?'

'Of course I am.' Sela pressed her hand against her forehead, trying to force her brain to work. She had not made a mistake. Her last words to her father were emblazoned on her heart.

She fought against the panic that threatened to engulf her. Forced air into her lungs. Stared blankly at the door. Her numb mind refused to take it in.

They had to be here. They simply had to be. There was a simple explanation for them failing to answer.

'Father? Kjartan?' she called louder this time and with greater urgency.

Her voice resounded out over the valley, came back and mocked her, each echo higher and shriller than the last. Going round and round until she thought she could stand it no more. She covered her ears and stared at the barred door, willing it to swing out and reveal Kjartan's welcoming smile.

'There is no one here, Sela, and no one has been here for some time.' Vikar's hand held hers, preventing her from pounding on the door again. 'The door is bolted from the outside. It cannot be opened from the inside. I do not have to be a soothsayer to be able to tell you that no one breathes within that hut.'

'But we had agreed. My father and I. This was where we were to meet if anything should happen…if the hall should fall.'

A great hole opened inside Sela and she struggled to breathe. She did not dare think about the possibilities. What could have happened for none of them to be here? She stared at Vikar and longed for the security she had felt in his arms this morning.

'This is where we were going to meet.' Her voice was a mere breath.

'You are positive of that? Confusion reigned in the hall yesterday.'

Vikar made no move towards her and she refused to beg. It was better this way. She would not do anything she later regretted.

'I know what my father and I agreed. It was almost

the last words I spoke to him. At the time, I never imagined that it would come to this.'

Sela hugged her arms about her waist as her mind conjured up images. A frail elderly man, a little boy and an aged woman. What chance would they have had against the *tottr* men and their demands? Against the other terrors of the forest? She should have been with them. She fought against the urge to collapse on the ground in a heap.

'It was only yesterday morning,' she said in a low voice. 'Only yesterday.'

'Shall we go in?' Vikar lifted the bolt and opened the door. His warm fingers went under her elbow, guided her forward. 'There could be many reasons why they are not here. It might have taken them longer than your father anticipated. Bose the Dark is wily if nothing else. He will be here. Trust me on this.'

Sela put a hand to her face and resisted to urge to tear her hair and scream. Vikar was right. She had no cause to panic. Her father would arrive in time. They could have been delayed for any number of reasons. She had to believe her father was a survivor and that he would fight to keep Kjartan and Una alive. She had to.

Sela's gaze swept the tiny hut, searching for any signs. At first glance, she could see nothing out of place.

She grasped the door frame for support.

How long would she have to wait? A day? Two?

Each breath she took seemed to take an age. Her heartbeat pounded in her ears. Every noise made her jump. How could she wait any longer? How could she not wait as long as there was breath in her body.

She had to believe.

Vikar went into the hut, bent down and examined the ashes, running them through his fingers.

'Someone was here, the ashes retain the faintest trace of warmth.' He looked up and his eyes crinkled at the corners. 'See, there are small bits of bread. Mice would have carried such things away.'

Sela nodded, as Vikar's voice flowed over her. Small crumbs of comfort, but he was trying. He understood what she was going through, and was not blaming her, or telling her that she had led him astray. Instead his voice was a soothing balm. When he was like this, she could see why it had taken so long for her heart to recover. Why, in the depths of the night for so many months, she had breathed his name. She pressed her fingers into her eyes and attempted to pay attention.

'There are three distinct footprints on the floor,' Vikar said, crouching down and running his hand on the floor.

'Where?' Sela forgot how to breathe.

'But there is no way of telling who was here.' Vikar looked up from where he crouched and the full greenness of his gaze hit her. 'You have to believe, Sela. They did make it this far.'

Her heart stopped pounding so loudly in her ears. Three sets of footprints. She offered up a quick prayer of thanksgiving.

She knelt down next to Vikar and examined the prints. Vikar was right. Three sets. She measured them with her palm. Two were larger, one a child's. Kjartan. It had to be. No adult would have a foot that small. Her finger trembled as she traced around the outline again.

'Thank you, Vikar. You don't know how much this means to me.'

She glanced up at him. All through out that day, she had told herself that with each step she took, she was getting closer to Kjartan. It had not mattered that she was going to have to come up with an explanation to Vikar about who Kjartan was. It simply meant she was going to see him. And now, she found the prospect of explaining beyond her.

'I had missed the footprints.'

'Ah, then you will admit that I am good for something.' A smile tugged at the corner of his mouth. 'A footprint finder.'

Her father, Una and Kjartan had been here, but had left. Her head began to reel. It made no sense. Maybe it was some other unknown band of travellers.

Her gaze swept around the sparsely furnished room, searching for any further clues. Any hints that it had been her father and Kjartan, and not some unknown travellers. Nothing appeared obvious, but then as she turned her head, the dull gleam of metal caught her eye.

'My father was here,' she said slowly, going over to the crude table that stood on the opposite side of the room. She tilted her head, searching again for the metallic gleam. She dug her fingers into a knothole on the top of the table.

'How can you say that with certainty?' Vikar came over to her. 'If you have some proof, show it to me.'

'Here.' Sela pulled the brooch from the knothole and turned it over in her palm. True, Kjartan and her father were not there to greet her, but they were alive. Alive. They had made it through the *tottr* men and the other dangers of the forest. Her fingers traced the familiar pattern. 'That is the gold brooch from his cloak. He always wears that. My mother gave it to him. It has Loki's face on it. She thought the trickster god would keep him safe. He always wears it.'

She paused, waiting for Vikar to say something. He stared at the brooch, winking in her hand.

'I should have seen it when you opened the door, but…' she said, filling the silence.

'You were upset.' Vikar finished her sentence for her. 'I believe it is your father's brooch. Your father was here.'

'Thank you.' She put the brooch back down on the table before she dropped it.

'Where is he now? Why has he gone from this place?' Vikar asked quietly. 'There is no sign of a struggle.'

Sela put out a finger and touched the brooch again. Made sure it was real and solid. The metal was cold. A shiver passed over her and she gazed around the room. There was nothing to show that there had been a struggle. This hut was a safe haven. Her father had always proclaimed it.

'I have no idea.' She hated the way her voice broke over the last word. She clenched her fists and started again, determined this time not to show her emotion, not to reveal the deep hurt she felt welling up inside her. If she started, she would have to explain everything, and she was not ready for that yet. She hated the way she wanted to trust him, wanted to forget that there had ever been anything bad between them. 'My father had to know that I would come, if I possibly could. Was it all for nothing? Has he abandoned me?'

She raised her eyes and met Vikar's. His gaze held a certain amount of compassion. Her throat closed and she lowered her eyes. She had expected many things from Vikar—annoyance, anger perhaps—but not sympathy.

'I don't understand,' she whispered. 'They had no reason to leave this place.'

It frightened her that she had no easy answers. What was worse, she could not even voice her darkest fear— why had her father taken her son with him? Did he have some darker purpose?

Since he had returned from Kaupang, and particularly in the last few months since his affliction had struck, sometimes he would look at her with dark brooding eyes as if his head was full of complex plots, plots that would swirl around her and had the potential to harm not only her, but also Kjartan. Sometimes she wondered if she recognised her father. Then her father would return to the man she loved and admired.

How could she confess this fear without arousing Vikar's suspicions? And if she did confess, wouldn't she be admitting what she had always denied to Vikar?

Vikar came and stood behind her, not touching her, but there. A temptation. She only had to spin around and bury her face in his chest. Sela dug her palms into the board as her whole body shook.

'You know that they made it here, Sela.' Vikar's voice rippled over her, and brought her back from that dark abyss in her mind. 'There will be a reason, if we can find it. Your father never does anything without a reason. Confide in me. Tell me his reason.'

She refused to cry. It would have been a little thing to wait for her. Her father must have known that she would face the giants themselves to get to Kjartan. The thoughts began to crowd around her, scream at her. She clasped her hands on either side of her head and willed it to stop. The clamouring thoughts became silent. She risked a breath.

'Yes, I know there must be a reason, but somehow it fails to make it any easier.' She tightened her grip on the table and felt a splinter dig into her hand as she held back a sob that threatened to overwhelm her senses. 'I am no further forward than if I had stayed in my father's counting room—your prisoner.'

Vikar made an irritated noise. 'There must have been a reason for them to leave. Can you think of one? Or is it that you don't trust me?'

'I wish they had waited.' Sela fought to keep her voice steady. She blinked rapidly and kept her vision on a small knot in the tabletop. A single drop splattered on the tabletop, staining it dark. She scrubbed furiously with the back of her hand. 'It would have made things much easier.'

'Yes, it would have.' Vikar reached over and picked up the brooch. He tossed it in the air before placing it in his leather pouch. His voice hardened. 'Did you make any further plans with him? What you would do after the hall was overrun and if you were captured?'

'Plans?' Sela stared at him in astonishment. 'I never thought the hall would fall, and I certainly had no idea who was sailing the ships. It was never supposed to come to this. You were supposed to see that we were willing to fight for the hall and depart.'

'But your father knew to wait for you here. No more tricks, Sela. The full truth.'

Sela went over it again in her mind. The whole scene. Examined it, but there were no clues.

'We discussed it. I told him, if the worst should happen, to take Kjartan and we would meet here. Then I left to see about the defences. I never saw… them again.'

'I see.' Vikar's face was solemn, but she thought she detected a touch of sympathy in his eyes. She could take many things from this man, but not pity. Sela glanced away and blinked hard, regained control of her emotions.

'You are wilfully blind,' she said when she felt she could speak without her voice breaking. 'This is the closest haven. He was under no threat. He had no reason to risk himself or Kjartan with another journey.'

'He obviously came here, but he left. You say that you had no other plans. You have not led me on some wild chase across the countryside.' He gave a short laugh. 'And against my better judgement, I believe you and your story. Your grief is too heartfelt to be feigned.'

'Are you offering those words as a compliment?'

'You may take it as such, if you need compliments.' A shadow of a dimple showed in his cheek. 'Shall my words become honey-sweet? Shall I say how your hair matches the ripen corn? How your lips are like ripe strawberries? How your eyes flash midnight blue when aroused?'

'I have never needed compliments.' Sela kept her chin high despite the warm glow his words caused. He was teasing her now, testing her. 'They have the tendency to fall off the tongues of people seeking their own advancement.'

'That's more like the Sela I know. Actions, not words.' Vikar gave a small laugh. 'Irritable, but determined. Always fighting, never needing the protection offered.'

Sela gave a small shake of her head. Not needing protection. Was that how he had seen her? And she had felt so vulnerable and alone in Kaupang. It was after that she had vowed that she'd never lean again. She would be the strong one.

'Why would he do such a thing?'

'Do what?' he asked and his words flowed over, holding her.

Sela regarded her hands. Everything she had held solid and secure seemed to be swept away. She forced her backbone straight, dug her palms into the wood of the table, hanging on for dear life.

'My father abandoned me, left me to my fate,' she whispered, saying out loud the words that were hammering in her brain. She had hoped that hearing them would make it more bearable, but it failed to.

'And it is unexpected.'

His breath fanned the back of her neck. A silent whisper that she had fought him long enough. That he offered a place of refuge. Something she could cling on to. It was all there in that breath, all there for her. He had not abandoned her during the journey. *He* would stay with her…for now…if she wanted…if she needed him. All this he seemed to offer.

'Yes.' Sela spun around and buried her face in his chest. She felt his arms come around her and his hand smoothed her hair.

'Hush, Sela, hush,' he said against her temple and pressed her head more firmly into his shoulder, cradling her. 'You must not exhaust yourself. This journey has been hard, there is no denying that. You don't always have to be strong.'

'I…I…' Her throat refused to work. She had been

standing strong for such a long time. And suddenly she did not want to be alone anymore. She wanted to be cradled, held tight. She was tired of fighting.

How long they stood there, Sela did not know. All she knew was that the uncontrollable trembling in her limbs stopped and she drew strength from his arms. She had not planned it, but somehow, for the first time in a long time, she did not feel as alone. She was powerless to move. She rested her head against his chest and listened to the reassuring thump of his heart.

Vikar's finger raised her chin so she was forced to look into the deep-green pools that were his eyes. Sela watched the changing colours in his eyes. 'They will be found, I promise you that.'

His lips lowered, touched hers. Instantly something flickered, changed. A great hunger grew within her, consuming her senses. She wanted to open her mouth, to take the kiss deeper, and to push away all the hurt she was feeling. But Kjartan's horse pressed into her side, reminding her of her responsibilities, and what had happened between them in the past. She was not ready to take the risk and return to the past.

Her hands came up, pressed against his chest and his arms fell away. He looked at her with a quizzical expression.

'Sela?' One word, calling to her.

'I can't do this. I need to find my father.' Her words were coming in gasps as if she had run a race. 'It is why I am here.'

'Why we are both here.'

She stepped away, shaken by her response to his nearness. She had thought herself immune to him, but even after that brief touch, she knew she wasn't and he was all the more dangerous for it.

It would be too easy to slip back into the past. The one before Kaupang, when she had found security in Vikar's arms, kindness in his smile and passion in his bed. A friendly face when she thought she was alone. The past she had left behind her. And yet its siren call echoed down the years, threatened to obliterate the hurt. She refused to return to that easier time, that fantasy garden of sunshine and sensation. The door had been barred and locked a long time ago. Her world was the present.

'There must be something I can do,' she said, crossing her arms, preventing herself from walking back into his embrace. 'A way I can find them. I have no wish to return to the hall…empty handed.'

Vikar tapped his forefingers against his mouth. 'Would your father have left a message? Something in case you were forced to reveal his whereabouts? Bose the Dark is a cautious man.'

Sela set her jaw and attempted to concentrate. She had to stop thinking about how it felt to be with him— the spark of comfort, the illusion of safety in a treacherous land. That way led towards heartache and betrayal.

'It is possible. I can read runes and message sticks. My father made sure of that. Women should know what the message says, instead of trusting the messenger.'

'A wise policy.' Vikar stared intently at her. 'One I always follow. Actions always speak the loudest.'

His words had more meaning than their current situation. Sela toyed with the neck of her tunic, temptation washing over her. She refused to let her mind go down pathways that led only to pain.

'I need to find my father. I need to find his message.'

Sela began to search the room, first walking around the room examining the walls, the floor and finally on her hands and knees, searching through the dusty corners. She had nearly given up hope when she discovered another of Kjartan's wooden horses in the corner. She lifted it up to the light.

The rune for waterfall was scratched on one side of this horse and on the other the symbol for farm. Sela closed her eyes in relief. She should not have doubted him. Her father had not abandoned her. He had left a message for her and in such a way that she need not tell unless she chose to, unless she trusted her companions.

Unless she trusted Vikar.

She glanced up and saw him standing there—fingers hooked around his belt, feet planted firmly. Standing there, but not moving. Waiting for her. Did she trust him? Her throat closed. Vikar was right—everything had changed since yesterday. The hall, her life all felt a long way away. She was alive because of him. But he was also the man who destroyed her life once, and could do so again. She had to think of more than her own desires.

'Did you find anything, Sela?'

'They have gone to the farm beyond the waterfall.' She held out the horse with the scratched runes. 'My father left this.'

'Are you sure they are there?'

'I believe so.' Sela fingered the horse. She found it difficult to say what she believed any more. She had thought her father would wait. There was no reason for him to be concerned about being followed or about the wild men, but he had left. 'It is sheltered and well equipped.'

'Can it be accessed from the sea?'

'From the sea?' Sela tilted her head. 'We normally have gone by the sea. Una used to take my brother and me when we were growing up. Una is some relation to the farmer's wife. Is there any reason you ask this? Are you intending to go back and sail there in one of your dragon ships?'

Vikar's eyes hardened. 'That is one line of thought. Are you certain your father will be there? Alone?'

'As certain as I can be,' she answered slowly.

'I sincerely hope that this is not some elaborate ploy of your father's. Sometimes, I think he forgets that *tafl* is merely a board game and that real people should not be moved like counters on a board.' Vikar slammed his fist down on the table. 'Ivar can cope if it is. He will have to.'

'Ivar?' Sela asked, tilting her head.

'Ivar the Scarred. He was at Lindisfarne with me, and came with me on this expedition. We were expecting to stay here only for a short time before continuing up to Tromso. A short stop to ease Thorkell's concerns.' Vikar put his hands on the table. His face had turned grave. 'He will be able to control the men.'

Sela tried not to think about Thorgerd and the other women, what might be happening to them at this very instant. How Ivar would be coping. Coping with the barrels of ale and mead. Coping with the demands of warriors. She knew what happened when a hall was sacked.

Those tales had not been legends.

She tried to tell herself that if she had stayed, she could not have done anything to help, but even still a twinge of guilt passed through her. There had to be something that she could do for her father's people, her people. But she found it impossible to think beyond her immediate problem of finding Kjartan.

'If you do not trust his leadership, then perhaps you should go back.' She forced her lips into her sweetest smile. 'You could reassert your authority before taking one of your dragon ships up the coast. The farm is two days' sail. One if you get a quick wind.'

Vikar lifted his eyebrow. He did not miss the slight emphasis on the word *you*.

'I trust Ivar's leadership, but until I have your father's formal surrender, the situation remains perilous. How many others might try for the prize under the pretext of liberating the hall for your father?'

'My father?' She looked uneasy. 'The hall was his whole life. He knows what men do when they sack halls.'

Vikar did not say a word. The way her eyes slid from him showed that she was entirely comfortable with the way her father had treated her. Moisture still glistened in her eyes. She had had a shock. The way she carried her body told him that. She would be easier to deal with if she complained, but if she did that she would not be Sela.

'How far is this farm from here?'

'A day's journey—a long day's journey.' Her eyes lit up. 'Do you mean to come with me?'

'Having come this far, it would be foolish to abandon the chase.' Vikar leant back against the table and dangled his foot. 'And I am strangely reluctant to shadow you again. If you go at all, you go with me.'

'You are planning to go with me.'

'It will take more than a day to return to the hall and outfit the dragon ships.' He gave a shrug. 'Besides, I have no guarantee that your father is at the farm.'

'It is where the runes say he is.' She started for the door. Her whole demeanour had changed. Before she had despaired and now she was full of a nervous energy and purpose. 'Shall we go now?'

'We will depart at first light tomorrow or not at all.'

'But…but…' She looked at him in dismay as she swayed slightly in the doorway.

'Exhaustion clouds your mind. We have travelled since first light.'

'If I did not know better, Vikar, I would say that you cared about my welfare.' She tried for an insolent smile but her lips only managed a ghost of the one he had expected. He resisted the urge to pull her once again into his arms. Never had he imagined that he would feel so protective of this woman. He wanted to fight against the shadows that held her in their grip. He wanted her to trust him with her secrets. He knew he could prevail, if she allowed him. But for now, he'd humour her, wait and watch for the opportunity.

'Someone has to. I can hardly have my guide dropping dead.' Vikar went over to the door and shut it. 'There are wolves and bears in these woods. Your wits must be as sharp as a newly forged sword.'

'I would be a fool to argue with that.'

'And you are no fool, Sela. Stubborn to the point of obstinacy, maybe, but not a fool.'

'Two compliments in one day, Vikar. You must be slipping.'

She bent her head and he could see where her blonde

hair had escaped at the back of her neck. His fingers itched to entangle themselves, but he held back.

'How are we are going to pass the time?' Sela asked after he lit the fire.

'I can think of one or two pleasurable ways,' Vikar said, watching the emotions flit across her face. '*Tafl*, for instance. You used to be quite an enthusiastic *player*.'

'It has been long time, Vikar.' Her voice was low. 'I am not sure I remember the rules.'

'The rules are simple, Sela.'

'They may have changed over time.' Her long lashes made smudges on her cheeks. 'I need to be sure.'

'We ought to wager. You used to enjoy wagering.'

'I used to enjoy many things.'

The fire crackled and popped. Vikar looked again at Sela. She was sitting facing him, her legs tucked under her. From any other woman, he'd assume that it was an invitation, but with Sela, he was frightened to take the chance. He leant forward, so that his forehead touched hers.

'What will you wager, Sela? What truth will you tell?' He placed his hands on her shoulders and felt her flesh quiver. His fingers brushed the flawless skin on her collarbone where her tunic had gaped open. A light, delicate touch. It gave her the chance to glance up and lift her lips. 'Confide in me.'

'I know your seduction technique, Vikar.' She leant back, breaking contact with a brief laugh.

'You never complained.'

'That was before.' She gave him a level stare, but Vikar saw her hand tighten on the wooden horse as if it were some talisman or shield to protect her from the desire that sung in her veins. 'If that is what you are after, we should go. I did not leave the hall to become your concubine.'

He rubbed his hand against the back of his neck. When was she going to trust him with the truth? And when was she going to see the truth? When was she going to tell him what she saw in the flames of the fire? He stood up and unbolted the door. 'Your virtue is safe with me, Sela, but perhaps you would care to chance it with a wolf or two.'

'You are right, Vikar. It has been a long day.' She settled herself down by the fire.

'Coward.'

She gave a soft laugh that echoed off the walls of the hut. 'You tried that trick once before as well. You forget we were married once.'

'I have never forgotten that.'

Chapter Eight

'Will there be supplies hidden here? Or will your father have taken everything? We finished the last of my food yesterday evening.' Vikar's low rumble penetrated through the fog of sleep that surrounded Sela.

She stretched. Her back ached from where she had lain near the fire. In the end she had shared a simple meal with Vikar and then her eyelids had drooped. Once in the night, she had half-woken to the howl of a wolf, but Vikar's reassuring bulk and regular breathing on the other side of the fire had calmed her and her eyes had closed again.

'My father has a policy of keeping the safe houses supplied, in case they have to be used suddenly.' She began to re-plait her hair, knew she was using it as a screen and was glad of it. 'I should have thought about it last night.'

'You had other things on your mind.' Vikar's eyes softened as he leant back against the table. But he made no attempt to move towards her. 'Where is the food kept? I tried the trunk earlier, but you obviously need a key.'

She went over to the trunk. She worked the lock, lifted the lid. 'Simple, if you know how.'

'Does you father delight in making things complicated?'

Sela studied the bottom of the trunk. 'My father believes in being prepared for the worst. He trusts very few and those he trusts, he tests.'

'Caution is good. Intrigue can have unintended consequences.'

'Like throwing you and me together.'

'Your father and I have had our differences over the years, but we have grown to respect each other's abilities.'

'I wouldn't know. He never spoke of it.' Sela concentrated on the trunk's contents—dried meat, salt cod and hard bread. Not exactly appetising or in a great quantity but sufficient. A veritable feast for a starving man. 'My father left some food.'

'Food *and* a coded message? He took the provisions from her. 'Where does the late and unlamented Hafdan fit into this?'

'Hafdan? He had no part in stocking the safe huts. He left.' Her head began to pound slightly.

'But why did he leave? To raid? And why raid to the south?'

'To find new trade routes. There is no mystery in that. Kaupang and its ports were closed. Our coffers were low.'

'And when did your father order the food to be brought here?' Vikar's voice was silky smooth, but there was no disguising the sharp-edged steel underneath. 'Before or after Hafdan left? How many other ships did he send away?'

'He will not have plotted with Hafdan the way you

suggest.' Sela swallowed hard, and tried to regain control of her thoughts. Her father would never have intentionally put her in this sort of danger. She was certain of that. 'My father is not like that, not like that at all. He cares about me…about everyone under his protection. He will be at the farm beyond the waterfall. I promise.'

'I believe *you* believe that, Sela.'

Sela forced the muscles in her neck to relax. The day before yesterday, everything had seemed so solid and secure. But this morning the truths wavered and changed like shadows from the fire. Would tomorrow cause her world to go upside down again? She refused to think about what tomorrow would bring. All she could do was concentrate on the solid things, not the shadows.

She forced her voice to be light. 'Do we eat here or shall we take it with us? There is more than enough to break our fast. We will have a long day ahead of us.'

'No, this time you do not change the subject. When did he stock this hut?'

'When he came back from Kaupang…he feared an invasion. Quite rightly, as it turns out.'

'Feared an invasion and yet sent his best warriors away. Think on that and tell me that you do not believe there is more to this than meets the eye.'

Sela rubbed the back of her neck. The shadows were crowding around her mind again, whispering.

'It makes little sense to me either now that you say that.' She pressed her palms against the table. 'I felt he put too much reliance on the sagas about his invincibility. I don't know if he actually came to believe them, or if he thought as Thorkell had not sent an expedition last year that he was weak-willed and would not do so. I was not privy to his private thoughts. He spent much of last winter with Hafdan. They quarrelled bitterly this spring.'

'What did they quarrel about?'

'His unjust banishment. Hafdan wanted to do something, but my father wanted to wait. He felt that Thorkell would need him again, sooner or later, particularly if the new trade routes were the success he envisioned.'

'Unjust?' Vikar crossed his arms and his face became hewn from stone. 'Your father was very lucky to have escaped with his life. I doubt that he intended to give Thorkell that option. And what he nearly did to Asa does not bear thinking about…'

Sela stared at him across the tiny hut, struggling for breath. The morning air suddenly seemed close and oppressive. She cursed her wayward tongue.

She knew that he would see things differently than she, but surely he had to understand what had happened. How her father had been duped. Her father had been too ready to trust. He had believed the stories of Sigfrid. Haakon had taken Vikar's part in the divorce, and her father had seen an opportunity for revenge. He had bitterly regretted it. Nothing had happened to Thorkell. Asa had enforced the banishment because she wanted to consolidate her power. It was all there for any who had eyes.

But she couldn't say the words.

'Come now, Sela. Let us not quarrel about this. Asa was nearly destroyed in the plot.'

'What are you more concerned about, Vikar—the threat to Thorkell's life or Asa's machinations nearly being exposed?' Sela tapped her foot, trying to hang on to her temper. Here at last was a truth that did not change. Always, Vikar was ready to take Asa's part. It did not matter what happened—somehow Asa was blameless and had to be protected.

Vikar lifted an eyebrow, and a strange smile flickered across his face.

'Your father attempted to poison my king, our king, the man who has kept the peace on this peninsula for nearly fifteen years.'

'You know that my father would never harm Thorkell.' Sela set down the bread, staring at Vikar in astonishment. 'He was like a son to him. A man he trusted duped him, fed him a tale. My father listened… because he wanted to…'

'You believe your father is innocent?'

'Thorkell had to do something, but my father retained his lands…. He remained jaarl of the north. Surely that should be enough proof for you. Thorkell plays a balancing act.'

'It was enough for you.'

Sela shook her head and turned back to the food, rather than face Vikar's accusing stare. The tale her father told had to be the truth. She needed it to be true. She had to believe in her father.

He spent years at Thorkell's side, never leaving except when she had given birth to Kjartan and someone had had to accept him into the world. The story he had concocted to tell his people why he should do the ceremony then sufficed—her lover was dead. And she knew he had kept her secret. She owed him much. He might not have approved of her actions, but he had accepted her decision. He wouldn't have lied to her about it.

Sela gave a sad smile in remembrance as she tried to weigh up who she believed—her father or Vikar.

In many ways the person she had thought she had married never existed. She had had a dream lover, one who vanished when the harsh light of the Kaupang court shone and she'd do well to remember that, not allow herself to be seduced into thinking he had changed, that somehow she had been mistaken about his intent all those years ago. He had only married reluctantly, because her father had forced the issue, demanded proof of his loyalty. Vikar hadn't cared for her. She had been used as a screen for Vikar's true intentions with the queen. She had been a glass counter.

'I was pleased to have my father back,' she said carefully in the long silence. 'For too long the affairs of state occupied his mind. He has grown old. You will find it hard to credit when you see him. His hair is white. Some witch cursed him and he finds it difficult to move with any great speed.'

Vikar stroked his chin. 'There is no use arguing with you, Sela. Your father is a god to you. You have always preferred to believe his tales. It is why you ended our marriage. You blamed it on shadows, but I knew the truth. I had served my purpose and your father had found another more malleable man for you.'

A white rage surged through her. It was Vikar who had discarded her! He had taken delight in making her wait, leaving her on her own while he spent time with Asa. She had suffered humiliation after humiliation until the weight had become impossible to bear.

'How little you knew me and my father! My father argued for me to stay married to you in those dark days in Kaupang. He begged me to, told me to think of the family.'

'What are you saying, Sela?'

'It was my choice and mine alone.' Sela paced up and down the small hut. Then she stopped and fixed Vikar with a level steely-eyed gaze. The time had come. 'It was your doing. You and the way you consorted with that witch. Any hour of the day or night, all she had to do was send a messenger and you left whatever you were doing to go to her side.'

'It was not that simple. I had duties. Asa relied on my counsel.'

'You abandoned me to the court. I heard you laughing about it to your cronies—that unsophisticated girl I married. She makes so many demands and doesn't understand the ways of court. Asa despairs of her.'

The words still had the power to twist her insides. She forced her head to stay high as she waited for Vikar's response. She fought against the urge to fill the silence with words. He had to speak.

'I have no memory of those words.'

'You wouldn't.'

'I am not denying I said them.' Vikar ran his hand through his hair. 'I have said a great many things in my life. I would never have said them to you.'

'No, it is just lucky I overheard them.' Sela tilted her chin in the air. 'My father said at the time that I should not worry, but a few days later I found Asa's love token in our bed...'

Her voice trailed away at his look of astonishment as if he had never heard the story before. He had to have known. She gritted her teeth and began to attack the bread, tearing with her hands.

'I had wondered,' Vikar said in a cold tone, 'if you still accepted everything your father told you at face value and now I know. You might say that you have grown and changed, but underneath, you remain the same blind woman you were in Kaupang.'

Sela froze. The bread dropped down on the table. 'My eyesight has never been questioned.'

'You blame Asa for the demise of our marriage?' Vikar put his hands on his hips. 'Despite what you might believe, Asa was a strong supporter of the marriage. She urged me to go after you, but it was too late. You had already left.'

'You mistake me, Vikar.' Sela crossed her arms. Her insides ached, torn asunder. How could she explain without giving away her secrets? She drew on all her hard-won strength. Forced her countenance to appear calm and collected. 'My resentment over her part in the demise of our marriage vanished long ago, her demands for attention, her need for your company, her desire to know if her threads matched.'

'Asa is lonely, a foreigner. She wanted to help you ease your way into court. She knew what it was like. Many times we spoke of your…misdemeanours and how they could ruin your chances.'

'Maybe if you had paid more attention to me, and guided me yourself, I would not have felt the need to act in the way I did.'

Vikar flinched and Sela knew her words had reached him. 'I do not deny that I was ill suited to be your husband, but you always resented Asa.'

'No, not resented.' Sela kept her voice quiet and calm despite the huge weight of hurt that was welling up inside her. 'You have no idea what the women's court was like, Vikar. You only saw the public face, that which Asa wanted the men to see. She is far from being alone. She and her women are a formidable cadre. Woe betide anyone who goes against her. I learnt that to my cost.'

Sela remembered how when she had first arrived Asa had snapped her fingers under Sela's nose and informed her that she could have any man she chose. Sela had not believed it then, but had found out quickly how innocent she was, and how little she understood.

'She is my queen—I owe her my loyalty.'

'You owe your king the loyalty.'

Vikar stood there opened-mouthed. 'Are you saying I would commit treason against my king?'

'Do you deny having an affair with her?' Sela asked, tilting her head to one side. This conversation was proceeding as her father had predicted all those years ago. He had been correct then. It was better that she had left without the confrontation. The girl she had been then would have been a quivering wreck. But now she needed to know. 'Do you?'

A muscle twitched in Vikar's jaw. He stood there, his face hewn from rock. 'I have never committed treason.'

. Sela stared at him, unmoved. 'I deserve an honest answer, Vikar, after what we have been through.'

'We are not married, Sela, you and I. Any answer I give you would seem false,' he said finally. A pained expression crossed his face and he gave a shrug. 'Mistakes were made, Sela. I do not claim otherwise.'

'You appear to have made a number of mistakes in your love life.'

'Some I regret more than others.'

Sela winced and examined the floor beneath her feet. She refused to ask what Vikar's life was like now. Or which mistake he regretted the most. 'I see.'

'Why are we speaking of this?' Vikar asked. He moved towards her, but made no attempt to take her in his arms. 'I prefer my past to stay behind me. Mistakes *and* triumphs. It is something I can't change. Skalds may sing all they want, but I want to live in the future.'

'And what does this future entail?' she whispered.

'I am the master of Bose's hall.' His voice was low and insistent. 'I am the jaarl of the north. I want to negotiate an honourable surrender for your father. It will save bloodshed. I want to look after my new people. My duty has not changed, nor my determination to do it.'

Sela wrapped her arms about her waist. 'We have a bargain, you and I.'

'We will discuss the exact arrangements after I meet with your father. But our bargain was to find your father here. We might have to…renegotiate the terms as circumstances have changed.'

'Then we are at an impasse.' Sela opted for a bright smile. 'I refuse to negotiate.'

'Are you offering me a challenge, Sela?'

'I would like the same terms as before—I am allowed to leave with my family.'

'We will discuss this after my meeting with your father, after I know what the true situation is—I can offer no more than that. You are welcome to leave now and take your chances if you wish.'

Sela pressed her lips together. She needed Vikar and his sword. The dagger he had given back to her yesterday morning would be no match for one of the wolves she had heard howling in the night. She would have ended up like that poor serving girl without his sword arm. She would be no good to Kjartan dead. She put a hand to her head, willed her thoughts to stop buzzing. 'We will speak of this after you have met my father, but I want to be with my family. Promise me that.'

'Sela…' Vikar reached for her hand but she withdrew it. 'I do not want to argue with you. My business is with your father. He must surrender. I will not have my people put in danger by his ambition.'

'I know my father is not perfect, Vikar.' Sela stared past him to the shadows. 'I told you I grew up.'

'You grew into your beauty.'

She knew the compliment was idle flattery. It had to be. All the same, her breath caught in her throat. 'I hardly think my attire has been conducive to that.'

'I would not be so sure, Sela. Your curves have filled out. And the trousers leave very little to the imagination.'

'I think I would like to leave as quickly as possible.' Sela drew her tongue over suddenly dry lips. Somehow the knowledge that Vikar had noticed her curves made a warmth flicker through her.

'Who are you more afraid of, Sela? Yourself or me?'

'I am not afraid of anything.' Sela took a step forward, tilted her chin into the air, dared him. Lied. 'You hold no attraction. Never did.'

Vikar's hands closed around her shoulders, pulled her unresisting body against his. He lowered his head and captured her lips, took flagrant possession of them. Devoured them, drew a sigh from her throat, demanded more.

A wild bolt of lightning shot through Sela. Something in her body flickered to life and responded to the urgency of his kiss, something so unexpected that she had considered it dead, but it wasn't. It had been hiding deep down within her, awaiting its chance. It curled around her insides, turning them molten, whispering that she should give in. She fought it, willed it to return to its slumber. She was through with such things and had been for four years.

She forced her body to ignore its natural inclination, to step away despite the heat searing through her. Her legs wanted to melt but she kept her backbone straight. She deliberately raised an eyebrow.

'What were you trying to prove, Vikar? Your mastery of the situation?'

'I did not hear any objections.'

'I am objecting now.'

'Truly?'

'Yes, truly.' Sela knew she said the words too quickly, before he launched another assault on her mouth, and her last remaining defences crumbled into dust.

'I think you lie.'

He rubbed the back of his thumb against her slightly swollen lips and Sela felt a pulse of warmth surge through her. An ache filled her and threatened to overwhelm her senses.

'And you know so much about me?'

'I know what your body whispers.' His voice rippled over her like smooth silk, calling her. She felt her nipples begin to contract as the heat within her intensified. 'We can stay here. Your father will not expect you for another day at least.'

'Your horde of seduction techniques ceased to astonish me years ago.' She plucked his fingers from her shoulders with the last ounce of self-control she possessed. 'You are very predictable, Vikar.'

Vikar rolled his eyes towards the ceiling. It had been a close call—either kissing her or strangling her.

He did not deny their marriage had failed in a large part because of him. He had married her for the wrong reasons—for ambition, because it seemed to be the right thing to do. Because he had wanted to please Thorkell. He had thought only of the prestige the marriage would bring and not of the woman that would come with it. One woman was much the same as another. But all that had changed after they'd married. Sela had had a special quality about her, but she was also unwilling to change, obstinate and stubborn. She refused to see where her loyalty lay. When she had left, he had let her go because it had seemed to be what she'd wanted. And the great emptiness inside him had subsided after a time.

He had thought himself entirely over Sela, but being here with her showed how much remained unsettled between them.

He wanted her. And had never really stopped wanting her. The realisation scared him more than he thought possible. But it also excited him. This time, they were both different. They had learnt from their past mistakes.

'I have no intention of surrendering to you again.' She assessed him with clear eyes.

'When you surrender, it will be complete,' Vikar said,

reaching for her again. 'We could be good for each other, Sela.'

'You never listen, Vikar.' The words were quick, but he had felt her lips move against his, heard the soft sigh in her throat as their tongues had slightly touched. She might fool herself, but she did not fool him. There was a hunger there.

'It depends on which part I am listening to—your mouth or your body. Next time, I will allow you to make the first move.' Vikar touched her cheek and felt the warmth of her. She jerked away as if his very touch burnt her. 'You need to decide what you want, Sela.'

'I want to find my father, and get rid of you.' Her eyes blazed. 'It is the only thing I desire. It is the only thing I want.'

'Do you believe that?'

'I do.' Sela's words were far too quick. 'I must go to him…to my father. I want to learn the truth about why he left here. It is important.'

Vikar gave a half-smile. He would wait and see how long it took for Sela's defences to fall. When it happened, she would come to him; she would beg for his kiss and he would accept her surrender. Graciously, but it would be total. 'It will happen.'

He took the bread and dried meat from the table, stuffed them into the pouch without looking at her. Then he headed for the door and sunlight. 'Are you ready to go?'

'The sooner we start, the sooner I will be finished with you.'

'Finished? We have yet to begin,' Vikar murmured as she stalked off.

Chapter Nine

Sela strode away from the hut with fast, furious steps. She had come so near to surrendering to his touch, to forgetting who he was and why he was with her. To forgetting her responsibilities. He with that smug smile, easy manner and oh-so-soft lips. She wanted to put as much distance between her and that kiss as possible.

He had attacked her home and forced her father and son to flee. He was her enemy and had been for a long time. The reawakening of this attraction towards him was nothing but an aberration brought on by lack of sleep and close proximity.

Not really, a little voice in the back of her mind whispered. It was an explanation of why she had not found other men attractive. And why she had actively sought to avoid other relationships. Somehow, Vikar was in her blood. But there was no future for them together.

She drew a deep breath of pine-scented morning air, and felt the promise of heat in the air. Her footsteps quickened and the trees cast barred shadows over her arms. She had thought the woods would be welcoming today, but they weren't.

She pushed a branch away from her face and stepped over a fallen log, swore softly as her toe hit a rock and the pain reverberated up her foot. But she didn't pause, she kept going forward.

The sound of the river cascading over rocks became clearer with each step she took.

'Are you trying to race me to this farm? Or is there something more?' Vikar caught up with her, matched her stride for stride. 'Why did you bolt out of that hut?'

'It is a long journey, and I had wasted enough time.'

'My time was far from being wasted.' Vikar put his hand on her arm. 'I want you to know that, Sela.'

'Good. The news improves my outlook no end.' Sela began to walk even more quickly until she was nearly running. It had ceased to be a race towards Kjartan, and had become a race away from the hut and her growing feelings for Vikar. She had considered the naïve bride dead and unmourned, but she appeared to have been merely slumbering, awaiting her chance to reassert her rosy view of life.

They trudged along in silence for a long while. The river, which had seemed so close, kept retreating. Sweat prickled Sela's neck, but she refused to stop.

'Pay attention to where you are going, Sela.' Vikar stopped and lifted his head. 'There is a heaviness in the air that I don't like. Is there another way?'

'I can hear the river. We shall be there soon and then it is not far. A waterfall is easy to spot.'

'Are you sure you are following the correct path?'

Vikar gestured towards a faint track. 'I believe we are going in circles.'

'There are no paths out here, Vikar. Only landmarks to navigate by,' Sela said impatiently. Didn't he understand? Once she was beyond the waterfall, her world would return to normal and the landscape would become a familiar one. She would stop being tempted by him and his lips.

She crashed through the undergrowth and heard a flock of wood pigeons rise in the air.

A strong, stomach-churning odour wafted towards them on the breeze, choking her senses.

'What is that stench?' Sela put her sleeve up to her mouth and tried to breathe through that.

'If you look, you will see, Sela.' Vikar put his hand on her arm, preventing her from going forwards. 'We can find another way.'

Sela looked down and saw the half-eaten carcass of a young boar on the ground. A small gasp escaped her throat. She stepped backwards and encountered the reassuring bulk of Vikar. 'I didn't see it.'

'Something killed it. Something devoured half of it.' Vikar's hand went to the hilt of his sword. 'It might be here.'

Sela cocked her head to one side, listening, but the small clearing was still.

'It has gone. The only creatures that will want this are the ravens and vultures.' Sela smiled at Vikar and pushed her hair behind her ears. 'No harm done.'

'It could have been worse. We will soon be at the river.' Vikar turned his back on the carcass. 'You should pay more attention.'

'In the future I will.' Sela skirted around the carcass

and turned her face to the sun. Now that she looked, she saw the bleached bones of many more animals. A killing ground. They should never have entered here. She fingered the hilt of her dagger. 'I think I caught a glimpse of the river through the trees. We are almost there.'

'We face one more foe.' Vikar forced her behind him with one sweep of his hand.

Sela paused ready to argue with him, then froze. A loud rasping noise filled the air, and then a low growl.

'Run, Sela! Run and don't look back! Make for the river another way!'

Her legs had turned to blocks of lead and she was forced to watch the scene unfold in front of her. Saw the large wolf jump in front of Vikar with its hackles raised and lips drawn back into a fierce snarl, pacing back and forth. Slowly she shook her head. 'If I go, we both go. Together.'

'Don't be a fool, Sela.'

'You would be,' Sela shouted back.

Sela heard the irritated noise as Vikar drew his sword, stood ready to face the wolf down.

'You are being a fool now,' she said in an urgent undertone. 'We both should go, together and without hesitation. There is still a chance we might escape. The wolf may just be warning us. He will make a show and then leave.'

She wasn't sure who she wanted to convince—Vikar or herself.

'It intends mischief.' Perspiration shone on Vikar's forehead as he made a pass with his sword. The wolf moved away from the sword, sat down on its haunches with his head tilted to one side. Then its pink tongue lolled out of its mouth and it licked its lips.

'It is trying to protect its food. If we back away... slowly...then both of us...' Sela started to move to her right, keeping her eyes on the wolf. 'Come on, Vikar. This is no time to play the hero.'

She took another step and the wolf moved his head, curled back its lips and gave a snarl that filled the whole clearing.

'Vikar!'

'Let me do it my way. Please, Sela! I know what I am doing.'

Vikar bent down, picked up a white bone and tossed it so it landed near the wolf with a soft plop. The wolf started to advance towards the bone, then stopped. Its yellowed eyes fixed on Vikar.

It began to move, creating a circle around her and Vikar. Tighter and tighter. Vikar turned, kept pace. Always facing the wolf. His sword was held in front of his face, ready to strike if necessary.

Wolf and man circled each other once. Twice. Three times. Probing, testing.

The wolf opened its gleaming teeth and, muscles rippling, sprang.

At the same instant, Vikar brought his sword forward, hit the wolf's back legs as the wolf missed and fell to the ground in a heap. It threw back its head and howled in frustration. Picked itself up, shook its fur. Began to circle again.

Sela remained where she was. Her mouth was dry. There was no opening. If she moved, the wolf would be on her.

'For Thor's sake, Sela, this is not a game or some court competition.' Vikar wiped his hand across his mouth. He gestured with his head. 'Get out of here while I have its attention.'

'I never said it was.'

'Go, so I don't have to worry about you.' He half-turned towards her. 'Please.'

Sela nodded, turned slightly. Her body felt like ice. She knew if she ran and Vikar held the wolf's attention, she could possibly make it to the waterfall and then to the farm.

But how could she leave him? How could she flee from here, knowing that she left him to a certain death? She stood, uncertain, torn between helping Vikar and obeying him. Wanting to do both, and able to do neither.

Paralysed.

Wolves were pack animals. It was only a matter of time before more wolves joined in, and then what chance would Vikar have? She wet her lips, knowing the choice had been made, feeling stronger for it.

'No, I remain at your side. We fight together.' She reached for her dagger, drew it. Grateful that Vikar had returned it to her the other morning. She looked for an opening. Vikar gave another furious look, gestured with his head.

'I can handle this.' The wolf paused in its pacing, snarled as Vikar lunged forward with his sword. The wolf retreated a few steps. 'Nothing to it.'

'Watch out!' she cried.

The wolf sprang a second time. This time, his aim was true and Vikar's sword went flying out of his hand as the impact of the wolf forced him to the ground. Vikar's cry of pain rang in her ears.

In slow motion, Sela saw the wolf begin to lower its head, saw the naked flesh of Vikar's throat.

Without giving herself time to think, she launched her body forward, and caught the wolf by the scruff of the neck, pulled. The wolf turned its head and its jaws snapped dangerously close to her face. She stabbed downwards.

The knife went into the wolf's belly, stuck. The howl of pain rang in her ears. She pulled back and stabbed again harder this time, raked downward.

The wolf turned towards her. Its foul breath covered her. And its yellowed eyes showed surprise.

She felt the weight of it turn on her, press her down. She forced her arm to stay straight, unmoving. It had to work. She did not know if she had the strength for another thrust of her dagger.

The wolf made a noise in its throat. It tilted sideways into her with its jaw gaping open. She struggled to breathe.

Perhaps Vikar had been right.

Perhaps she should not have tried. She had only endangered them both. A failure once again.

The world went dark and fur filled her mouth, but there was no pain, just a heavy weight. A total silence flowed around her, contrasting with the growls that had so recently filled her ears. Death? Not while she still could fight!

She struggled, pushing against the overwhelming weight, certain the wolf's fangs would bear down on her throat but unable to move the weight from her chest. She tried to twist her hips, but the weight of the wolf pinned her to the ground. She kicked with her feet.

Then, suddenly the weight was lifted and blue sky showed above her. Vikar's sword gleamed silver in the light.

'The wolf breathes no more—do you?'

'Yes.' Sela lay there, gasping for breath. She was alive. Alive. She put her hand to her face, and breathed in the sweet air, unable to move. Alive when she had been so certain that she had been dead. 'Yes, I live.'

'When it is the end of the world, and Fenis the Wolf comes, I know who I want by my side.' Vikar held out his hand. His words flowed over her like a soothing balm. A very large part of her wanted them to be true.

'I suspect Fenis would be a much harder proposition,' she said, rolling over on her side and shielding her eyes. She refused to let Vikar know that she had wanted those words to mean something. It was how the trouble had started the last time. She had always turned his words over and over in her mind, searching for hidden meanings, demanding to know what he was truly trying to say. Then they would fight. She was not going back to that past.

'Is the wolf dead or simply injured?' she asked.

'Very dead. Your aim was true, Sela. None of Odin's warriors could have done it better.'

The sun was behind Vikar, concealing his expression. She tried to move her fingers and toes, then her limbs, and found they all worked and were without pain. Her escape had been total.

But the wolf's teeth had actually sunk into Vikar.

She looked towards him, her eyes devouring his form, shoulders, chest and legs, searching for a sign that the wolf had not done serious damage. His right sleeve showed patches of dark blood. His? The wolf's?

'Vikar,' she said slowly, thickly, and found her voice would not work. Wordlessly she held out her hand and hoped that he would understand.

Vikar knelt down beside her. He knelt down before her much as a warrior kneels before his king. 'I owe you my life. My sword had gone and I had no shield.'

'Anyone would have done the same.'

'Not everyone,' came the soft reply.

His green-eyed gaze caught and held hers. She swallowed hard and tried not to remember how firm his lips had felt against hers and how secure she had felt waking up in his arms the other morning. The longings his earlier kisses had stirred, longings she had tried to ignore, but which flooded through her. She had lied back in the hut. She was attracted to him.

She did want him, but it would be a mistake to act on her desire. She was no longer an impulsive child, but a grown woman. Responsible for more than just her own body.

'You would have done the same for me.' She made a dismissive gesture with her dagger. 'Forget it. I already have.'

'I owe you my life, Sela. It is something that is not easily forgotten.'

Sela gazed into the green pools that were his eyes and knew that she had lied to herself for years. She did care about this man, and had never stopped caring. It was what made him so dangerous.

'Then next time, don't attempt to throw it away so quickly and on such a little thing.'

'I will remember that.' His eyes began to dance. 'I had thought to save you from harm.'

'And I saved you.' She returned his smile with one of her own, amazed at the bubbly feeling that was coursing through her system. 'I guess I will never learn.

I should have listened to your good advice and escaped. I could be halfway to my father by now, instead of lumbered with a Viken warrior.'

'Lumbered?'

'No, not lumbered.' Sela paused, and searched for the right words. She had no appetite to use words as barbed arrows. 'I need your skills, Vikar, as a fighter out here to survive. My father set me an impossible task. One I could not have accomplished without you.'

'I owe you a life-debt, a debt that I intend to pay.' Vikar touched her shoulder. His hand appeared to sear through the material to her cold flesh. Sela shivered slightly, resisted the urge to move closer. 'I mean that truly.'

'You owe me nothing of the sort.' Sela pushed back her hair, tried to concentrate on something other than his face. She didn't want to think about life-debts or who might owe what. 'It was my fault in the first place. I did not watch where I was going, and stumbled on this… this feeding ground.'

'Are we to argue about that as well?' Vikar raised an eyebrow as he rose. 'You seem intent to argue about everything else today.'

Sela gave a small shrug, and started to rise. His warm fingers came instantly to her elbow. 'We have fought so long and hard that I have forgotten what our original quarrel was about.'

'No doubt some infraction of mine. I am not sure I was ready for the ties of marriage. I had anticipated a very different sort of wife.'

Sela examined the toe of her shoe.

A different sort of wife. She knew the sort he had needed. The young woman she had been then had had many faults, had probably been incapable of being the accomplished court hostess that he had desired. She doubted if she could be such a thing now. However, at least she knew that it was beyond her capabilities and she had no intention of adding the skill to her repertoire.

'We both had expectations that the other failed to fill.' She wiped her hands against her trousers. 'You are right— we should leave that particular quarrel behind us.'

'I am willing if you are.' He held out his hand. 'To the future, Sela and not the past.'

Their fingers touched. She drew back her hand too quickly as heat travelled up her arm.

'Done.' She shielded her eyes and looked in the direction they needed to go. Tried to think of her responsibilities, who was waiting for her. 'We need to cover quite a bit of ground, if we are to make it to my father tonight…'

Vikar pursed his lips, lips that her own mouth remembered far too well. And somewhere in the distance a skylark trilled its song. Liquid. Free. And full of life. A call to adventure.

'Are you injured?' he said finally, breaking the silence. 'Your trousers drip with blood.'

Sela look down and saw the dark patches spreading over her clothes.

'It is wolf's blood rather than my own. In many ways, I am pleased my brother did not live to see what I have done to his favourite pair of trousers. He would have probably skinned me alive.'

'Your brother always did have an exaggerated sense of his own self-importance.'

'Can you imagine what his face would have been like? And how he would have sounded?'

'Yes, I can, but you are evading the question, Sela. How great are your injuries? You took quite a blow when the wolf fell. How far can you comfortably travel?'

'I am possibly sporting a few bruises, but otherwise I am fine.' She made a show of cleaning her dagger on the green grass and then replaced it in her belt. 'My brother taught me that the first thing one does after a kill is to clean the blade. He eventually allowed me to join the hunt, after he was sure that I could follow his direction and I had nagged and nagged him. My father was away in Kaupang at the time.'

'You did the right thing.'

She sat back on her feet and glanced up at Vikar. His face was ashen and he appeared to be holding his arm awkwardly. 'You are in pain. The wolf bit you.'

'Nothing that won't heal. It could have been much worse.'

In the distance a wolf's howl sounded. Sela shivered and reached again for her dagger. Having faced one, the thought of encountering a whole horde made her blood run cold. She *knew* how lucky she had been.

'Do you think there will be more wolves?'

'They generally hunt as a pack.' Vikar gave the dead wolf a prod with his toe. 'This one acted on his own. It is hard to say if it was left here to guard while the others were out hunting, if it was an opportunistic scout or if it had been shunned by its pack.'

'I don't want to stay here and find out.' Sela looked to where the wolf lay. Its coat was glossy, but even now that it had breathed its last, the fierceness of its face unnerved her. What if her dagger had missed? A shudder ran through her.

'I would prefer to put some distance between us and this feeding ground. And you have not answered my question. Should we try for the farm, or attempt to find some safe place to rest? I defer to your knowledge of how much longer we have to travel.'

Sela glanced down at her bloodstained trousers. They were an excuse. She knew that. She had no desire to destroy this fragile thing that had sprung up between them. And she knew she was not ready to face what was to come—her father and Kjartan. The truth about Kjartan's parentage.

What if they weren't there? If she had to face yesterday all over again? Today had been traumatic enough.

Cowardice or self-preservation?

She looped her hair back around her ears. She'd play for time, and hope for a miracle. 'Not in this state…it would make my father worried.'

'We can't camp out at night, not with wolf packs on the prowl.'

'There is a cave behind the waterfall,' she said slowly. 'My brother and I discovered it once. We used the farm as summer pasture for the cows and sheep for a few years.'

'And is this cave behind the waterfall safe?'

'It will provide us shelter for the night, a chance for us to recover and I can see to your wound.'

'Wound?' Vikar moved his arm back and forth. 'I told you it was the merest scratch.'

'You are not a good liar, Vikar.' Sela put a hand on his arm and watched his face crease in pain. His lips appeared to have a whitish tinge to them. 'And that is not just wolf's blood on your shirt. I saw his jaws on your arm when you dropped your sword.'

'You are too observant at times, Sela the Wolf Slayer.'

Vikar draped his good arm about her shoulders and brushed the top of her hair with his lips. Her body quivered and she swallowed hard. She moved out of the shelter of his arms.

'I think I like the title,' she said, sticking out her chin and adopting a pose. 'It has a certain ring to it. Do you think the skalds will use it in a saga? Sela the Wolf Slayer.'

'You always did want to become a warrior.' The dimple flashed in his cheek. 'Always ready to play the more masculine games like racing. I remember how disappointed you were when I had to forbid you racing on horseback. It was not seemly, Sela. Not at court. You always wanted to defy convention. The rules are there for a purpose. Women are to be protected.'

Sela sobered, checked her movement. Her heart began to thump loudly in her ears.

Was that how Vikar had seen her?

A woman who had no desire to be feminine, or to be protected. How wrong he had been. She had wanted the things that any woman wants—a home, children, a husband who respected her. When she had asked for his protection, for his help navigating the currents of court life, he had not given it, not in a way she could understand. When she had made mistakes, he had ignored her. She had only tried racing the horse to make him pay attention, to provoke him. It had not worked. All that she had experienced was his cold fury.

'I have not raced for some time. Not since…'

'Since when?' Vikar's voice was soft and insistent.

'Since I grew up.'

She turned and gave Vikar a brilliant smile, but the

smile faded slightly at the expression in his eyes. The light that had been there earlier had dimmed. She knew she should tell Vikar about Kjartan, but the words refused to come. She wanted to put the past behind her. She would find the words after they arrived at the waterfall.

Another wolf howl rent the air, echoed around them, held by the trees. It sent a shiver down her back.

'Shall we go?'

'Yes. I am ready.' As they left the field, Sela took one more glance back at the dead wolf in the shadow of the tree, then she turned her face towards the sun. 'We will spend the night at the waterfall.'

'When you said a cave behind a waterfall, I had envisioned a small damp thing with barely enough room to stand up in.' Vikar looked about the large cavern as they came through the curtain of water.

The front third was slick from the spray, but there was plenty of dry space at the back. He did not have to stoop until he was nearly at the back wall. There appeared to be a vent for air. It would mean they could make a fire here.

'You underestimated me.' Sela laughed and flicked her water-slicked hair back from her face. She stood next to him, close enough that he could see the droplets glistening on her face, begging to be tasted, tantalising his lips. 'You always did.'

'Did I, indeed?' Vikar inclined his head, giving her the opportunity to move away from him. She was skittish like a young horse. He had frightened her before at the hut. He had allowed her to escape, but Thor had placed another opportunity in his path. 'I learnt the hard way to underestimate you at my peril, Sela. You have grown into a woman of many talents.'

She remained where she was, looking at him with her blue eyes. He cupped his hands on either side of her face. Knew how her lips would taste. Cool. Delicious. Like ripe strawberries on a summer's day. Knew that he wanted to do more than taste them.

Her skin trembled beneath the pads of his fingers. Reluctantly he made his hands fall away.

They had come far today, but she had to want him. She had to make the choice. She had to make the first move.

He knew he was playing a high-stakes game of *tafl* with her, and he did not intend on losing. Her surrender would be worth waiting for.

'You are cold after coming through that waterfall.' He gave one last touch to her cheek, allowed her to turn her head to his palm, but she held her body still, unmoving. 'The shock is starting to set in as well. There should be a fire. I do not think the smoke would overpower us.'

'I will manage.' She kept her head high, but her eyes were wary. If he gave her an excuse, she'd retreat somewhere he couldn't follow. He had let her do that in Kaupang. It had seemed the right way then. It no longer did. 'I always do.'

'I will get a fire started.' Vikar looked around the bare cave. He would create some distance between them and see if he could approach the problem in another fashion. 'There is barely enough wood in here to start a fire, let alone provide enough heat to warm you up.'

'Where do you propose getting the wood?' Sela tried to make her words sound normal, but she was aware of every move his body made, was transfixed by the shadows that played across his face.

She had come very close to kissing him, had wanted to. Her body was infused with a stinging disappointment.

He had not wanted her. Instead his thoughts were of firewood and other mundane things. Practical things. Even now he was moving about the cave, speaking about where the fire should go and what food they had to eat. What had passed between them at the hut was gone.

She struggled to pay attention. A great cold weight seemed to be developing in the centre of her being. She knew it had very little to do with the outside air temperature or the ordeal she had been through, and everything to do with Vikar's rejection.

Vikar headed towards the curtain of silver water.

'Are you leaving?' She hated the way her voice sounded needy. The cave suddenly seemed a large and forbidding place. She wanted to ask him to stay or to take her with him. But she could not ask the question.

Four years ago she had needed him, wanted him to return with her to their lodgings after several of the court ladies had mocked her dress sense and he had refused. They had fought in front of everyone. It had been the beginning of the end. Even now the humiliation of that evening made her insides squirm. She had sworn that she would never put herself in that sort of position again.

'I mean it is sensible to have a fire,' she said slowly and carefully. 'I had not realised what a chill I would get. Give me a chance to get my breath back and I will help you gather the wood.'

'I will return with some wood. There is no need for

both of us to go.' Vikar's voice was gentle as if he were speaking to a child. 'If we are going to spend the night here, I would like to be comfortable.'

'Should I be doing anything? Your arm…'

'Wait.'

'I am not very good at waiting,' Sela said. 'Remember? I like to be busy doing things.'

'That is something of an understatement.' Vikar inclined his head. 'You must not doubt—I will return. I plan on returning. I have always planned on returning.'

He vanished through the wall of water before she could protest more.

Sela put her fingers to her lips. Vikar's words meant something more.

Had she misjudged him all those years ago?

The signs of his defection had all been there. She had not needed her father to point them out. Vikar had started staying out late and only returning when he knew she would be asleep. When she had tried voicing her fears, and asking for reassurance, he had brushed her aside. The ready excuses had dropped from his lips like ripe cherries on a summer morning—why Asa needed him, why he had to help and how Sela had to understand.

She sat back on her heels and listened to the sound of falling water.

That past was long behind her. She had grown up. Sela's hand brushed Kjartan's horses. She had responsibilities. But was she clinging on to her past like Kjartan clung on to his horses? He had left them for her to find. Now, she had to leave her past behind.

Her desire for Vikar was nothing new. It was from the

past, and she needed to put it behind her, before she did something foolish…like confiding her secrets.

When he did return, would he try to cajole her, to get her to reveal things best kept hidden?

Sela tapped her fingertips against her mouth. Earlier she had struggled with the temptation to reveal her secret. With each passing moment, the risk became greater. She had to find a way to distract him. She would have to take action and ensure her secrets were protected. She would strike first, but not immediately. Vikar was no fool; he would suspect something if she was too overt. She had to remain in control. It was the only way—to lay ghosts to rest and protect her future.

With quick footsteps, she walked over to a small ledge and secreted the horses. Tonight had nothing to do with Kjartan's heritage, and everything to do with his future.

It was the only way. She had to protect her son. And, more importantly, she had to protect her heart.

Chapter Ten

Vikar stepped through the curtain of ice-cold water, half-expecting Sela to be feigning sleep.

She wasn't.

She was sitting quietly, hands on her thighs, watching the water. He dropped the wood with a crash, but still she sat there. Ignoring him? Waiting for him? What game was she playing now?

Vikar regarded her profile, considered his next move.

Tonight, Sela would tell him why her father had abandoned her. Her story only gave the appearance of being complete. Now, after what they had been through, she would tell him every secret.

He would make her reveal her hidden truths. She was not indifferent to him, and he would not hesitate. And after he had learnt the truth, then he would consider what his next step would be.

The only thing gathering wood had shown him was how much he desired her. This morning's kiss haunted him. One touch, one taste of her lips, was not enough. He wanted more, but she had to give them willingly.

Even taking a plunge in an ice-cold pool had failed to dampen his ardour. But it would have to wait.

He wanted her surrender first.

This time, he would not be the one to ask, to seduce. He had sensed her desire earlier. He would wait.

Two could play at this game, but there would be only one winner: him.

He turned and left through the curtain of water, without saying a word.

'Have you brought in a whole forest?' she asked when he returned. Her hair was neatly plaited; her face sparkled with drops of water as if she had bathed in the waterfall.

'Enough for tonight, I have no desire to return to the forest later if our supplies run low,' he said, trying not to think about what bathing with her would be like.

'You appear to have thought of everything.'

'I like to think so. Enough wood to keep us in this cave for days.'

In reply, her tongue caught a droplet of water that clung to her lower lip.

He arranged the pieces of wood on a makeshift hearth, held on to his self-control, reminded himself of the promises he'd made. She needed to come to him. 'I should be able to get the fire going in no time.'

'If you wish; you must not hurry on my account.' Her lashes swept over her eyes, making dark smudges against flawless skin, skin that begged to be touched.

Vikar breathed deeply and knelt down. With practised movements, he used his piece of touchwood to capture the spark and then light the twigs and sticks. Small movements but ones that allowed him to regain some measure of control. In no time, a fire blazed out.

The light made it appear as if precious gems lined the walls—a room fit for a king…or a seduction.

'When I was a girl, I wondered what this cave would look like with a fire.'

'Does it meet with your expectations?'

'It surpasses them.' She toyed with the end of her plait.

'Did you never think to come back after you grew up?'

'I had…other responsibilities.'

'And what made you grow up?' Vikar asked softly and willed her to answer the question.

He waited and watched.

Twice she started to speak and appeared to change her mind, coming towards the fire and warming her hands. The area around her mouth went pale in the flickering light.

'I hadn't realised I was so cold,' she said finally.

Silently, Vikar cursed. What had caused her wariness to return?

'Are you all right, Sela?' he asked. 'Is there anything you need?'

'You have given me what I most wanted—a warm fire,' she said with more than a hint of laughter in her voice. 'Isn't it strange how, sometimes, you don't even realise what you want until it is there in front of you, staring you in the face?'

The tension went out of Vikar's neck. He risked a breath—she had been cold, that was all. He would wait and then try again. Patience. Unhurried. 'No mystery about that. Wet things can cause a chill.'

'You are right—wet things can cause a chill. It was sensible to get the wood. My clothes will be dry in no time…Vikar.'

Vikar turned from the glowing blaze to look where Sela knelt, and wished he hadn't. The water had moulded her clothes to her curves, curves that haunted his dreams and waking thoughts. She looked like one of the sirens from the sagas, enticing him with her dark blonde hair, and her eyes peeping out from under her lashes.

Was it deliberate?

Vikar rejected the idea as fanciful. She had never used her feminine wiles during their marriage. Although she had been an enthusiastic if inexperienced bed partner once she was there, Vikar had always known he was coaxing her into bed. He was not going to repeat his past mistakes. She had to show him that she wanted to be in his arms.

He planted his feet firmly and crossed his arms over his chest.

'Sela…' he started and his voice sounded thick to his ears.

'Shall we see about that mere scratch on your arm? I saw the size of the wolf's teeth.' She stood up and moved away from the fire, towards him with out-stretched fingers and a determined look on her face. Vikar's stomach clenched. He felt the same sickening sensation that he always did before battle. He wanted to get this right. He wanted her to trust him for more than just one night.

'It's nothing I assure you.'

He knew if she touched him at all the temptation would be too great. It was one of the most difficult things he had ever done—to wait and to watch.

'Let me judge that.' She put her hands on her hips,

but her eyes flashed with hidden mischief. 'Will you take off your shirt, or do I have to help you?'

'I am capable of doing it myself,' he mumbled, trying to keep his thoughts straight, and not be distracted by her nearness.

'But I want to help.' She ducked her head. 'You have not gone shy?'

'Me? Never.'

'Then stop being such a baby.'

Without waiting, she freed his tunic from his belt and lifted it upwards. Her fingers brushed his skin and sent ripples of pleasure through him. She lingered just fractionally on his chest. Vikar drew in his breath and kept his body still, waiting to see what she would do, if it was intentional.

'You carried all the wood with that?' Sela's eyes grew wide as she saw the gash.

'I told you it was no more than a scratch.' Vikar flexed the muscles in his arm, tried not to think about her fingers stroking his naked flesh. It had been far too long. 'No lasting harm done.'

'I would hate to see what you thought a real wound was like. It appears I knocked it slightly when I took your tunic off.' The colour on her cheeks flared.

'Touchwood will make the bleeding stop.' His voice sounded stilted to his ears.

'Touchwood? How can that help with wounds?' Sela tilted her head to one side. 'I have heard of many things in my time, Vikar, but never touchwood as a cure for wounds.'

'A trick I learnt from Haakon's new wife,' Vikar explained, relieved to have something besides Sela's lips to focus on. He was in danger of reaching out and pulling her into his arms, in danger of forgetting his plans. 'It stems the bleeding very quickly. She managed to save Haakon's elkhound that way, after they had encountered wolves.'

'Haakon's luck holds. A talented healer is to be prized.'

'She is.' Vikar looked to where the fire made shadows on the cave wall. 'More than that, she is an astonishing person. The change in Haakon since she came into his life has been astounding. He lives for Annis and his marriage.'

'I find that hard to believe. The Haakon who was always the first to arrive at any feast and the last to leave? Are we speaking of the same man? The one who went to Lindisfarne with you?'

'Maybe he was missing something in his life, and found it in Annis. You could say that she healed his spirit.'

Vikar looked at Sela, and willed her to understand what he was saying. He had puzzled over it, how his old friend could suddenly be so contented and happy, but there was no doubt Annis and the baby she carried had added to Haakon's life. When he had seen them together, he had realised that something had gone from his own life. How he needed something more, wanted something more, and had come looking for it.

'Is that her name—Annis?' Sela wrinkled her nose. 'It is unusual, but pretty.'

'Northumbrian.'

'Ah, that explains it. I would like to speak to her some time about the different healing methods. I find it useful to learn…' Her voice trailed away as she dropped her hands to her sides. 'I suppose I am unlikely to encounter her where I am going.'

'It is entirely in your hands.' Vikar watched her,

willed her to understand the unspoken message. 'What is the true reason why you never returned to Kaupang?'

'I spent some of the unhappiest times of my life there.'

Vikar flinched as her barb stuck, paining him far more than his wound. The past was not something he could undo, however much he might wish it.

'It is a place, nothing more or less.' Vikar carefully kept his face blank. The unhappiest she had ever been and yet he knew there had been good times, if only she'd care to remember. 'It has much to recommend it. The court is there with its entertainments.'

'There are other places I want to go and experience,' Sela said slowly. 'I grew weary of entertainment. Each day passed much as the one before, another piece of juicy gossip, another scandal to uncover, another humiliation to be endured.'

'I had not understood you hated it so much.'

'I dislike feeling confined.' Sela gestured with her arms. She gave a quick smile. 'In Kaupang, I was like a bird, beating my wings against the bars of a cage. People expected me to act in a certain fashion, to speak certain words, to wear specific clothes. It became so it was difficult for me to breathe.'

'And have you found happiness here?'

'I like to think so.' She paused. 'Yes, I am certain of it.'

'You will have to tell me the secret.'

'It is my secret.'

'Secrets are meant to be shared…between *friends*. You told me that.'

Her lips parted and he willed her to say it, to finally surrender. Then she closed her mouth, shook her head. 'Not this one.'

Vikar forced his attention away from her. He had nearly been there. She wanted to confide in him. He could feel it. He crumbled a piece of touchwood and started to apply it to his arm as he considered his next move.

'Allow me.' She took the fine dust from him, put it in his wound. Vikar tried to concentrate on something other than the slender fingers that were stroking his skin.

'There, now, it is much better.' She looked up at him and the smile on her face faded, replaced with something else. The fire played across her features, turning them gold. He doubted that Sif, Thor's wife, could have been more beautiful, more desirable than Sela was, standing here in the firelight with her hair softly curling about her face. He felt his control beginning to slip. He wanted her, but it had to be on his terms.

'Thank you.' Vikar forced his hands to fall to his sides. She had to give him a sign that she was willing to surrender to him, that she would share her secrets with him, that she wouldn't leave again. 'As you can see, the bleeding has stopped. I will recover. You will not get rid of me that easily.'

'Having saved your life, I would be disappointed if the wound had proved serious.'

Her fingers lingered on his forearm. He used his other hand, and held them there. She kept them there for a few heartbeats longer and then withdrew them, looked up at him with parted lips.

'Would you?' His voice had thickened considerably. He felt control beginning to ebb from him.

'Sometimes, it is easier if you have help.' She lifted a shoulder and her creamy neck was revealed.

'It depends on the sort of help.'

'Vikar…' Her voice was no more a whisper. Vikar felt his insides clench with anticipation, but he needed to hear it from her.

'What is it that you want, Sela?'

'You,' she whispered and curled her arm around his neck, pulled his lips to hers. 'I want you.'

'For how long?' he whispered and his breath filled her mouth.

'For as long as it lasts,' she replied against his lips.

'That could be a lifetime.'

Or just until dawn, she thought. 'I am no soothsayer.'

Something flickered in his eyes. Triumph? Passion? He gave her no time to wonder as he lowered his head and took possession of her mouth.

She opened her mouth and allowed their tongues to meet and explore. He tasted sweet and clean like river water. His hand came around and held her head, entangled his fingers in her hair.

'I am incapable of retreat, Sela,' he said against her mouth. 'If you mean to tease and torment, tell me now. And it ends. I mean for this to last.'

'I know what I want, Vikar.'

'Show me.'

Her hands came up and met the warm skin of his chest. A warmth fluttered inside her, grew and expanded until she was not sure what was providing the most heat—she or the fire. All she knew was this primitive urge sweeping through her.

'You are wearing too many clothes. Let me see you. Let me reveal your body.' His voice rippled over her as he tugged at the bottom of her tunic.

She went to help, but his fingers brushed hers away

and removed the tunic, freeing her body from its confines. She hesitated, wondering if she should react modestly, but decided against it. She was no blushing bride. Instead she stood there proudly with her shoulders and her back straight as his eyes slowly feasted on her breasts. She watched her nipples contract under the intensity of his gaze.

His fingers slid over her, travelled downwards until they cupped her breasts. He rubbed his thumbnail against her nipples, made them pucker tighter.

She reached out, did the same to him, heard with satisfaction the sharp intake of his breath. His skin was smooth against her fingers.

Without warning, he lowered his mouth, captured a nipple, tugged and sent a spasm of pleasure through out her body.

Her hands came up and buried themselves in his thick hair, now dark from the water. Held him there. Then she trailed her mouth down his neck to his chest, and tentatively touched his nipple with the point of her tongue, felt it contract, become taut and heard his indrawn breath.

A surge of satisfaction filled her. She could do this. She would remain in control.

'You should have the trousers off as well,' he whispered as his fingers travelled inexorably lower, gliding over her body. 'I wouldn't want you to catch cold.'

'Yours are still on,' she reminded him with a husky laugh.

'Not any longer.'

With one fluid movement, he divested himself of the trousers. Stepped away from her. Stood there in front of her as the fire made golden patterns on his skin.

She had thought that she knew what he looked like, knew the faint tracery of scars he had received over the years, remembered the feel of his skin against hers. But she knew, looking at him, that her memory had not done him justice. He was fashioned like some broad-shouldered god. A faint sprinkling of hair covered his chest and led her gaze lower. His rampant desire was revealed to her.

Her hand reached out, hesitated, but then went forward. Touched his arousal. Hot. Firm, but as smooth as the most luxurious fur. She glanced up and saw something flare in his eyes. She was doing this to him. He desired her, and her alone.

A wave of triumph swept through her. Her fingers closed tighter around him. Traced his hood with the edge of her finger before stroking the full length of him. A growl of pleasure emerged from his throat.

'Do you like?' she asked.

'I like very much, but if you continue that way, it will be over before we have properly begun.'

'And that would be so bad.' She pressed her lips to his throat, intending to trail them down his body, the way she remembered him doing to her years ago.

'I want to savour you, Sela.' He leant forward and put his hands on her hips, drew her body to him. 'Allow me to give you pleasure as well.'

He positioned her hips against his, sliding her up and down. The hardness of him rubbed against her trousers, pressed forward and into her, causing the material to tighten over the nub of her most sensitive flesh. At the gasp of pleasure, he continued to rub up against her while his fingers caressed the ever-tightening points of her nipples. She shuddered. The small fire inside her had rapidly grown and radiated outwards, flaming out of control. All she could concentrate on was the growing pressure between her legs.

A small moan rose in her throat as he tantalised her, holding her lightly against him, stroking her body, demanding a response, receiving one and then demanding another. He was playing her as a skald plays a harp. This had ceased to have anything to do with keeping secrets and everything to do with experiencing the satisfaction his fingers promised.

A shiver coursed through her body and she knew it had nothing to do with the dampness of her clothes. Heat pulsated inside her, warming her from within. A raging fire, scoring her, demanding she divest her remaining garment. Her fingers grasped ineffectively at her trousers.

'I told you that wet things would make you cold,' he growled in her ear. 'Will you take them off or shall I assist?'

'You.' The whisper hung in the air. 'You take them.'

His fingers grasped the fastenings, fumbled, and undid them on the second attempt. A smile tugged at his cheek. 'I had never thought to undo trousers before. You will have to forgive my…inexperience.'

'There is a first time for everything.' She gazed at him from under her lashes, willing him to continue. Her entire body tingled with anticipation.

'That is one way of looking at it.'

'It is the only way.'

He gave a soft laugh and went back to work, easing the trousers slowly down her hips, her legs.

'Your skin tastes sweeter than honey,' he murmured

against her belly as his lips followed his hands, skimming the surface of her skin.

Her legs became like water and she struggled to stay upright as her body remembered the passion from years gone by. How his fingers had worked a certain magic on her that made her forget everything in the world but him.

She wondered if he'd notice the changes in her body. How her hips had become fuller, and her breasts larger? Would he notice she had carried a baby?

She waited for him to say something. To notice. But his hands continued to stroke her body, light fluttering caresses, followed by a lingering of his tongue. She looked up at him and saw only passion in his eyes. Decided that it didn't matter. The only thing that mattered was him and what he was doing to her.

When they were together like this, she never had any doubts or fears. Those had come later when she was alone, waiting for him to return.

Her hands gripped his shoulders for support, and he gently scooped her up and laid her down.

'Such smooth skin deserves fur to lie on, not hard stone,' he said.

'The fire has given warmth to the stone.' She knew that it did not matter where she lay. The only thing that mattered was him and this fire that was raging inside her.

His eyes were like polished emeralds. Emeralds with a flame hidden within their depths, reflecting the tongues of desire that were shooting through her being. The sort of eyes that she knew she never wanted to look away from.

The pads of his fingers stroked her body, sliding gently as if she were made of some precious glass. Evoking the past they had shared and making promises for the future, promises of pleasure that her body wanted him to keep.

All the memories of the times before crowded back in around her. Captured her and tantalised her body. She knew what was coming next and, because of that, her body reacted more strongly.

She had forgotten how good this could be. It was as if she had been living some sort of half-life, more asleep than awake. Now every fibre of her being rejoiced in being alive once more.

The passion they had shared engulfed her, but equally there was a new urgency about it, as if it had not lain dormant all those years, but had grown and demanded something more. It had become a raging hunger.

Her hands reached up and encircled his neck. She brought his mouth down to hers and recaptured his lips, explored the texture of his mouth. She felt the weight of him on her, trapping her, but calling to something primitive within her.

'Vikar, please.'

Her breath had started to come in small pants and she barely recognised her own voice. Her hips lifted, inviting the length of him to enter her. The only thing she knew was that she wanted him inside her, filling her, making her whole.

He nodded, seemed to understand.

His fingers parted her thighs with a great urgency. She lifted her hips to welcome him. He entered with a rush and then lay there, deep inside her.

She looked up at him, and the unexpectedly tender expression on his face caused her to still. His hand stroked the locks of hair from her face.

'I have missed this…with you,' he said. 'I hadn't realised how much.'

'I have as well.'

Gently she began to move. His rhythm echoed hers, built until, together, she heard the cries, felt the shudders and had the world made new.

Much later Sela opened her eyes to see that the fire had burnt down to ash and the waterfall had turned a sort of silver-grey. She started to slip away, but Vikar's arm tightened around her and held her against him. She saw his eyes watching her with their deep-green gaze. There was a question in them that was quickly masked.

A tremor of panic went through her. The night was over, and in the morning—regrets?

She wasn't entirely sure that she wanted morning. Wasn't sure that she wanted to face whatever was out there for her, but she knew that she could not stay here forever.

'The sun is rising,' she said, nodding towards the waterfall.

'Is it morning already?'

'You can see the light. The night is nearly over.'

His hand ran down the length of her. 'A pity. I enjoyed the night. I had wanted to continue on and on. Can we ask the sun to wait?'

'The night is made to provide pleasure. With morning comes responsibility.'

Responsibility. What were her responsibilities? His hand stilled on her stomach. It was not as smooth as he remembered. In the half-light, he could make out a network of silver scars. He rolled away from her, allowing the cool air to rush over him. He needed to think clearly.

Before they arrived at the farm, he wanted to know the truth. Last night, he had been distracted, but this morning, he would wring it from her. She reached for her tunic. His hand caught hers, prevented her from moving.

'Wait.' There was a different tone to his voice. Half-command, half-plea.

'Is there a problem?' Sela looked directly at him, her brow furrowing.

'When were you going to tell me that Kjartan is your child?' he asked softly and saw her flinch.

'Is it something you needed to know?' she asked. Her hand went to cover her stomach and her eyes widened.

'It is something I would like to have known.'

Vikar concentrated on the roof of the cave, picking out the little indentations, taking deep, steadying breaths while he waited for her answer. Willed her to share her innermost secrets. She said nothing, only looked at him with big eyes.

Sela's silence confirmed his sudden fear.

She had not planned on telling him. She had intended to keep it a secret. She'd had a child with some unknown man, some lover who had unlocked her hidden places. She had never been this uninhibited before with him. Had she been, he doubted he would have had the strength or the desire to leave her bed. Even now, he could feel his body beginning to harden, wanting her again, wanting to put his mark on her and erase all memory of other men.

With each passing breath, he felt more anger towards her unknown lover, the one who had given her a child, a child so precious that she had dared risk her life crossing that ravine to keep his wooden toy.

'Is your only answer going to be a question?'

'Why is it important now?' He could hear the sorrow in her voice, and wondered what the father must have meant to her. He had been blind before. He had thought she'd wanted to get to her father, but it was her son. It had to be. It was the only explanation. 'Why have you asked?'

'I suspected before, but seeing your body like this has convinced me.'

'My body?' Her hands tried to shield her nakedness from his gaze. He grabbed her tunic and tossed it to her. She caught it and instinctively put it on, hiding her body from his gaze. He reached over and pulled his damp trousers on. 'Why should seeing my body make you ask this question?'

'You are fuller about the hips and your stomach has a series of silver scars.' Vikar curled his lip back. 'Did you think I wouldn't notice?'

'I was not aware that you noticed much about me when we were together.' Her eyes blazed out at him. 'I had not given it much thought. Does it make much difference?'

Vikar felt his jaw tighten. Had he failed that much as a husband? Of course he had noticed her body, had rejoiced in it, but she had always appeared modest, not like the way she had behaved last night. He had never imagined the passion that had lurked within her.

He tried to control his temper, the sudden surge of jealousy that filled him.

What had happened to this lover of hers? Why had this unknown man been able to unlock her passion when he himself had clearly failed all those years ago?

'Are you seeking to deny it?' he asked the back of her head.

'Kjartan is my child,' she said and stood up to face him. 'It is nothing I have ever denied. I would never deny it.'

'Why is he with you instead of his father?' Vikar searched her face, but it provided no clues. 'Why did your lover desert you?'

'His father and I were no longer together when I gave birth.'

'He left you?'

'I left him.'

Sela stared directly at him, her eyes furious, her jaw clenched. What had this man done to her? Vikar felt the urge to run him through for hurting her, for leaving her with a baby. The man should have fought for her. He would have.

'Did he come after you?'

'No. He never did.'

'Did you tell him where you were?'

'If he had wanted to find me, he would have known where to find me.' She gave an eloquent shrug.

'But you knew you were going to have his baby?' Vikar looked at her in astonishment. 'And you did not seek him out?'

'Yes. I had my reasons. It seemed to be the only thing to do. I did not want to risk—'

Vikar put up his hand, stopping the flow of her words. He knew the tradition of the Viken. She must have feared her lover would not accept the child and the child would have been exposed.

'What did your father think of this? How did he feel about your lover?'

She blinked twice and seemed confused. 'My father has very little to say about him. Now. He adores Kjartan, wants the best for him.'

'It begins to make sense.'

'What does?'

'Why your father left you unprotected. Why he never allowed you to return to Kaupang. Why he abandoned you to your fate. He was ashamed of you and your child, your child by your untrustworthy lover.'

Sela stared at Vikar in astonishment.

'Ashamed of me? Ashamed of Kjartan?' Sela shook her head in vigorous denial. She bit her lip before she continued. She had thought he would guess, but he hadn't.

She would have to tell him, but not now, not when he was in this mood. He would not believe her. If he saw Kjartan, then she could begin to explain what had happened. If she told him now, the chances were that he would deny him.

'I will explain about Kjartan, if you wish, but I should like you to meet him first.'

'Why do I need to meet him?' Vikar remained motionless. 'It is obvious what happened.'

'Is it?' Sela pressed her hands together. She had no idea why Vikar felt the need to play this sort of game. He must have guessed. 'Tell me what your conclusions are. How have I led my life since we last met? Why would my giving birth to Kjartan have anything to do with my father's actions in the past few days?'

'You had an affair.' Vikar's eyes became hooded. 'Your father disapproved and ended it. He accepted the child, but has ceased to protect you as much as he once did. You rebelled. He sought to punish you. I have seen it happen before, Sela. It is sad, but true.'

'Aren't you interested in Kjartan's father?' Her voice showed her astonishment, despite her best efforts.

He believed she had had an affair. Truly believed it. She fought against hysterical laughter.

She had no idea why he should think that, but it might mean Kjartan could remain with her. He might be willing to let them go. She damped down the hope. She would wait and see how he reacted when he first encountered his son. If he guessed, she could not deny his parentage, but had the gods fed her a scrap of hope?

'Do you not want to know who my lover was?' She rolled the word 'lover' stretching it out.

'Not particularly.' Vikar's mouth thinned. 'You say he has departed from your life. I cannot understand why a man would, but that is a matter for him.'

'If that is your decision. But I do wish you to meet Kjartan. We can speak then.' She fought to keep the pleading out of her voice.

'Let us speak no more of this.' Vikar put his hands on his hips and his eyes narrowed. Sela recognised the stubborn set to his jaw. 'My business is with your father, not with your son.'

Chapter Eleven

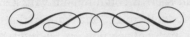

Sela stepped through the curtain of water and into a world remade.

She had thought that everything would return to normal in the morning, leaving the cave behind, but the colours were sharper, the pine scent in the air stronger. A rainbow she had not noticed before shone in the spray. Her senses tingled with it. Beyond all reason, she felt thoroughly alive.

It gave her hope that everything would turn out perfectly. She wanted to believe that like this sparkling morning somehow her destiny would turn out bright and shining.

She gave a small sigh. She had thought that she'd given up believing in happy endings, and making glorious halls in the skies, but this morning her mind was alive to the possibilities.

Finally everything in her life appeared to be heading towards a glorious future.

'We need to turn our faces to the sun and keep going,' Sela called. 'We should be there before noon.'

'You forgot something.' Vikar came through the water. The droplets of water sparkled in his hair like diamonds. Sela resisted the temptation to pluck one of them to keep.

'I don't think so.' She put her hands on her hips, leant forward. 'I remember *everything*.'

'Kjartan's horses.' Vikar held them out. Two wooden horses cradled in his hands. 'I discovered them on a ledge.'

'Thank you.' Sela took them. A lump rose in her throat. She had been so busy with her thoughts about the future and its possibilities that she had forgotten her responsibilities. How had that happened? Her fingers curled around the horses. It would not happen again.

'Did you mean to leave them?'

She shook her head and placed them snugly in her belt. 'I wanted to put them somewhere safe…last night.'

'Ah, you were frightened that I would want to burn them for firewood.' Vikar dropped a kiss on her nose. His smile made her insides turn over, but there was something else deep within his eyes.

'Not that.' She shook her head, aware the dreams were building quickly in her head. She had thought last night would have quenched her desire for Vikar, but her passion for him appeared to have grown rather than diminished. Equally she knew that she was poised on a knife's edge. Too much lay between them for her to want anything more than what they had just experienced.

'The reason doesn't exist any more. I am pleased you discovered them. It saves me having to come back here.'

'Don't you want to return?' His green eyes twinkled as he ran a finger down the curve of her neck, sending ripples down her spine. 'Here I was already plotting how to entice you back.'

'I want to face the rest of my life.' She tucked her hair behind her ears, felt the warmth of the sun and the sudden weakening in her knees. 'Kjartan is waiting for me at the farmhouse. He has never been away from me for so long before.'

'And your father.' A muscle jumped his jaw. 'Your father will be there.'

'Yes, my father. We will find them today.' Her voice shook slightly. And the unspoken question hung in the air. Would they? Could she face it if it was another empty building? She pressed her hands against her eyes, and willed the dread to be gone. She forced her lips into a trembling smile. 'Won't we?'

'I hope so, Sela, I hope so.' Vikar's fingers were warm under her elbow, supporting her.

'Sometimes, all you have left is hope,' she whispered.

'And, sometimes, it is enough.' His fingers fell away from her elbow. 'You have to believe, Sela.'

Sela's breath caught in her throat. She waited for him to say something more, but a raven cawed loudly.

'It is time we were going.'

'Yes, we have wasted enough time here,' Sela said, starting to climb the hill.

'Sela, whatever we experienced here, it was far from a waste of time.'

Sela's footsteps faltered, missed a step. She glanced back. Vikar stood there with the faint breeze ruffling his hair. Rugged. Determined. Her fingers curled into fists.

How far was she prepared to go to fight for her future? She forced her gaze forward.

'I stand corrected,' she said quietly.

'Mor, Mor.' Sela heard Kjartan's excited shout before she saw him. 'You came.'

Her heart constricted and tears formed in her eyes. He was here and he was safe. All her fears had been for nothing, and she had achieved everything she wanted. Dreams could come true. He was here, at the farm beyond the waterfall. She had not even dared think about where he might be if he wasn't. She had forced herself only to think of the next boulder in front of her.

She began to run, heedless of Vikar, heedless of everything except her son. She heard a cry and knew it came from her throat.

Her son was here, and whole, and not lying injured or dead on some lonely mountainside, exposed with his shade condemned to walk the earth until the final battle between the gods and the giants.

Her mind took in everything, devouring the details, the blond hair, the green eyes, the soft pink skin—before her eyes misted up and the world blurred. She inhaled deeply, enjoying that scent of young child that was Kjartan.

Kjartan launched himself towards her. She caught him in her arms and turned him round and round. Devoured him again. Then hugged him close.

If she could, she'd never let him go. There were so many things she wanted to say, but most of all her heart rejoiced because he was here alive and she had feared that she was destined never to set eyes on him again.

'I have been so worried about you,' she said, pressing

her lips to his temple, savouring his childlike scent, his
soft, blond hair. Him. Her son. 'I have missed you so
much. You do not know how I worried. How I longed
to see you.'

Kjartan's brows drew together as he wriggled out
of her grasp.

'But, *Mor*, I'm safe. I was with *Morfar.* We played a
game. He promised we could play it again soon.' He put
his fingers to his lips. 'Shh, or the *tottr* men will hear
you, Una says, but *Morfar* says if she's not quiet, he will
call the *tottr* men to come, eat up Una. Una, shh.'

He gave a merry laugh as if it were a big joke and
mimed walking on tiptoes with his finger to his lips. And
to him, she supposed it was.

A cold chill ran down her spine.

Her father had most certainly known that the *tottr*
men were real, but had Una? Had her father's words
frightened the elderly maid?

Her father would never have carried out the threat.
She was certain of that. He loved Kjartan and always
strove to keep him safe. Would he have sacrificed Una?
A deep chill went through her.

She looked up, watching the white clouds against the
blue sky and ruthlessly suppressed the doubts. She had
to trust that her father had not allowed Kjartan or Una
anywhere near that awful place. She would not think
about it. She trusted her father. He had been true to his
word and had kept Kjartan safe.

She put her hands on Kjartan's shoulders and looked
him up and down, reassuring her mind that he was there,
real and solid and not some waking dream.

'I declare you have grown in the last few days. You

are getting big, young man.' Sela brushed a lock of hair, hair that was the exact same shade as Vikar's from Kjartan's forehead and remembered what he had been like as a baby—weak and helpless—and how she had worried that he would not live out the winter.

'Soon I will have a real sword. *Morfar* promised.'

'We shall have to see about that.'

Sela let her hands fall to her sides. He was growing up. How long would he stay her little boy? And how long before he would have to begin his training as a warrior? It was his destiny to be a warrior, she knew that. Every boy had to become a warrior, win his sword and his honour.

Her father could not instruct him, not in his current condition, and all his warriors were scattered, his allies gone. The problem remained. It was a decision she would have to make in the days and weeks to come, but Kjartan would have to begin. Somewhere. Soon.

Sela straightened her posture. This journey had changed in more ways than one. She would have to face realities that she had not wanted to admit to before. The world around her was changing, and she could not hold time still. However much she might want to.

'*Mor…Morfar* promised.'

'Your grandfather should not make promises without speaking to me.'

Kjartan stuck out his chin, becoming a miniature replica of Vikar. The resemblance was so great that she expected to hear a sharp intake of breath behind her. He must guess. It was obvious to any who used their eyes.

She should have told Vikar last night, when he had given her the opportunity, but his words had been so biting and condescending. She had reasoned that he wouldn't have believed her—not without the evidence of his own eyes. And now, she waited for the inevitable question. Vikar remained silent, watching her and Kjartan from hooded eyes. Their gazes locked, but he did nothing.

Kjartan tugged at her tunic, and brought her attention to back to him.

'A real sword. When we get back to the hall, *Morfar* will find Uncle Eric's sword. I proved myself w-w...' Kjartan's brow wrinkled with concentration and his hands bunched into his fists. 'A worthy champion, he said. I will be a warrior soon. A great warrior.'

'A real sword? We shall see about that.' Sela patted his shoulder as a stab of ice ran through her. What had Kjartan's journey entailed? What plans did her father have for him? She wished he had spoken with her first.

'*Mor*, please, a sword.' Kjartan's face looked up at her.

'I have found something else. A few items I think you misplaced.'

She held out the horses and watched Kjartan's eyes light up. He reached out and fingered them as if he couldn't quite believe it. Tears came again to Sela's eyes. She blinked hard, and knew that Vikar watched Kjartan's joy as well.

'You found both! I told *Morfar*. Silly *Morfar* not to believe. He didn't believe you would come here. I believed.'

'Your grandfather seriously underestimates your mother's abilities,' Vikar said, coming to stand beside Sela. 'I have heard quite a lot about you, Kjartan.'

Kjartan made no reply, but tucked his head down. He turned his horses over and over and his bottom lip stuck out.

'Kjartan, mind your manners. This is someone I would like you to meet—a great warrior,' Sela said, stumbling over the last word.

The words—your father—stuck in her throat, choked her. To say them aloud would mean to lose Kjartan, and she found herself incapable of that finality. She wanted Vikar to know and yet… She'd wait until Vikar guessed or at least looked at her with a question in his eyes. It was all she could do after last night. He had seemed positive that she had taken a lover. *Her!* The question had to come from him. It had to. She was unable to gamble Kjartan's future in that way.

'Kjartan, it is an honour to meet you.'

Kjartan continued to keep his head down and turned away from Vikar. Vikar raised an eyebrow. Sela gave a shrug and a little laugh. 'He is only young and he has had a traumatic few days. Give him time. He normally chatters away to anyone who is in earshot.'

'When did you arrive? Was it a hard journey, Kjartan, for you and your grandfather?' Vikar asked.

Kjartan shrank back against Sela's leg, hiding his face and putting his thumb in his mouth. His big eyes looked appealingly up at her.

'Who is that?' he asked in a trembling voice. 'Why is that man here?'

'Because he is. Because he helped me to find you.' Sela kept her voice even. She looked between Vikar and Kjartan, helpless. She had expected Kjartan to behave.

'I don't like him.' Kjartan's bottom lip trembled.

'Send him away. Make him go away. *Morfar* won't see him. Won't see anyone.'

'Kjartan!' Sela stared at her son in astonishment. He was never like this. She had expected... She bit her lip. She wasn't sure what she had expected, but not this.

'I am a Viken jaarl and I wish to speak with your grandfather. I will speak to him and he will listen to me.' Vikar bent down, so his face was on Kjartan's level. 'I have come a long way. Take me to him. There's a clever boy.'

'I will not!' Kjartan reached for his wooden dagger, stood there. Green gaze met green gaze, neither backing down. A lump formed in Sela's throat. 'My father is a great warrior and I will be one soon. I am not afraid. Go away. Bad man.'

Sela went still. She knew her father in his prime would not have accepted such words from a child. If Vikar raised his hand... She swallowed hard and saw Vikar's fingers reach towards his belt. Time might yet remain.

'Kjartan! You must not say such things. Apologise now.'

'I will not!' Kjartan stamped his foot. 'Because I'm not afraid.'

'Really?' Vikar lifted an eyebrow, but his eyes were like cold glass. 'Foolhardiness will not give you a long life. And a great warrior should learn courtesy. Someone should teach you manners.'

'Vikar, forgive my son.'

Sela moved between Kjartan and Vikar, shielding Kjartan with her body. If Vikar found out about who Kjartan truly was and publicly rejected him, Kjartan would have no future as a warrior. He would have no place in Viken society. Vikar wouldn't be so cruel, would he?

'He is young and has been through an ordeal. He is overly tired and has no idea what he is saying.'

Vikar looked at her and Kjartan with sceptical eyes, but he did nothing. Sela propelled Kjartan forward.

'You will apologise, Kjartan. You speak to adults with a civil tongue.'

Kjartan's face took on a mutinous expression, one that reminded Sela of Vikar when his will was thwarted. One unyielding face meeting another. Kjartan flushed slightly.

'Sorry. Thank you for bringing my mother here,' he said in a small voice before hiding his face again in her trouser leg. 'You're not bad. You're good.'

Sela glanced at Vikar and hoped it would be enough.

'He certainly appears to have inherited your impudence as well as your looks, Sela.' Vikar gave a short laugh. 'There is no mistaking his parentage. He is you all over again.'

Sela opened her mouth, but Una hurried up, her face creased with worry and her shawls quivering about her.

'Una, it is fine. Kjartan is here with me,' Sela said. 'It is good to see you.'

'My lady, my lady, you have arrived.' Una grabbed Sela's hands. 'I prayed to the gods that you would arrive today. You had to arrive today.'

'Is there something wrong?' The back of Sela's neck prickled. She should have hurried yesterday rather than stopping at the waterfall. She could not, however, undo the past. She had to remember that Una often exaggerated. 'Why did I need to arrive today? Was my father planning on travelling somewhere else?'

'I have been praying to the good goddess Frejya that you would arrive.' Una appeared close to tears. 'Bose the Dark had one of his turns early this morning. I fear the journey was too much for him. I fear…the worst.'

'Vikar, wait here. Speak to Kjartan. I am sure he would like to hear about your dragon ship.' Sela shoved Kjartan slightly towards Vikar. Maybe if they became friends, then she could explain… 'You will like him, once you become acquainted. I know you will.'

Sela began to run, covering the distance between her and the small farmhouse with great speed.

Her father was lying in the best bed with the farmer's wife standing next to him. The clean but sparsely furnished room had a fire lit in the centre despite the heat of the day, and her father was swathed in furs.

Her father's skin was much more yellow than when she'd last seen him and his eyes were sunken. She hated to think what the effort to make his way here had cost him. All because she had been unable to control the men at the start of the fight. Did he blame her?

'*Far, Far*, I am here. I have arrived safely.' She brushed her lips against his withered cheek.

'Daughter,' he croaked out and his claw-like hand came up to hold hers. She nodded towards the farmer's wife, who made a brief bob of her head and disappeared out of the room. 'You did make it.'

'I did with Vikar's help,' Sela said quietly. 'I owe him my life. I would not have survived the forest without him.'

Her father's hand plucked at the fur covering him. 'Vikar is here? You brought that man here? To this sanctuary? My one remaining refuge?'

The accusation was there in his voice. She had failed. It stung to know he blamed her. Would he have preferred her to perish? She refused to believe that of her father.

It was merely that she had not explained the situation properly. Once he knew how Vikar had saved her life, then he would see.

'He guessed which way I would try to escape...' Sela paused and wondered how much she should tell her father. There were certain aspects of the situation that he did not need to know. 'He captured me when the line broke and the hall fell. Gorm fell, *Far*. His sword is broken.'

'Gorm had lived a good life, but I shall miss him.'

'Vikar was the one who forced me to surrender. I had to. I had to save what remained of our men.' Sela paused, willing her father to make some sign that he understood why she had done that. 'I refused to tell him where you were. He imprisoned me in the strong room.'

'Continue.' Her father made an imperious gesture. 'When I know everything, I will make my judgement, daughter. I am not an unfair man, despite what some might say about me.'

Her father was silent as she related the tale. He merely raised his eyebrows and pulled his lips down into a mutinous expression when she mentioned the *tottr* men and their escape, and how they had approached the hut from a different direction.

'*Far*, why did you come here?' Sela asked. 'I had expected to find you at the hut.'

Her father gazed up at the roof of the farmhouse for a long time.

'It was necessary.' He turned his face towards her and reached out his fingers. She gave them a small squeeze.

'*Far*, you don't know what it was like to arrive there and discover you had gone.' Sela withdrew her fingers.

A small touch of his hand failed to banish the memory of her despair. 'I need to know more. Please.'

'I had considered that Vikar might wish to see me, child, when I escaped. I have no wish to speak with him on such terms.'

'How did you know I was with him?'

'Him or someone else.' Her father moved his hand slightly. 'The hall had fallen. I feared you might be taken, and my fears proved accurate. Much to my regret. Perhaps Gorm was right. Perhaps it is best to die with a sword in your hand.'

Her father collapsed back against the pillows and appeared to go to sleep. Sela listened to his steady breathing and struggled to control the hurt that flooded through her. He was ill and did not comprehend what she had said. Later, when he woke again, they would talk and he would see she had acted correctly. She was ready to slip off when he opened his eyes again and stared directly at her.

'Why did you bring Vikar here after I left you that clue? You should have gone back to the hall. I expected you to go back.'

'I had very little choice…Kjartan…you.'

'You did. Daughter, I am ashamed of you.'

Sela leant forward, so that her face was close to her father's, so that he could read her lips. '*Far*, haven't you been paying attention to what I was saying? He saved my life several times. I had no choice, even if I wanted to make one. I owe him my life. I had to make sure you and Kjartan were safe. He has promised…'

Her father made an irritated noise in the back of his throat. 'If I was the man I once was—'

'If you were the man you once were, you would not have left me to guard the hall.' Sela stopped, appalled at her words. The accusation seemed to hang in the air. She had not meant to say it. '*Far*, I did not mean that. We agreed on the strategy. You did the right thing. It is not your fault that the hall fell in the manner it did. It is entirely mine.'

'You are right, Daughter, I should have argued with you. My own feebleness was no excuse for cowardice.' Her father's voice trembled. Old. Weak. Tired. Here was not the father she knew.

'You have never been a coward, *Far*. Never that.' Sela shook her head, willed him to believe it. 'None of your men would call you that either.'

'What men? Where are they? Where have they gone?'

'*Far*, it is in the past. Leave it there.'

'I should have faced them with my sword in my hand. You should have demanded it.' His head collapsed down on his chest and the light went out of his eyes. 'I have thought about this, and about other mistakes in my life. But I cannot undo the past.'

'Neither of us can.' A wave of tiredness hit Sela. Her head began to pound and all she wanted to do was curl up in a ball. But it was impossible. Vikar would have to be faced, and she would have to tell him of Kjartan's parentage. She would have to find a solution to her problems on her own.

'Daughter, give me some time and I will make it up to you. It was never my intention that you should have to go through this, that you should be put in any danger.'

'I know that, *Far*.' Sela felt her throat close around the words. 'Thank you for saying it.'

'You are a good woman, Sela. I know what you have been through. Trust me on this and trust me to see you right.'

'I have no idea what you are talking about.'

Her father closed his eyes and his voice became slurred. 'You need a strong man, Sela. I am determined to find you one. Hafdan—'

'Hafdan is dead, *Far*.' Sela kept her voice steady. 'He died attempting to raid a Viken estate, violating our truce with Thorkell. He never went to Permia. He brought this on us.'

Her father's face drained of colour. 'Dead? Hafdan? Who killed him?'

'Vikar. He attacked the farm where Vikar and his felag were.' Sela pressed her hands to keep them from trembling.

'That was reckless of him. The gods have duly punished him.'

'Did you know that Hafdan would do this? Did you agree to the plan?'

Her father turned his face from her. 'I wanted what was best for you and Kjartan.'

'That is no answer.'

'It is the only one you will get.'

'I have come to speak with you, Bose the Dark.' Vikar's clipped tones came from the doorway. Not a single syllable held warmth. 'You will not escape this time. I have given you long enough with your daughter. It is time.'

Chapter Twelve

Sela regarded Vikar's stern face. She found it hard to reconcile the warrior who filled the entrance with his hand on the hilt of his sword blocking out the daylight with the tender lover of last night.

Which one was the true Vikar?

Where was the man who had cradled her last night? Had he used her? Had she trusted an illusion?

Their journey had finished, the truce was over, and she found she wasn't ready for it to end. She wasn't ready for Vikar to become the ex-husband who had destroyed her world again. She wanted the man she had depended on to see her safely here standing before her. The man who had given his cloak to save a boy's beloved toy would understand about her father, but would this warrior?

With an effort, she pushed away her concerns, and concentrated on her father. Her first duty was to her father. He had had enough shocks today.

'Who is it, Daughter?'

'I will take care of this.' She pulled the covers up to his chin. 'You rest and we will speak more about this later.'

'You are a good daughter.' Her father gave her fingers a squeeze. 'A man could not ask for a better one.'

'Sela, why am I waiting?' Vikar thundered. 'Your father cannot hide forever. He must face what has happened.'

'My father is ill. You can speak with him later when he has recovered a bit. I have just told him about Hafdan. They were close.' She advanced towards Vikar, blocking his way, intending to bodily shove him out of the room, if he did not take the advice.

What right had he to barge in here and make demands?

She had planned on calling him in after she was certain of the situation. She bit her lip. The journey was over. The truce had finished. They had returned to warfare, only she discovered it was not what she wanted.

'I will speak with him now. It is why I journeyed here. If he is alive, and can speak…'

'Give him some peace.'

'Very convenient timing.'

'Let him rest and then he will be fit to speak with you.' Sela held her hands under her chin and willed him to understand, just as he had understood about her fears on the journey.

'Let me speak to him and judge. I have had him play the illness trick before in Kaupang. Your father has played me once too often, Sela.'

Vikar moved his hand as if to sweep her aside, but Sela planted her feet more firmly. His eyes were hard lumps of green glass and showed none of the compassion she had seen before. They swept the room, coming to rest on the bed. Her father gave a small moan and appeared to sink lower down amongst the covers.

It was a small thing, surely Vikar had to understand.

Her father could not go anywhere. What difference did it make if he said his piece now or at twilight?

'On what we went through together,' she said, 'I beg you to wait.'

'We made a bargain, you and I,' Vikar reminded her, but he did not move towards the bed. 'My sole purpose in coming here was to speak with your father. That has never altered.'

'I have held to it thus far.'

Vikar's lips became a thin, white line, but he said nothing.

Sela turned her palms upwards in a gesture of supplication. She hated to beg, but she wanted some sign of understanding and co-operation. This was about more than Vikar speaking to her father. This was about them, about Vikar trusting her.

After all they had experienced, did he really think she would lie to him? With Kjartan she might not tell the whole truth, but she wouldn't lie.

'Should you not have trusted me to keep it?' Her voice caught. She swallowed hard and lifted her head as high as it would go, forcing her voice to be dignified. 'You will have your chance.'

'I know Bose the Dark of old.' There was no softening of his features. 'You have not seen how he operates. How he slides away into the shadows, leaving others exposed. He did the same to you—left you exposed at the hall, left you to make the trek over the mountains on your own.'

'I have not been at court for years, but my father is what he seems—ill. The shades of his ancestors hover around his bed.'

'How do you know?'

'He appears weak and feeble. His skin is yellow.' Sela gestured towards the bed. 'Look at him. The scent of sickness hangs around him.'

'I made that mistake two summers ago. He was ill in bed or so I thought. Hafdan told me. Ill with little hope of recovery,' Vikar said, his lips turning downwards. 'I left and later discovered he had gone behind my back and taken the best trade route.'

A sound of muffled laughter came from the bed. Sela frowned.

How ill *was* her father? Was he simply tired from his long journey, and seeking to exploit it? The story Vikar told seemed genuine enough. But this was about more than trade routes. She hesitated.

'He is proud of his cunning. Loki with all his tricks is his personal god. But this time, it is different. He has been through much.'

Vikar reached out, pulled her towards him. She could see the hollow of his throat.

'After what we have been through on this journey, do you truly trust your father to be honest in all his dealings?'

'I trust my eyes.' Sela shook her head and stepped away. 'My father is in no state to converse. Please, Vikar.'

'I have had enough of this prevarication. Your father appears well enough. He will speak with me.' Vikar brought his fist down onto the palm of his hand. The sound reverberated throughout the room.

Her father made a noise in the back of his throat. It could have been agreement. Sela hesitated, glancing between the two men.

'Sela…' Her father held his hand. 'You are a good daughter.'

'My father wishes to say something.' Sela kept her head upright.

'I will see what he says.' Vikar's expression remained wary.

Another snort of laughter emanated from the bed.

Vikar made a bow, more suited to the rigours and rituals of court life than the confines of this farmhouse. 'What say you, Bose the Dark—will you speak with me, or do you hide behind the skirts of a woman?'

'I will speak to him, Sela…alone, if you please.' Her father's hand clawed at hers. 'You understand? Alone!'

'But I—' Sela pressed against her father. She wanted to be there. Her father was not strong enough to manage this. She had to protect him, and make sure that Vikar did not bully him.

'Sela, I promise you that your father will be in the same health when you return. I only wish to speak with him.'

'Are you sure that is all?'

'I give my word on it. You may have my sword if you wish.' He drew his sword and held it out to her. 'Take it. Keep it for me.'

Sela regarded the hilt with its rings. She knew what he was offering her—the assurance that he would not attack her father. Only a few days ago, it would not have been enough. Now it was too much. It angered her that he felt the need to offer it. She straightened her back, pushed the hilt away.

'Your word will suffice.'

Vikar regarded her for a long time before he slid the sword back into its hilt. 'It is good to know you trust me.'

Trust him? Far more than she had believed possible.

Somehow, she had to discover a way to prevent what was between them from being destroyed.

'Your son wishes to see you, Daughter. He has been asking after you. Day and night—where is my mother? Why can't we wait for my mother? Your son wishes to be with you.' Bose waved a hand, dismissing her before she could say another word.

'I saw Kjartan before I came in here. He was all full of praise for you.'

Her father struggled to sit up. His face changed slightly.

'When you are dressed like a woman, then we can speak, but not before. I can barely tell you are my daughter.'

Sela stared at him. His words cut deeper than she thought possible. But after he had been cursed, his mood would change suddenly and without warning.

'*Far*, I had no choice. I did what I had to do. We spoke of this before.' The tears pricked the back of Sela's eyelids. She had expected a warmer welcome. Of all the people in the world, her father ought to understand what she had been through, what she had suffered. How she had suffered for his sake.

'Did you?' Her father cocked his head. His smile turned cold, reminding Sela of ice at yuletide, when the winter was at its harshest. A shiver ran through her. She tried to remind herself that her father had agreed to the plan, endorsed it, but the thought provided little comfort. 'Or did you simply make rash decisions and lose me my hall? If I had my strength back, you would regret it. You will regret it. You do not defy me.'

'Bose the Dark, I warn you…' Vikar's voice boomed, halting her father's bitter outpouring. 'You will not raise a hand to your daughter. She has behaved better and with more courage than most men. What are you seeking to prove—that you are the master here? Your daughter has never denied it.'

Sela bit her lip. A wave of happiness washed over her. The words were unexpected. *Thank you*, she mouthed.

Vikar gave a nod. 'What say you, Bose the Dark, to that?'

Her father regarded Sela with a jaundiced eye and down-turned mouth. 'Warriors need to speak here—when you have earned the right, you may join in.'

'I earned the right over the last few days.' Sela stared directly at Vikar and dared him to say differently.

'Sela,' Vikar said quietly, 'you were the one who tried to convince me that your father was ill, too ill to speak with me. I think now of how much more it will distress him if you stay.'

'I will withdraw as you both wish it.' Sela lowered her eyes. She refused to show how much her father had hurt her. She had never thought that he'd speak to her like that. The last time he had spoken like that was when she said the rumours about Vikar were untrue. And then, the following day, she had discovered the love token. 'I wish to spend time with my son.'

Vikar waited until he heard the click of the door. Sela had left, and now the real business was at hand. Matters had to be settled between Bose and him. He wanted answers, answers that Sela might not want to hear.

He regarded the ill man on the bed. In the little less than a year since he had last seen him, Bose the Dark had become an old man. Vikar had no doubt from the way he struggled to sit up that Bose was not long for this world. But why had he not wanted to go to Valhalla? Warriors only reached Odin's feast by falling in battle.

'You have me at a disadvantage, Vikar.' Bose turned his gaze on him. 'I had not expected you for a few more days.'

'You expected me?' Vikar stared at Bose in disbelief. He knew the man to be wily, but could he have seriously expected him? Most warriors would have been too content to feast and enjoy the fruits of victory. 'Your soothsayer must be excellent to predict such a happening. I should like to meet her some time.'

'You or someone else. I needed no soothsayers to tell me that I would be pursued…eventually. There are some who still call me friend and who would seek to aid me. But I think they would be thinking of their own coffers.' Bose shrugged and his frown increased. 'You are here now, so what does it matter when I expected you?'

'You must formally surrender the hall to me.'

'Did not my daughter do that?' Bose shook his head. 'You are getting lax, Vikar. I always demanded the leader swear an oath on my sword. She had my sword, or so Una tells me.'

'Your daughter surrendered, but I wish you to surrender as well.' Vikar held out his sword. 'I too know of your *friends* and their ambitions.'

Vikar stared hard into Bose's watery eyes. For a man so weak in his body, his will remained incredibly strong. Where Sela used hers for the good of others, her father thought little of anyone but himself. Vikar wondered why he had not realised that until now. Sela and her father were like two sides of a silver coin from the Holy Roman Empire.

'Oh, very well.' Bose waved an impatient hand. 'I

will do as you say. It has very little meaning, my surrendering the hall. Little meaning at all, now that Hafdan has perished. But if you insist on the formalities…'

'Does it?' Vikar held the sword steady, pointing the hilt towards Bose. He willed him to do it, and to accept his protection.

'You hold the hall…now.' A faint glimmer of a smile crossed Bose's face. 'I am an old man without warriors. How can I ever hope to regain it?'

A cold prickling went down Vikar's back. What Bose said was true, but there was more to this than an old man whose hubris and pride were so great that he thought his hall could not fall. Vikar knew he should feel triumphant. He had achieved the impossible, but he could not rid himself of the feeling that he and Bose were somehow playing a very high-stakes game of *tafl*. But how could he lose? What did Bose still possess?

'I intend to hold it for ever. Once a thing has come into my possession, I am reluctant to have it go.'

'An admirable quality.' Bose cleared his throat. 'I once believed as you do, but then age came creeping on its paws and I became as you see me—an empty shell of a warrior, living off the benevolence of a woman.'

'You should never have let your warriors go.'

'You think I had a choice?' Bose plucked at the furs. 'Perhaps you are right. Perhaps I seek too much. I wanted the best for my daughter, for my grandson.'

'You have no choice now. I will have your surrender.' Vikar held out his sword.

Bose's words were barely audible. He pushed the sword away and wiped a hand across his brow.

'There, I have done it. My humiliation is complete.

May it bring you little joy.' Bose stared at him with furious eyes. 'Are you satisfied? Will you leave me in peace to live out my remaining days? This farmhouse is small, but it is adequate for my needs. My daughter and her son can reside with me.'

'No.' Vikar replaced the sword in its hilt and enjoyed the look of dismay on Bose's face. Had the wily old man really thought that he would be left in peace? Vikar had learnt the folly of that mistake many years ago. 'I have other uses for you. Do them, and we will be finished, you and I.'

'What more can I do for you? You have all my jewels, the vast majority of my lands. What more do you wish to take from me?'

'I intend to marry your daughter.'

'And she has agreed?'

'She will agree.'

'You may marry her, if you can. She is stubborn. Takes after her mother.' A small shadow of a smile crossed Bose's face. 'I wonder why I had not thought of marriage to you before? Such a simple solution to a seemingly intractable problem.'

'What exactly have you been plotting, Bose?' Vikar leant forward. 'Rumours have reached Kaupang about strange activities in your area.'

'How can a man like me plot?' Bose regarded the ceiling and gave a half-shrug. 'As you can plainly see, I am as helpless as a newborn here, entirely dependent, completely at your mercy.'

'It would make a change.' Vikar hooked his thumbs in his belt. It was as if another piece had moved on the *tafl* table. Only time would tell if his king was seriously threatened. 'I have my doubts that you would ever be at anyone's mercy.'

'Times change.' Bose's eyes grew shadowed. 'Never grow old, Vikar. It is very lonely, being old.'

'I suspect I will discover the truth of that statement.'

The rook fell silent and Vikar began to wonder if Bose had fallen asleep.

'What do you think of Sela's child?' Bose whispered as Vikar was about to leave.

Vikar froze. He refused to let Bose goad him, refused to show the jealousy he felt towards Sela's lover. The lover who had abandoned her but who had also unlocked the passion in her. He forced his features to remain bland and gave a careful shrug.

'That she had a child out of wedlock is no concern of mine. Neither of us has a perfect past. He will be provided for. I assume the father isn't living.'

Vikar watched the elderly man for any hint, but Bose tapped his fingers and pursed his lips, the expression of a man who has spent his life in the service of kings, a man who played *tafl* with an unerring eye. Vikar fought the urge to shake him and demand a name.

'Very magnanimous of you, Vikar. Very noble. Spoken like the honourable warrior I know you are,' he said, finally breaking the silence.

'I shall take that as a compliment.'

'If you wish.' Bose gave a rattling laugh that turned into a wheeze. 'You've spoken with her about the child's father, then?'

'We have had words. She told me her lover left her before the child was born. I would have run him through had I known. I wonder that you did nothing about it.'

'This should prove to be most intriguing…most intriguing indeed.' Bose gave another of his rattling laughs.

Vikar stood there, fuming. The feeling of being outmanoeuvred yet again overwhelmed him. He longed to ask for more information, but to ask would mean giving Bose power over him. He smiled. He would curb his impatience and wait. Bose wanted to tell him, was desperate to tell him. He would tell him in the end.

'Then *Morfar* said we were going. It was very early and Una made a fire to cook my porridge.' Kjartan leant forward, his eyes shining with his tale of adventure.

'Did you see any wild animals, any at all? Hear any animals?' Sela hardly dared ask the question. To even ask it meant giving voice to the fears that had plagued her.

Kjartan shook his head, smiling.

'Nothing, but I would have been ready. I had my sword.' He withdrew his short wooden dagger and held it up in the air as if he were ready to strike. 'Why do you think I used to be frightened of the woods? They are quite a friendly place as long as you say the proper spells.'

A chill went to Sela's inner core. Spells were no protection from danger, but she had no wish to dent his confidence. It was one of the things she hated most about being a mother—wanting to keep her child from hurt, but equally wanting to give him the experience he needed to grow up.

'There is good reason to be frightened of that place.' Sela pushed her hair behind her ears. She knelt down beside and kept her voice low. 'I have had many adventures. Come, shall I tell you of them?'

Kjartan nodded. He slipped his hand in hers and settled himself on her knee, his head resting against her breast, his hair the very colour of his father's. She put her arms about him. 'I had wondered, *Mor*, I had wondered.'

Sela paused and thought about how to begin. She would have to tell Kjartan who his father was. And it would have to be done carefully, gently. She would have to prepare him for the future.

'It all began three days ago when the sails were spotted—'

'Come now, Kjartan.' Una bustled up, her arms laden with cloths and her head scarf quivering. 'It is time for your nap. You can see your mother later.'

'Una.' Kjartan gave a plaintive wail. '*Mor*'s telling me a story.'

'He can stay up a little while longer, I have just arrived, Una.'

'My lady, I must insist. Kjartan is overly tired. He is like you were—always needing a nap at mid-day.' The elderly woman's lips turned down in disapproval.

'Yes, but I had hoped...' Sela allowed her voice to trail away as Kjartan began to rub his eyes. She was being selfish. Kjartan showed clear signs of being exhausted. She had been lucky that Vikar had reacted so well to Kjartan's earlier outburst. He might not be so forgiving after he had spoken with her father.

'And in any case, the sweat bath has been heated for you.' Una made a clucking noise in the back of her throat, as if Sela was a child no older than Kjartan rather than a fully grown woman who had survived a perilous journey. 'I felt you would want to clean yourself after your travels. Make your hair nice. I declare you have let it become badly tangled. You appear to have forgotten much of my teachings, Sela.'

Travels. Una made it sound simple. Sela regarded the older woman. Was it worth explaining to her that all the outlandish stories she had told about the *tottr* men had a basis in fact? How much had Una known? How many other secrets was she privy to?

Sela looked down at her hopelessly stained trousers and tunic. 'Do you have anything else for me to wear? What good is it to bathe if I have to put the same garments on? Or do you intend for me to wrap up in a blanket until these are washed? My father wishes me to dress like a woman, but his mind wanders, I fear. Where could I find such clothes here?'

'I have managed to procure some garments from the farmer's wife. She is quite happy to give them to you.' Una thrust a pile of clothes and two small brooches into Sela's arms.

Sela nodded.

The woman would expect some sort of favour in return. Her father and Vikar would be still talking, still negotiating. If she did have her bath and change, she would have an excuse to go back and discover if Vikar had found his answers and delivered Thorkell's message. Then she would hold Vikar to his promise: that he would allow them to leave, unmolested.

She cast her eyes towards the mountains. But without retainers, and a ship, how could she get her father to the land her mother had left her? How could she ask that of him? And what about Kjartan? Who could she get to train him? Could she bear to send him away? And how could she face a future without Vikar?

Sela straightened her back. She would decide that after she had had her bath, once her mind was rested. But she had to decide and it had to be done. Today.

Chapter Thirteen

Sela rested her head back against the warm, stone ledge of the crude bath-house, allowing all the tension and anxiety to seep out of her. It was no more than a simple hole in the ground, lined with stone and covered with a leather roof, but it was hot and served its purpose. With a bundle of birch twigs, she idly scraped a bit of dirt from her forearm, closed her eyes and allowed her mind to drift.

She should move, get up from the warmth and take a plunge in the lake. Take the plunge in her life and go to Vikar. She might be able to bargain with him, offer to be his concubine for a while, and then retire with her father and Kjartan. It was one solution. He certainly had not seemed averse to her back at the waterfall.

But how was she going to explain about Kjartan?

She knew he said that the boy's parentage did not matter, but ultimately it did. Kjartan needed to be trained as a warrior, and that time was coming far quicker than she had imagined. She should have taken the initiative earlier. But she had hesitated and the first meeting had gone badly. She had seen that. Vikar had not been enamoured of Kjartan and his manners. He had not looked at her with questions, but with disapproval. And what if Vikar rejected Kjartan? What if he did not believe her?

The thoughts buzzed round and round her head and she would no sooner settle on one solution than she would reject it. And her mind kept returning to last night's events, kept remembering again what it was like to experience Vikar's touch.

A cool breeze rippled across her skin. Her eyes flew open and her hands groped for a cloth to cover her naked body. A dark figure stood on the threshold. Her breath caught in her throat and, for a heartbeat, she wondered if her mind had conjured him up.

'Vikar?'

The word was no more than a breath, but she could see the dimple appear in his cheek.

'Your nurse said that I would find you here, but she failed to mention your state of dress.'

Sela's fingers trembled against the cloth. No illusion, then. And she discovered that she was not ready to confront him with possible solutions. She did not want to discuss the future; her body wanted to return to the waterfall. Silently she cursed Una and her interfering ways, while outwardly she strove for as normal a voice as possible. 'Did she, indeed? You should have knocked.'

'If you hadn't wanted company, you only needed to have latched the door,' Vikar pointed out with maddening directness.

'I did not invite you here.' Sela tried again. She nodded towards the door. It would be for the best. They needed to have things settled between them. She had to make sure her son and father were safe before she thought about her own needs. 'You are not welcome.'

'When has that stopped me?' He crossed the space between them in two strides. His breath fanned her cheek. 'Are you really going to deny me a chance to bathe?'

'After I finish.' Sela made one last attempt at rational thought. His nearness was doing strange things to her insides. 'The stones will retain their warmth.'

'And do you?' Vikar did not move from where he stood. 'Do you retain your warmth?'

'I have no idea what you are talking about.'

'I think you do.' Vikar lifted her chin so he was staring directly into her eyes. 'What we shared last night was only the beginning.'

She wrenched her chin away. 'What happened last night was an ending, not a beginning. Our worlds are far apart, Vikar.'

'Not so very far apart. You are here and so am I.'

'It makes no difference.'

His cool hands reached out and his fingers caressed her nipples, turning them to hardened points, causing spasms of pleasure to ripple through her body.

'Are you really going to lie to me, Sela? Are you going to deny what your body desires?'

'My father…Kjartan…' Her voice sounded thick to her ears.

'Both are asleep. Your nurse and the farmer's wife are having a good gossip. I believe they are related. And the farmer is busy with his livestock.' Vikar crossed back to the door and secured the latch. 'However, I find it is always best to take precautions.'

'Precautions?'

'Precautions. *I* have no wish to be disturbed unnecessarily.'

'You wish to speak to me.'

'You might say that. We could speak.'

'Allow me to get dressed.' Sela's hand reached for the pile of clothes, fumbled and sent it toppling to the floor. She bent down and the cloth she was holding up slipped a bit. She glanced up at Vikar. He was but a shadow in the tiny room. Dark, dangerous, but her body was irresistibly drawn to him. His hand unerringly lifted her up and the cloth she was holding fell to the floor with a soft sigh.

'Leave it,' Vikar commanded.

She stilled, every nerve in her body straining to be with him. It was as if the fantasy she had played over and over in her mind had come to life. But there was a difference between fantasy and reality. She found her body swaying towards him, ignoring the commands from her brain, ignoring the reasons why she should keep her distance.

'Now, where were we?' Vikar placed his hand on her shoulder, cool against her slick skin. 'Ah yes, first things first. I believe your body was demanding my attention.'

She knew she ought to protest, but a little voice in the back of her mind asked if this was not what she wanted, the very thing she desired. But there were too many things between them, things that had to be said and decided before she could experience this again. It was wicked of her to want this, wicked of her to desire him like this, to keep him in ignorance.

'We need to speak,' she said thickly, forcing her mind from the way his lips felt against her throat as his hands drew her unresisting body closer. 'We need…'

'I know,' he whispered against her lips. 'And we will speak later, but right now I want to devour your body. It is by far the most important thing I have to do today.'

Later. A little word, but one that carried meaning. She would ensure they spoke later.

She gave up her mouth, yielding to the pressure, allowing his tongue to penetrate the inner recesses. The cool taste of him filled her senses while her hands clutched his shoulders for support.

She was taking the path of least resistance. She knew that. She knew if she were honest and forthright that she'd tell him about Kjartan, and beg for his forgiveness. But she couldn't take the chance, didn't want to take the chance. She was being a coward not telling him. But was it so wrong of her to want this one last time together?

Afterwards, they'd speak and she'd find a way to confess. But for now she'd savour the sweetness of his touch.

She closed her eyes as the sensation from his hands filled her, prevented her from thinking clearly. His fingers caressed her, moved down her body, until they cupped her backside and pulled her closer to him, so close that she could be in no doubt of his desire for her.

'You are not dressed for bathing,' she said as the rough wool from his tunic brushed her bare breasts.

'You may be right.' His mouth nipped her chin, and she wondered why he was in such an expansive mood. Had her father given him everything he had asked for? He rubbed his thumb along her swollen and aching lips. 'But I am dressed for this.'

His mouth trailed down her body in a long, slow descent, pausing to encircle her nipples and to render them hardened points of pleasure. He suckled and encircled them again. When she thought she could stand no more, he moved farther down. His hands held her hips so she was unable to move even had she wanted to.

'Vikar,' she breathed his name as his tongue teased her belly button, sending wave after wave of searing heat through her. The sweat bath had been warm before, but it was nothing compared to the fire that was growing inside her.

He took his time, every piece of her skin meriting his attention. Her hands dug into his crisp hair, and then moved to clench the wool of his tunic. She pulled at his shoulders, wanting him to remove it so she could feel his skin against hers.

'Later,' he murmured against her belly as he knelt before her. 'Patience. We take this one slowly. Your pleasure first.'

His breath fanned her triangle of curls before his tongue nudged apart her lips, delved and discovered her pearl-like centre. Suckled and sucked. Her body started to move, but he held her firmly in place, kept her there. The pulses grew within her, increasing with each pass of his tongue, until, with a mewling cry, she shattered.

He glanced up and gave a satisfied male smile. 'You like?'

She nodded imperceptibly, took a step backwards and nearly fell as her legs threatened to buckle.

He lowered her down on the warm, stone floor and removed his tunic. Her hands pushed his away, worked feverishly to remove his trousers. They fell to the ground and he kicked them away. Then he positioned himself over her.

'Is it better now?'

'You will find it easier to…bathe.'

His husky laughter echoed throughout the small room.

'And how does one bathe here?'

'The same as one bathes anywhere else,' she replied with an echoing note of laughter. 'One sweats, scrapes off the sweat and then goes into the lake.'

He gathered her in his arms, but rolled over, so she was on top. 'This way, I think. You call the rhythm. We will work together on that sweat.'

She moved backwards and took him inside her, felt his hips lift up to meet her. She rocked back and forth, watching his face in the pale light and saw his look of satisfaction. They went faster and faster until the crest hit her and their cries intermingled.

Afterwards, she lay there against his chest, listening to the steady pounding of his heart, trying to get her breath back. She ran a finger down his side. 'That's one way to work up a sweat.'

'Much the most preferable way.' She felt the low rumble of his laughter and raised her head to see the smile on his face.

'I shall take your word for it.'

'What would you have done, if I had not interrupted your bath?' he asked, threading a lock of her hair through his fingers. 'What were you planning to do before you were…detained?'

'I was getting ready to take a quick plunge in the lake,' she said. 'It is what I always do after my sweat bath.'

'Good, then we go together.'

'What do you mean?'

'Holding hands, we jump.'

Laughing, enjoying being with him and not wanting the time to end but knowing somehow it must, she was determined to hang on to it while she could, to make a memory.

He took her hands, pulled her up beside him as he undid the latch.

She laughed and beat on his chest, but his arms tightened about her, holding her there. 'People will see.'

'They are busy,' he growled in her ear. 'Take the risk, come with me.'

The idea appealed to her sense of fun. Illicit and yet innocent. 'I will,' she said, raising her hand to his face. 'Together.'

'Together.'

They ran and leapt far out into the pond. The water was cold against their skin, washing away the sweat and the dirt. She sank down to the bottom and came up again, spluttering with laughter. She splashed a wave towards Vikar, covering his chest.

'You will pay for that,' he said, wiping the droplets of water from his face.

'Will I?' She raised an eyebrow. 'Make me.'

'I intend to. I will exact a penalty.'

'I'd like to see you try.'

'Try? Woman, you should know that I will succeed.'

She pushed her hair from her face, and looked into his eyes. Her breath stuck in her throat. He was magnificent, bare-chested. His shoulders were firm but capable, his chest covered in a network of scars.

'You are very beautiful.' Vikar caught a droplet on the end of his finger. 'See what you do to me.'

His hands reached out and pulled her against him. She felt his rampant arousal press against her belly, inviting her, demanding. Warmth started to spread through her.

'Here?' she gasped.

'Here. It is your…penalty.'

'In the open? In the water?' She glanced about her and a loon rose in the air, but there was nothing else. A *frisson* of pleasure ran through her body, the temptation beckoned. One more time and then she'd bargain. 'Shall we?'

'Trust me. We can and we will.' He put his hands on her hips, lifted her. 'Wrap your legs about my waist and hang on. Let the water support you.'

She put her hands on his shoulders, and settled against his arousal. The entire world had narrowed down to this one point, this one man. He put his hand on her hips and began to sway. Her hands gripped his shoulders, trying to keep her body steady.

The water swirled around them. Holding them. She heard his voice and felt him shudder as she thought she could bear it no more.

She allowed her hands to slip and leant back, buoyed by the water, but still joined with him. Her hair floated around her and a deep contentment filled her. She stayed there for a long time, and looked up at the blue sky.

Finally she straightened with trembling limbs. Her entire body felt refreshed. It was as if she were poised on the brink of something new and different. She had found a solution to her dilemma. It would work. It had to work.

'What happens next?' she asked, smiling as she wrung the water out her hair.

Vikar reached out, and, capturing her cheek, traced the path of a water droplet. 'We get dressed; we talk.'

* * *

Vikar waited until they had both dressed and Sela was putting her hair into a loose plait. He stood just inside the bath-house, finishing dressing, watching every move she made. The door was open, and the light trickled onto her skin, turning it golden.

He had not intended to make love with her, but it was for the best. She could not hide behind an indifference. There was a passion between them, and, in time, he would wash away all memories of other men.

He would wait until she had finished plaiting her hair and fastening her brooches and then he'd inform her of their future.

They would wed.

She smiled up at him, caught him watching her do her hair and her smile became that of a cat who had stolen the cream. She stretched slightly and the cloth tightened about her breasts. A sensuous move, calculated, designed to inflame his senses.

'If the position of your concubine is open, I would be happy to fill it.'

Vikar's fingers missed his belt. He heard it thud as it hit the stone flooring. Concubine? She had misunderstood.

'You are not going to be my concubine, Sela. That position is not open to you.'

'But…but…' She made a little helpless gesture. 'What we shared out there…just now. Surely…'

'You have forfeited the choice, Sela. You will be my wife.'

'Your wife?' Her mouth fell open and her eyes widened. She shook her head as if her hearing was troubled. 'Your wife? What mischief is this?'

'I have spoken with you father. He agrees it is the best solution to our present problem.' Vikar looked at her in surprise. She had to understand the honour he was according her. It was the perfect solution for him. The fact that they had renewed their passion for each other made it much easier. Surely she was not going to deny the attraction?

'Does he, indeed?' Her eyes narrowed. 'How clever of you both to settle my future without consulting me.'

'You need a protector. The situation remains the same.' Vikar reached out to draw her into his arms, but she pulled away and stood with her arms wrapped about her middle. 'Our remarriage solves many problems.'

'And what did my father say about…Kjartan?' Her voice was small as her hands toyed with the end of her plait. 'What provisions did you agree together? Or am I to remain ignorant of those as well?'

'I will treat Kjartan like my own. Of course he cannot expect to inherit and once we have children…'

Vikar stopped and waited for the thanks. Her devotion to her son was without question and the boy, although impudent, appeared resourceful. He would make a good warrior, given the right training. He was being more than generous. Kjartan was her lover's son, not his. He had done the right thing, so why was she staring at him with accusing eyes instead of murmuring her undying devotion?

'What is wrong, Sela? Surely you cannot expect him to have precedence. He was born out of wedlock.'

Her white teeth caught her upper lip. 'He was conceived in wedlock.'

Vikar went still. The warm hut became icy cold. He

shook his head. He had to be hearing things. Sela had never married again. She had said so. She was single. Had married the once. Had only been married to him.

She could not have taken a lover while they had been married, could she?

He tried to say something, but discovered his voice refused to work and only a hoarse gasping sound emerged. He swallowed hard, refilled his lungs with air and tried to see beyond the red mist that had descended upon his vision.

'You had a lover when we were together in Kaupang?' Vikar asked through gritted teeth, daring her to answer. She remained white-lipped and silent, standing there proud and defiant. He took a step towards her. 'Who is he? I shall take pleasure in running my sword through him. I never imagined that I wore the cuckold's horns.'

He stood there, hands flexing at his sides, struggling to contain the wild fire of rage that was rushing through him. He brought his shoulders back, drew on all of his years of training, and still he felt his control slipping.

'Whose son is he, Sela? Who are you protecting?'

'He is our son—yours and mine, Vikar.' Her quiet voice filled the room, echoing off the stone bench. 'He was conceived when we arrived in Kaupang. I have never lain with anyone else. *I* never dishonoured *you* in that way.'

Vikar shut his eyes and tried to comprehend her words. Kjartan—*his* son? *Their* son? Impossible!

The air was too close in the small hut. His mind reeled and he could not concentrate, could not think let alone speak.

He stumbled outside, clutching the side of the doorframe, and filled his lungs with several deep breaths of pine scent and sweet, clean air. The smoke in the hut must have addled his brain. He could not have heard her correctly. Idly he watched a loon take off and land as he tried to make sense of her announcement.

Kjartan his? Why then did she hide him?

She had to be lying. She must have had a lover. She had to have been faithless. And yet, he wanted to believe her, to believe the impossible. He walked to the lake's edge and splashed cold water on his face. And the notion refused to leave him.

She had no reason to lie. None at all. It would be far easier for her to claim that Kjartan was some other man's son. And the more he thought about it, the more he knew that she had to be telling the truth. He had not seen the resemblance when he met the boy, but then he had not been looking for it.

'Vikar?' she called quietly from the doorway of the hut. 'Do you understand what I am saying? Kjartan is our son. I gave birth shortly after I returned from Kaupang. You know as well as I that I had no other lover there.'

Vikar turned and saw that she had finished dressing and now resembled every other Viken woman, like the Sela he remembered from Kaupang, rather than the woman who had saved him from the wolf. Perhaps she had been the illusion.

'Kjartan is my son, and you never told me,' Vikar said, slowly as the comprehension dawned. And he found he wanted to believe it with every fibre of his being. He had no family, no one to pass the stories of his father and grandfather on to, but now he did.

He had a son! Someone to sing his saga to. A child of his own.

'I discovered I was pregnant the day I left you.' Her quiet voice broke over him.

'You knew you were pregnant and still you left?'

'Yes.' Her voice was not more than a breath. She pressed her hands together, held them up. Unshed tears turned her eyes into pools. Vikar turned his head.

'How could you?'

'It seemed like the only thing to do after discovering Asa's love token. I did send a message. I sent a rune with Hafdan. He handed it to you. He told me how you went white and then turned on your heel.'

'Hafdan gave me no rune. He gave a message, said with a curled lip, demanding that I go straight to your father's lodgings and apologise to your father. I told him that I would not be Bose the Dark's lapdog. Your father and I had had words in Thorkell's chambers earlier. We fought. He left.' Vikar fingered his jaw. 'We had a score to settle, he and I. That day he won and left me with a broken jaw.'

'I asked for you to come, but you never came for me. You gave me no explanation. Hafdan said that you laughed.' Sela came around so he faced her. 'You must believe me.'

'You never asked. Your father did. There is a difference, Sela.' Vikar crossed his arms over his chest. 'By the time I could move, you had gone. Vanished.'

'We shall have to disagree on the circumstances. My father told me you went to a feast that night—sang and danced. Made jokes about me.'

'And you believed him.'

'I had every reason to believe him. I knew your be-haviour from previous nights.' Sela's voice was quiet. 'I left the next day. You had forfeited all rights.'

'You hid my son from me.' Vikar struggled to control his renewed anger at her. 'Deliberately concealed him! Wilfully concealed him!'

'It was not something one sends in a message.' She wrapped her apron-dress about her hands. 'I intended to tell you…but you never came to see me.'

'You left the next morning.'

'Asa told me that it was best to go.'

'Asa?' Vikar pressed his lips together, remembering. She had been pleased with herself in those days after Sela had left—sending healers, enquiring after him. It had been easier to let Sela go and bask in the attention.

'I had gone to her.' Sela stood in front of him, her arms wrapped about her waist, but her head up and proud. 'I am not proud of what I did, but I had to know. I showed her the token. She confirmed everything.'

'She did?' Vikar stared at Sela in astonishment. 'Ev-erything? How could she?'

'You know her way—the little sighs, nothing direct.' Sela gave an eloquent shrug. 'I had had enough hu-miliation. She was welcome to you.'

'But it was my son you carried.'

'How was I to be sure that you wanted him?' she asked quietly, her words cutting him more effectively than any blade. 'That you would look after him? Asa gently told me that you found it hard to go to my bed. Why would you want my child?'

'Not want him?' Vikar stared at her. A deep anger filled him. How dare she say such things about him?

How could he not want a child? A child of his flesh? He shook his head, pitying her.

'And what if it had been a daughter—would you be saying the same things to me?'

'How little you know me. My own flesh and blood, Sela. You only had to send a message and I would have been there. It was my right to know.'

'I had planned on telling you…you must believe that!' Her mouth twisted and her eyes became clouded. 'Circumstances intervened.'

'When? When were you going to tell me?' Vikar leant forward, so their faces nearly touched. 'It is not as if you couldn't have found me. I was at Kaupang. Your father and I had many disagreements.'

'I did not keep track of your whereabouts. Why should I make a trip to a place that only holds bad memories, on the presumption you might be there?'

Vikar slammed his fists together. He wanted to shake her out of her complacency. She had done this deliberately and, what was worse, she'd had no intention of telling him before today. Until he informed her of his plans. She had been content to let him think Kjartan belonged to some other man. She would have taken him away. The earth tilted slightly. He was within the shadowlands.

'Kjartan must be four years old. He is long past weaning. He should have been sent to me. I should have been there when he was born! You know the customs of our people.'

'He's three. He will be four in a few months' time.'

'How many other people know?' Vikar's gaze fastened on her deceitful eyes. 'How many others? Your father? Hafdan? Thorkell? Who knew?'

'My father. My brother and his wife before they died. My maid. I swore them to secrecy.' She raised her eyes, the studied expression of innocence. 'My father thought it best under the circumstances. You have to understand what it was like.'

Her father. Vikar stroked his chin. Yes, he could see that. Bose the Dark armed with knowledge, waiting until it became advantageous to impart it. No wonder he had chortled earlier. Bose had once more taken him in. He had been blinded again.

Wherever his thoughts led, they kept coming back to one inescapable fact—Kjartan was his son. And she had thought so little of him that she had hidden the boy, would have gone on hiding him. Everything they had shared on the journey out here had been a lie.

He was tempted to shake Sela, to make her see what she had done, but it was no good. He had never raised a hand against a woman and he did not intend to start now.

He turned on his heel and began to walk away. Away from her. Away from what he thought they had shared.

'Where are you going?' She ran up and caught his arm.

He shook her off. 'To see my son. To see what is to be done with him. It is my right as his father.'

'Kjartan doesn't know,' she said and the sob was clear in her voice. She moved in front of him, blocking his way. He attempted to go round her, but she moved in front of him. 'He is only little. He has never done you any harm. For pity's sake, spare him.'

Vikar froze. He looked her up and down. He could still see the redness of her lips where they had kissed. She had betrayed him in the worst possible way. His insides felt worse than when he had seen his father killed as a young boy. He had believed in his father, but his father had lied to him, told him not to worry, that he would return, that it was only a little dispute.

'You have not bothered to tell him who his true father is?' Vikar tapped his fingers against his thigh. 'Who, pray, does he think his father is? Odin? Thor himself? A passing pirate? Who? He must have asked. What tale did you spin for him?'

She flinched as if he had slapped her and he felt a certain amount of satisfaction at the impact that his words had had. But he knew nothing could compensate for the deep hurt that ached inside of him.

'A great warrior. That was all he needed to know,' she whispered. 'I used to tell him tales of his father's daring deeds. I wanted him to be proud of him, of you.'

'Why not tell him the truth?

'How could I tell him that you abandoned us before he was born? That his own father could not be bothered with me?' She held out both hands in supplication. Tears swam in her eyes. Vikar reminded himself that she was not to be pitied. She had done this to herself. 'I could not risk you rejecting the life I carried. I wanted to give him a chance. I regret nothing.'

Vikar ran his hand through his hair. He had never abandoned her. Not in the way she meant. He had left her to her own devices. He had been annoyed at the strictures Bose had tried to place on him, annoyed that she had placed her father above him. Ashamed that he had married her for the wrong reasons. The marriage had soured, but at no time would he have abandoned his son. It was unthinkable.

A living child? He knew some men might have, but he abhorred the practice.

'Your memory differs from mine.' He made a stiff bow.

'You said you didn't want children the last time we quarrelled.'

'I have no memory of that.' Vikar shifted uncomfortably. Their quarrel had been bitter. Accusations had flown on both sides. Words said that had not been meant, nor that he could take back. Truths best left unspoken. He flinched, remembering the look of anguish she had given him, when she'd pleaded for him to return to her bed and he had refused. 'We both said things we regret. I would never deny a child of my own. You must believe that.'

'What was I supposed to think? I had a duty towards my child.' She kept her head high. Tears shimmered in her eyes. She was proud and defiant, despite what she had done. 'I regret nothing. Kjartan is a credit to you, to us.'

'You can justify your behaviour to yourself and to your father, but you can never justify it to me.' Vikar pointed towards where a curl of smoke rose against a clear blue sky. 'That is my son asleep in the house. *My* son. No other man's.'

'He is mine as well.' Sela put her hand on his arm, holding him back. 'Remember he is innocent. He is just a boy.'

'Move out of my way.'

He shook her hand off and stormed away up the slope, turning his back on her and her deceitful, self-serving lies.

Chapter Fourteen

Kjartan was sitting in the dust of the farmhouse door, playing with his horses when Vikar reached him. Vikar regarded the boy dispassionately. His blond hair flopped over his forehead and there was an intense look of concentration on his face. He had Sela's hands, her slender build, her hair. Everything about him screamed that Sela was his mother.

Vikar shook his head. There was nothing about him in Kjartan.

Then the boy glanced up, smiled. Vikar caught the full force of his eyes and wondered how he had been blind before.

Kjartan was his. He did not belong to anyone else. Could not.

Vikar's insides twisted as the realisation swamped his senses. He could only stand there stunned, staring at the boy, savouring his hair, his eyes. His son. His flesh and blood.

He had no immediate family but this boy. Vikar

clenched his fist. Sela had denied him the opportunity to be a proper father.

When Vikar made no move towards him, Kjartan turned back to play in the dust, oblivious to Vikar's inner turmoil. His little song about the horses marching up the road, searching for a way home, for their father, reached Vikar's ears. Stabbed Vikar somewhere in his chest.

He started to rush forward but then checked his movement, forced his feet to stay still, kept true to his discipline and watched the boy. He had no wish to frighten Kjartan. He simply wanted to get to know him, to learn his ways.

They had years to catch up on. Years lost to them.

Vikar swallowed the lump in his throat. He wanted to bring him up to be a good warrior. A thousand plans rushed at him. Kjartan should never have to suffer the way he had suffered. He wanted to tell him stories about his family, show him how to use a sword and teach him how to ride a horse. But most of all to instill in him that being a Viken warrior meant more than just waving a weapon about. All the things his own father never had taught him.

He stood, watching the boy, not moving, simply taking everything in.

'I am playing with my horses,' Kjartan said, looking up again. An entreating smile crossed his face. 'Do you want to play with me?'

'Yes.' The one word was all he was capable of.

'You can use this one. He is my favourite.' Kjartan held out the horse Vikar had saved from the *tottr* men. 'He was a very naughty horse, running away from me, but *Mor* found him and brought him back. He's safe now. He's with me.'

Vikar cast his eyes up to the skies blinking rapidly, but a single tear escaped and trickled down his cheek. With impatient fingers he pushed it away. He doubted if he had ever cried in his life. Not even when he had seen his father's broken body lying on the ground after the berserker had killed him. But a simple request from his son and he found it impossible to speak. Vikar drew deep on his discipline and regained control.

'I would like that very much.' He knelt down in the dust with Kjartan and took the horse. He turned it over in his hand and remembered how he given his cloak for it. He was pleased he had done it without knowing who it truly belonged to. He could understand in a small way why Sela had risked her life for the toy. 'I have many horses in my house, but none as fine as this one.'

'Real ones?' Kjartan's eyes shone. '*Mor* promised next birthday I could have a pony of my own, a golden-maned one.'

'I am sure that can be arranged,' Vikar said. Mentally he went through his horses. There was at least one that would be a suitable mount for Kjartan. He would make sure he had the proper training. He touched Kjartan's hair with a finger. Light, soft and totally like Sela's. 'Should you prove an adequate horseman.'

Kjartan's green gaze pierced him. 'Some day I'll be a great warrior like my father and I will need a horse.'

'I am sure you will be.' Vikar barely managed to say the words.

'*Mor* said you are a great warrior, a great Viken warrior. Do you know him? My father?'

Tears blurred Vikar's vision. 'We've met.'

* * *

Sela stood, looking out at the lake. Its surface was glass smooth. There was no sign that she and Vikar had ever been there. Had ever experienced such pleasure.

She stuffed her hand in her mouth. All that was gone. She hadn't even realised that a bond had been growing between them until it had been severed, leaving behind an awful aching and emptiness.

Worst of all, she wanted that bond to be there, for them to be a family. Such a thing would be impossible now. She knew that. There would be no happy ending to her saga. There couldn't be. She had cheated both Vikar and Kjartan through her own selfishness.

Vikar would not let Kjartan go.

Why should he? How could he?

Kjartan was his son and, under Viken law, the law of the north, Kjartan belonged to him. She had no right to him. Vikar could take him wherever he wanted. It was the day that had woken her from her dreams in a sweat. It was the day she had dreaded facing. She had thought that somehow, if she tried hard enough, she would never have to, that Kjartan's parentage would remain a secret.

All the careful safeguards she had built around her heart were gone. And in their place was a quivering wreck.

Her jaw tightened. After she had killed the wolf, Vikar had said that he owed her a life-debt. She would ask for it to be repaid. It was the only way. She could not face seeing Vikar with another woman, Kjartan growing up without her. But he might still let her and her father go. She could start a new life somewhere, try to rebuild something from the shattered remains that were once her life.

Her fingers curled around a pebble, and she was tempted to throw it in the lake. Instead she placed it in her pouch. A reminder that she had started a new life, one where her heart would have to be made of stone.

With quick steps, she made her way to the farmhouse.

Laughter assaulted her ears. Vikar and Kjartan sat in the dust, playing horses, their two heads together, the set of the shoulders the same. She wanted to bury her face in her hands and weep. Kjartan seemed to have accepted everything. And, of course, Vikar could provide far more than she ever could. Only she wished that somehow it did not mean that Kjartan would have to go away.

'*Mor, Mor*!' Kjartan raced up to her, his eyes glowing. 'This man knows my father. He says that he is a truly great warrior. He knows many stories about my father, and he's promised me a horse, a real horse.'

Sela put her hands on Kjartan's shoulders, and knelt down so she could look him in the eye. She tilted her head to one side. Vikar had not told him.

What game was he playing now?

Surely he was not going to refuse to recognise him. She sent a prayer up to any god that might be listening. They had to forgive her. Kjartan could not bear the cost of her mistakes.

'Kjartan…' She paused and glanced towards where Vikar stood with the wooden horse in his hand, waiting. She tried to speak, but her throat refused to work. There could be no mistakes. She summoned all her courage. 'This man, Vikar Hrutson, is your father.'

A furrow appeared between Kjartan's eyes as if he were having trouble understanding her. He wrinkled his nose and shook his head ever so slightly. Sela took a step backward. He had to accept the truth of her words. For Vikar's sake. For his own.

She glanced again at Vikar and willed him to make it easier for her. Pleaded with him to understand and not to punish her child, *their* child for the mistakes she had made. Then she waited for what seemed like an eternity.

'Yes, Kjartan, I am your father.' Vikar looked from the little boy to Sela. He walked purposefully over to Kjartan, and made the traditional sign of acceptance on his forehead. 'I will deny you to no man. You will learn to be a warrior and make me proud. You are Kjartan Vikarson.'

Kjartan's eyes lit up, brighter than the torches on Thor's feast day. He let out an excited squeal and threw himself at Vikar. 'My father, truly?'

'Truly.' Vikar caught him in mid-air, circled with him and then gently set him down. 'Truly, you are my son.'

Sela released a breath as a weight rolled off her back. Vikar had accepted him. He would look after him. After their time together she believed his words. Relief flooded through her and at the same time her heart ached as though it had broken into shards, too numerous to count, so many that she knew it would never be whole.

'Thank you,' she breathed.

'You should have more faith in me, Sela.' Vikar's eyes were cold, green glass over Kjartan's head. It was hard to imagine that they had ever held any warmth in them. 'I never abandon my family.'

'I will hold you to your declaration, Vikar Hrutson.' Her father's voice rang out from the doorway. He was leaning on a stick, but there was a crafty look to his face.

'I need no holding. I have never shirked my responsibilities and I have no intention of doing so.' Vikar put his hand on Kjartan's shoulder, drew him close. 'This is my son, my only son, and I will bring him up to be a Viken warrior.'

'That is good to hear,' her father responded.

'Why did you mislead me about Kjartan's parentage, Bose the Dark?' Vikar asked.

'Yes, *Far*, why did you?' Sela asked, putting a hand on her hip. 'Who were you trying to protect?'

'If your former wife made no attempt to convince you, and you did not believe the evidence of your own eyes, what good would the word of an old man be?' Her father began to cough. 'I am not in the habit of making things easy for you, Vikar.'

'I expect I should take that as a compliment, rather than an insult.'

'You would not take kindly to my smoothing your way. You made that quite clear once.'

'I have always stood on my own two feet. Never asked for handouts.' Vikar's eyes blazed.

'*Far*, you should not be up and about.' Sela went forward to lead him back into the house. Today had been traumatic enough without a fight between her father and Vikar.

'What, and miss the revelation?' Her father's eyes shone with mischief. 'This has improved my mood no end. Far better tonic than any soothsayer's.'

'You *knew* Vikar would find out?' Sela asked in amazement.

'The truth always comes out...even if it occasionally needs a bit of help.'

Sela went cold and then dismissed the thought as

pure fantasy. Her father was doing his usual trick. He was trying to make it seem like he'd had something to do with the situation when he had done nothing at all.

'Kjartan, take your grandfather back to his bed, I wish to speak with your mother,' Vikar said in a persuasive tone, but his eyes were hard.

Kjartan appeared ready to protest but he took one look at Vikar's face and went over to his grandfather. 'Come, *Morfar*, you go back to bed and, if you're very good, I will tell *you* a story about Loki and how he tricked Thor.'

'I do believe I have heard that tale somewhere before,' her father said with the utmost solemnity. Sela hid a smile behind her hand.

'A good choice, Kjartan,' Vikar said. 'Your grandfather would do well to ponder Loki's fate.'

Bose grimaced, but said nothing as he allowed Kjartan to lead him in.

Sela waited until they had disappeared inside. Despite everything, Vikar had some common sense. There was no need to discuss anything in front of Kjartan. The last thing she wanted to do was upset her son. But things had to be decided. Kjartan's future was at stake.

She only hoped that Vikar would understand. She needed a few days with Kjartan, to prepare him for what was to come, and for her to store a lifetime of memories.

'Thank you,' she said into the silence. 'Thank you for what you did just now.'

'For what?' Vikar's eyes were wary. 'What have I done to unintentionally please you?'

'For acknowledging Kjartan. For promising to bring him up as a warrior.' Sela hesitated slightly. She took a deep breath, and kept her shoulders upright. Later within the privacy of her own sleeping place, she would give way to tears. 'I know you will keep that promise. I know you will look after him and see that he becomes a proper warrior, rather than being allowed to run wild.'

'And you thought I wouldn't?' Vikar gave a short bitter laugh and shook his head.

'I feared the worst of you, but I can see that I was wrong.' Sela ran the toe of her boot along the earth. She had to be honest. It might mean the difference between a warrior's life and neglect for Kjartan. 'I can admit that.'

'This must be a first—you admitting to a mistake.'

'I always try to accept responsibility.' She raised her head and stared back him. 'I have never run from them.'

'Haven't you?' he inquired softly.

'I want what is best for my son, Vikar. It is all I have ever wanted.'

'As do I.' Vikar ran his hand through his hair. 'Kjartan will find a fair father in me, I can promise you that. He will be brought up according Viken custom as the son of a jaarl.'

'I am sure he will.'

Sela's throat began to close but she kept her head high and proud. She refused to cry. Not in front of Vikar.

This way, at least, Kjartan would have a secure future with a powerful father to smooth his path. She could only hope that when he had grown to manhood he would come looking for her, that he would not forget his mother. Her heart ached to think of it, seemed to break into another thousand shards.

'You should have no questions about it. I pledge to you that he will want for nothing.'

The pain at the back of Sela's head grew. There was no point in prolonging the inevitable. She had to know when the parting would come.

'As you have what you want from my father and you have discovered my secret, I presume you will want to be away from here as quickly as possible.'

'I wish to get back to my men.' Vikar pursed his lips. 'I have never made a secret of that desire. The farmer has a vessel that he is willing to part with for a handful of silver. His son is using his other one for a fishing trip. My men need to see that I have been confirmed as the lord of the northern lands. With a fair wind, it should take no more than a day or so, the farmer tells me.'

'And you plan to leave?'

'On the morning tide.'

'As quickly as that?' She fixed her gaze on a point somewhere in the distance. She had hoped for a few days.

'The boat is seaworthy and small enough for me to handle.'

'How…how do you know that?'

'I did not trust the farmer's word and had a look at it before I discovered you in the hut. My plans remain unaltered.'

'And you will take Kjartan with you.' Her throat tasted like sawdust.

'Having just acknowledged him, can you doubt my intentions?'

'No, I had no doubt.' She gave a small shrug of her shoulders. Then, unable to stop her words, she made one last attempt to appeal to Vikar. 'Perhaps I had a small hope. He is a young boy. When he is ready to be trained…'

'His training will begin as soon as possible, Sela. It

should have already begun.' Vikar's gaze narrowed and he once again became the warrior. 'You know that as well as I do. He is weaned. Your duty to him is finished. Allow me to do mine.'

Sela nodded. She checked that breath was filling her lungs and her heart still pounded. Each word was like a dagger but it was not unexpected. It was the thing she had feared most since she had given birth. And now that it had happened, it was far more awful than her worst imaginings. She was losing not only Kjartan, but also that bright, elusive peace she had found with Vikar. It was far worse than when she had left him in Kaupang.

She drew a shuddering breath. Now was the time to ask for his clemency, to demand on his life that she and her father be allowed to retire to her mother's old estate. Her father deserved some dignity in his final days. She had to say the words now, before her nerve failed her. But now that future stretched out ahead of her—colourless, devoid of life, empty. So very different from the way it had appeared this morning. Some day, she might be able to make sense of it all.

'You will hold to your truce with me. You will let me and my father go. You promised you would not force me to return to the hall.'

'Our truce ended days ago, Sela.' A muscle in Vikar's cheek twitched. 'I said that we would speak of it when we arrived here. And we have.'

Sela took a step backward, stumbled and fell to the ground. She ignored Vikar's outstretched hand and rose to her feet.

'What do you intend to do with me?'

'That is a question that needs careful consideration.'

Vikar stroked his chin. 'We will marry when we return to the hall.'

'Marry?' Sela stared at him in astonishment. Of all the punishments he could have devised, marriage was surely the worst. 'You cannot mean to marry me.'

'But I do.' His voice sent a chill down her spine 'We will marry and stay married. There will be no divorce this time.'

'But why?' Sela stared at him uncomprehending. Why did he wish to marry her? She had to keep her heart from whispering that perhaps he cared about her. That somehow this had nothing to do with Kjartan, and everything to do with her. 'I hid your son from you.'

'Precisely.' The word was clipped and cold.

'I don't understand.'

'We have lain together.' Vikar ticked the items off on his fingers as if he were counting furs or other items for sale. 'I have spilled my seed inside you. Several times. By your admission, you have no other lover at the present time.'

'Is that supposed to be a compliment?'

'You may take it for what it is,' Vikar replied. 'The truth. We marry on the next feast of Freyja.'

'I do not see what difference that makes. We lay together. The last final flare of passion. A mistake on both our parts. Finished for ever!'

Something blazed in Vikar's eyes briefly and then was hidden. Gone in less than a heartbeat. His face had become a warrior's mask and Sela wondered if she had only imagined the expression of pain.

'I do not have the time to argue with you. Arrangements need to be made.' Sela turned to go before she broke down and begged him. Her throat was as dry as sand. She wanted him to deny her words, but how could such a denial come?

'You could be carrying my child.' Vikar's hand encircled her wrist like a shackle. 'I have no wish for history to repeat itself. I learn my lessons, Sela.'

'I would send the child to you.' Sela tugged at her wrist but his grip tightened. 'I promise you that on my life, on my son's life.'

'Do not tempt me.'

He released her so quickly that she stumbled away from him. She rubbed the red mark with her fingers, trying to get the blood back into her hand. He started to stalk off. If she let him go, she knew that she'd have truly lost him. She could not bear it.

'Please, you must believe me,' she cried, running forward and catching his arm. 'I know now that I was wrong in hiding Kjartan from you. If you understood the circumstances…'

'I have no reason to trust you after how you have behaved, but in this, I do believe you.'

Sela found she could breathe again. Her head sank on to her chest. He knew that she was not so far consumed in hate and desire for power. He knew she would never contemplate risking her son's life. It was a small thing, but it was important.

'Then why marry me? Why not wait until you know if I carry your child?' Sela hated the way her voice trembled on the words. She was not sure how she would feel if she found out that she carried his baby. Could she face giving birth again, only to give up her child? She knew she had poured all her unwanted love into Kjartan.

'I know the law the same as you—children inherit from their fathers, but a mother may inherit if her children die. I want you in a safe place. You have the potential to be a great heiress, Sela.'

'How dare you even think such a thing? I would never do something like that.' Sela stared at him astounded. 'How could anyone think that?'

'You wouldn't, but would your father? You tell me why he sent Hafdan away. Tell me who informed Thorkell all was not right on his northern border. Who insisted that I come north? I wanted to send one of the other younger jaarls like Haakon's half-brother Thrand, but Thorkell insisted. Even if I had not encountered Hafdan, I would have encountered Kjartan.'

Sela fell silent. She wanted to say that her father would never contemplate such a thing, but after today she had no idea. Her father would have left her to die in the forest if it had suited his purpose. He had changed from the father she remembered. But she was not prepared to admit it to Vikar.

'My father…' she began, and gathered her wits about her. 'My father has but a little time left to him on this earth. You can see how ill he is. He loves Kjartan. He risked his life for Kjartan. The reason he was not on that battlefield was because I made him promise to look after Kjartan.'

'You wanted to hide Kjartan from me.'

'At first I did. I had no idea how you would react. My son is very precious to me, Vikar.'

'You wanted to deny him a father.'

'If I had truly wanted to do that, would I have told you about the second horse?' Sela held her breath and waited. 'As you said, everything changed.'

'I need a wife, and the alliance will help keep the peace in these lands.' Vikar gave a slight shrug. 'My earlier reason for marrying you has not changed, despite your attempt to avoid such a thing.'

Sela winced. She had thought that some sort of affection had been built between them, but it had been an illusion. Her secret had shattered everything. She drew the shreds of her dignity around her like a cloak. 'I see. I will make you a good wife. But you must do one thing for me.'

'And that is?'

'I want some measure of freedom. I have no wish to return to Kaupang. My father will not be well enough to travel in any case. Allow me to remain at the hall. You will need someone there to look after your interests.'

Vikar's smile increased. 'No, you have earned no measure of freedom. You will marry me even if I have to carry you shrieking to the altar. We will exchange the rings. My son's future depends on it.'

'You leave me little choice. I will marry you, Vikar.'

The words seemed to stick in her throat. This morning, she would have said them joyfully, thinking that there was some chance of happiness, but now, she knew that it would be a life sentence whichever way she turned.

'It is good that you have decided to be sensible for once in your life.' Vikar's countenance held no joy.

'When will the wedding be?'

'It will take place after we return to the hall. I want no man to say that I have not freely won claim to it and to all of your father's possessions.'

He turned his back on her and stalked off.

All her muscles strained, urged her to run after him

and demand on the life-debt he owed her that he change his mind. She looked at the pebble, then threw it far away from her. She couldn't do that. She had to take this chance and believe somehow her life would turn out better.

'*Far*,' Sela said as she re-entered the farmhouse to find Bose in the act of climbing back into his bed. 'How much did you overhear?'

'My days of listening behind doors have long gone, daughter.'

'You cannot fool me. I know you positively revel in listening to other people's secrets.'

'But I am good at keeping them.'

'Until it serves your purpose to reveal them.' Sela crossed her arms. 'Why didn't you tell Vikar who Kjartan was?'

'That was a matter between you and him. It pleases me that it is finally resolved.' Her father gave a half-smile and tapped his nose. 'It has been on my mind these past months, ever since I became afflicted.'

'You never said.'

'You do not know all my secrets, Sela.' His face became sombre and his watery, blue eyes slid away from her. 'It is better that way.'

A shiver passed through her. All his secrets. She had encountered several of them on the journey.

'You mean about the *tottr* men.' She tucked a stray lock of hair behind her ear. 'You should have told me they were real.'

'Would you have believed me if I had?'

Sela shook her head. 'But what else haven't you told me—what other things are you hiding?'

'They are my secrets to keep.' He leant forward slightly. 'Believe me, Sela, when I say that I had every confidence in you getting through that forest. You are resourceful.'

'With Vikar's help.' Sela could not prevent the catch in voice. A wave of tiredness washed over her. Her entire body was numb. All she wanted to do was curl up in a small ball and sleep for a hundred years.

'Will he allow us a few days to rest?'

'Vikar wants to leave on the morning tide.'

'And there is no persuading him, I suppose. Una has not had long with her cousin. She might object.'

'You have never taken notice of Una's objections before.'

'If I had…' Her father lifted his hand. 'It is nothing, Daughter, but give me a reason. Why do you agree with Vikar? Why do you wish to leave this place?'

Sela put her hands under her chin. She could hardly tell her father that she wanted to put as much distance between herself and the place where she and Vikar had made love as possible. 'I want to return to the hall. There are the dead to honour, and the injured to look after. The people there still look to me.'

'Some days, I wonder if you are not all your mother's daughter. She was concerned about such things.'

'And you only sought power,' Sela murmured under her breath.

'What did you say, Daughter? My hearing is not as acute as it used to be.'

'I said that it is time we got you to bed. It will be a hard journey. Vikar is determined that we should all return with him.'

She moved to help him and his hand clawed at her arm, forcing her down to him

'I expected this,' he whispered hoarsely. 'Vikar has proved a formidable opponent.'

'This is not a *tafl* game, *Far*.'

'No, but as I grow older, I wonder if the gods do not play *tafl* with us humans. Moving us around on the board. Giving us success or failure as they see fit.'

'*Far*, you never had much time for religion.'

'It is one explanation.' Her father looked directly at her and his eyes seemed old. 'When you are cursed like I am, the gods give you a lot of time to think.'

Her father settled into his bed and signalled that she should help arrange the furs.

Sela looked at him. She had always defended him before, told her brother's wife that she was wrong to resent her father. That he meant well.

But how much had he planned? Had he sent word to Thorkell? Did he know that those ships from Thorkell were coming? Had he guessed that Thorkell would send Vikar?

She attempted to dismiss the thought as unworthy. Her father would never have taken such risks. But she paused in smoothing the fur about him, unable to fully banish it. There were parts of his life that she knew nothing about.

'Vikar is taking Kjartan to Kaupang.'

'It is right and proper. Kjartan deserves his birthright. He is the son of one of the most important jaarls in Viken. You have denied him for far too long.'

Sela dropped the fur with a plop and sent it sliding to the floor. 'Me? *Far*, you know the full story. You agreed with me and what I did. You said that it was the only way.'

'Circumstances change. I greatly fear I misjudged your former husband.' Her father gave a long, shuddering sigh. 'I have lain awake at nights, thinking. It was wrong of me—what I did.'

'What do you mean?'

'I should have stood with my sword and shield strapped to me. I shall now suffer the icy torments of Hel because I allowed you to stand in my place.'

'I highly doubt that, *Far*.' Sela brushed her lips against his withered cheek. 'You are too cunning to get caught there.'

Her father laughed.

'Now, go to sleep, because in the morning we have a boat journey. We must return to the hall.'

'I shall be a prisoner in the hall I built with my own hands.'

'You will be a guest, an honoured guest.'

'You have a lot to learn, my girl, if you believe that.'

'I have already learnt a lot. More than I wanted to. I am no longer the naïve, young woman that I once was.' Sela smoothed the wrinkles from the skirt of her apron-dress. 'I will leave you now and see to Kjartan. He will need to be prepared for the journey.'

'He is an excellent traveller. Your son is a credit to you. You were right to take on so much of his education. Una complained about it, but you were right.'

'He reminds me of his father.'

Her father's eyes narrowed.

'Do you have feelings for Vikar?' The question was sudden and shot like a knife through her heart.

'Of course not,' she lied and hurried from the room. She stopped and laid her face against the cool wall of the farmhouse, seeking to regain control. She knew her father had seen something in her face. Her feelings for Vikar had never gone away. They had stayed there under the surface, like a spring waiting to bubble up.

Vikar was right when he'd said that she had run away. This time, there would be no escape.

Vikar finished checking the ropes of the small trading vessel. They would hold. With the few improvements he had made to the way the sail was rigged and a fair wind, he had every hope of reaching Bose's hall before nightfall the next day.

In the back of his mind, he could not dismiss his instinct. It had saved him before and it would save him now. The victory was far too easy. It was as if Bose wanted him here.

He stretched and looked up at the yellow light that pooled from the farmhouse. He would sleep here tonight—away from the others, away from Sela.

Today had gone very differently from he had planned. He had gained a son. But had Bose the Dark intended this all along?

'Am I fitting in with your plans, Bose, or disrupting them?' Vikar asked into the growing darkness. 'And where does your daughter enter? Is she part of your game or is she playing her own? Her own, I think. It is why you were willing to sacrifice her.'

He fingered his sword. 'Our game is not yet over, Sela. You may think you will win your freedom, but there is still everything to play for. And I mean to win.'

Chapter Fifteen

'*Mor, Mor*, I can see the raven gables!' Kjartan called from where he stood at the prow of the boat. 'We are home.'

Home, but not really hers any more. Sela raised her eyes towards where the gables just peeked out over the trees as Kjartan chattered away about the dogs and cats he had missed, the friends he wanted to play with and the things he was going to do now that he was home.

Soon the green slope would appear and the hall would be fully revealed. Always, when she returned to the hall, she looked for the silver raven gables. They had always been a sign of home, and when she had returned from Kaupang, of welcoming refuge. She felt nothing of this as she looked at them today. She saw the signs of age, of wearing—one of the ravens had lost a beak, another had a split head. Worn out, tired and in need of repair.

The hall had ceased to be safe.

It no longer belonged to her. It was not a refuge, but a prison. It had been a place that she had run to when the world had turned out to be different from what she had expected. She was through with hiding herself away from the world.

She steeled herself, hating what was to come. What scars of battle would be visible first? Or would they be invisible like the scars on her heart?

'The hall stands. This is good,' Vikar said as he moved about the boat, tightening a line here, letting out the sail there, always strong and capable. He was in total command. 'We will have the formal surrender when we land.'

'You doubted that it would stand?'

'Not doubt, but I had concerns.' He shielded his eyes. 'I have learnt to distrust when things are too easy. I have always had to fight for my victories, for the things I believe in.'

Vikar's hand brushed her elbow as he reeled the sail in tighter, changing the course of the boat. The unexpectedness of the touch caused a small tremor to flicker through her. Ruthlessly she damped it down and focused her attention on his words. Concerns. Fighting for victory.

She gave a short, bitter laugh and pressed her palms into the railing, concentrated on the practical rather than the faint hope growing inside her. The thought that she might be carrying another child of his had taken root, refused to go away, and she knew she wanted it to be true. It frightened her how much she wanted it. She wanted to see the pride in Vikar's eyes when he held a baby of hers in his arms. She wanted to show him that she could learn and that she would trust him with her children.

'Are your warriors that ill disciplined?' she asked to take her mind away from the future. 'Perhaps you should not have left them, then.'

'I have no doubts about the discipline of my warriors. Ivar is a more than adequate leader of men. That is why Thorkell gave us joint command of the *felag*.' His face became angles and planes. 'Hafdan and his warriors might be dead, but your father had other allies. Was this a trap set to spring?'

Sela frowned and listened to the water lapping against the hull of the boat. She knew what he was saying. Sela's stomach churned. She had seen enough blood over the past five days for her to wish never to see any again. She watched the waves lap the boat as they glided ever closer to the shore. 'My father's allies melted like snow in May once it became clear that he had lost his power.'

'Is that what you believe or what you know for the truth?' Vikar tilted his head to one side as he assessed her with cool eyes.

'It is what I believe.' Sela leant forward as her heart raced. He had to trust her on this. It had to be true. The alternative was too gruesome to contemplate. 'Hafdan knew there was nothing for him here…after…well after the argument. He was ambitious and wanted to prove his worth. My father allowed him to go.'

'Allowed?' Vikar raised an eyebrow. 'How exactly did he allow?'

'He was hardly in any fit state to protest.' Sela stared out as the raven gables drew closer. The hall with its imposing frontage was now clearly visible. Was it true that her father had built it on the bones of *tottr* men? She shivered slightly. And she knew the time had arrived to speak her other fear. 'My father is nearing his end.'

'All the more reason for Hafdan to stay. He could have been jaarl. You are unmarried.'

'I had refused him. Several times.' Sela wrinkled her nose. 'I'd call him a pig of a man, but I would be being unkind to pigs.'

'On that one point, I would agree.' Vikar fingered his chin. 'Hafdan has always deferred to your father.'

'And you never would. He asked but a little loyalty from his son-in-law. Would it have been such a great hardship to support him in the king's council?'

'My judgement is my own. Your father knew that and then he asked me to change. I refused.' Vikar's gaze was on the horizon, but Sela thought she detected a tinge of regret.

'My father had nothing to do with Hafdan leaving. He wanted him to stay, but accepted his need to go.' Sela tightened her grip. A small splinter pricked her, but she ignored it as she tried to forget Hafdan's leer. 'Why must you persist in this fable of yours? That my father has planned all this.'

'Because he has proved untrustworthy in the past. I dislike accepting what he wants me to believe. Why did he escape?'

Sela glanced back to where her father sat, eyes closed, his face in the sun. If he felt her father untrustworthy, what must he think of her? Vikar's rugged profile gave no hint. 'My father had no ulterior motive. He left the hall to protect Kjartan. He had no thoughts about returning to power. There is no need to humiliate him.'

A corner of the sail fluttered free, and the boat shifted. In the front Kjartan and Una gave small squeals—Kjartan's of delight, while Una prayed to the gods to save them. Sela braced herself as her body collided with Vikar's. His arm went around her, held her steady for a heartbeat and then let her go. The unexpected contact sent warm tingles throughout her body.

'Who alerted Thorkell to Hafdan's departure and why?' Vikar asked as he recaptured the sail and righted the boat. 'Thorkell sent us north for a reason. A few more days and we would have walked into a trap.'

'I have no answer for that, and neither do you,' Sela said with more conviction than she felt. All through the voyage she had been over and over the questions as well. She had no firm answers and nothing she was comfortable with. All she knew and could hang on to was that her father would never willingly put her in peril. 'Thorkell has many who are willing to whisper. He learnt from my father that knowledge has value.'

'Deep within me, I know your father is involved and my men will not be safe until his people see him surrender, until they realise that there is a new power in the north.'

Vikar's profile was hard and Sela struggled to see the man she had shared the outward journey with.

Had he vanished for good?

Sometimes on this voyage, she had thought that she'd caught glimpses of him as Vikar bent over the ropes or straightened the sails. Several times, she'd felt his eyes burning into the back of her neck, but when she turned, he was always busy with something else.

Her imagination, just as it had been all those years ago when they were first married. Only her longing for him had not decreased with time.

Sela dug her nails into her palms. She had to remember what had happened then. How he had proven less than reliable and had gone off without a backward glance. His story of Hafdan's beating was too easy. It did not explain his behaviour beforehand. It did not explain the love token or why he had refused to take any notice of her. She had to retain control of her wayward heart.

There was too much between them to hope that somehow they could find their way back to what they had briefly shared on the journey. Somehow, she had to carve out a new life for herself, protect her father and her people and enjoy the limited time she had left with Kjartan. Most of all, she wanted to discover a way to do the impossible—make Vikar love her the way she cared about him.

'*Mor*, *Mor*, come watch with me!' Kjartan called out, waving his wooden horse above his head.

'Be careful, Kjartan.' Sela rushed forward to hold him back.

As the boat came close to the shore, a horn's blast echoed out over the fjord, sending a flock of seagulls wheeling in the sky. Vikar felt his muscles begin to relax. The horn was from his dragon ship. No trap. Dozens of people rushed down to the water's edge. Ivar plunged into the sea and grabbed the rope that Vikar tossed out.

'Allow me to offer some help, friend.'

Vikar jumped down and joined him in the water. Together they pulled the boat to the shore. The cold water kept his mind from the way Sela's apron-dress hugged her curves. He had found the proximity to her much harder to bear than he had anticipated. He had even discovered that he was jealous of his son. Jealous of what they shared and jealous of the way Kjartan commanded her attention. He wanted her to look at him, but always her gaze was towards her son.

'It is about time, Vikar. I had begun to think you might have finally encountered the frost giants or Fenis the Wolf.' Ivar clapped his hand against Vikar's back. 'It is good to see you looking well, and with all our escapees in your care. You must be congratulated.'

'It will take more than a wolf to stop me,' Vikar replied in a mild tone.

'Did you encounter many on your journey? Vikar, I will insist, this time you must hire a skald to put poetry into your tale.'

'A man should have a saga for his sons. You may be right, old friend, it is time I considered it. For too long I have ignored my saga.' He glanced up to where Sela stood with her hand on Kjartan's shoulder and noticed her cheeks had flushed slightly. It could be wind burn. But his blood leapt at the sight of her reddened lips. He ruthlessly turned his attention away from her.

'How goes it? Have you subdued the hall?'

'Guarding the hall has been an easy task, Vikar.' Ivar smiled and Vikar could see the shadow of the handsome man he had once been. 'I have enjoyed sampling the kegs of ale and mead.'

'Not so ale-soaked that you have forgotten to keep guard, I hope? Have there been any strange movements? Unexplained sightings in the nights?'

'You must think I believe the skald's tales.'

'I have learnt that they may have more truth in them than I had ever considered.' Vikar ignored Ivar's sceptical expression. 'Bose likes to dress the truth up as fiction.'

Ivar's face became wreathed in a smile as he peered in to the boat. 'I see you have accomplished your mission. Are you going to take him in chains to Thorkell?'

'I found Bose the Dark alive and have returned him here to formally surrender the hall to me.' Vikar looked at his old friend. 'Did you have doubts?'

'If any man could do it, you could.' Ivar fingered the scar on his face. 'When will the formal surrender take place? It needs to be done quickly.'

'Now.'

Vikar gestured towards the elderly man, frail but fighting his infirmity with every breath of his body. Vikar knew that Bose was determined to return here—but to die in his old hall or for some other darker purpose? He had not unravelled that particular spool of wool yet. But nothing had happened to make him trust Bose any more. 'If you please, Bose the Dark…'

Bose gave an irritated sigh. He wrapped his cloak about him and stepped from the boat.

'Be careful, *Far*.' Sela's words floated on the breeze.

'I am no infant to be wrapped in swaddling clothes, daughter.' Bose turned back towards the boat. 'I know what I am about.'

'As do I,' Vikar said. 'We will have this done properly, Bose the Dark. I will make peace with you.'

'If that is what you desire…some men prefer war.'

'There is much to be gained when the peace is on my terms.'

Vikar held out the hilt of his sword. A pained expression crossed Bose's face. For a heartbeat, Vikar wondered whether he would do it, or whether he would prefer death. He willed him to take the hilt and make the sign. Vikar knew he could not cold-bloodedly kill Sela's father. He only hoped that Bose did not realise that.

Then, just as Vikar was sure he would challenge him,

Bose appeared to change his mind. He lifted his head, made the sign and the ceremony of surrender was over. Peace would reign.

Vikar's shoulders relaxed as he slid the sword back into its sheath. He had won. He had gained control of the north lands, and he would protect them for his son.

'The hall is yours...for as long as you can hold it.' Bose gave a short laugh and his eyes slid away from Vikar. 'This hall has a tendency to test its owners. There is something about its foundations, or so the skalds tell me.'

'I intend to hold it.' Vikar fingered the hilt of his sword. 'And tales told by skalds do not frighten me.'

'They should. They frighten me and I know the truth of them.' The wind blew Bose's hair, but his eyes seemed fixed on some far point. 'You should learn them, and respect them, if you wish to safeguard this land for your son.'

'I have met the legends. Men of flesh and blood do not scare me.'

'My blood and sweat built this hall. It takes a man with courage and vision to hold it. I thought I had it, but other matters called me and it slipped from my grasp. Will the hall become an empty shell without laughter, without love?'

'I believe I have what is required. I know what this hall needs.' Vikar stood straight and realised he did know.

Bose's eyes raked him up and down. He fancied that he could see the respect grow in Bose's eyes. 'You are made of stern stuff, Vikar. Sterner stuff than your father.'

Vikar blinked. He had expected Bose to say many things, but not this. 'I was unaware that you were more than acquaintances.'

'We had our differences, Hrut the Bold and I, but I respected him.' Bose pursed his lips. 'He should never have fought that berserker. I warned him against it, just as I am warning you now. You should heed my words. This hall has mouldered in the shadows for too long. It needs a strong arm and a stout heart.'

'I have spent my life undoing my father's mistakes. I believe I understand what drove him and I have learnt from him.' Involuntarily Vikar's fingers tightened their grip on his sword. 'I had his sword remade.'

'And your own mistakes?' The words were a whisper on the wind. 'Will you have your son deal with those? Will he have to remake your sword? Will the son be like the father?'

'I will deal with them when I have to.' Vikar looked to where Kjartan stood, his blond fringe blowing on the breeze. 'My son will be proud of his inheritance.'

Bose gave a nod as if he approved of Vikar's response. Vikar frowned. He did not require Bose's grudging approval.

'The ceremony is finished, Bose. When I want your guidance, I will ask for it.'

'All the same, you will need the gods on your side to hold this hall.' Bose spoke in an undertone. 'I have counted your men and your dragon ships.'

'I had enough men to take it, and I shall hold it.' Vikar met his eyes. 'It is mine by the right of sword.'

'I once thought that way.'

Suddenly the effort appeared to be too much for Bose and he crumpled. Kjartan's nurse came up and supported him. Her dark eyes flashed. 'Do you not know how he has suffered?'

'My father must rest,' Sela said at his elbow, suddenly there, her presence filling his senses. 'The voyage has been hard for him.'

'The difficulty was entirely of his own making. He should have stayed here.' Vikar forced his mind to stay on Bose, rather than on wandering to her lips and remembering her cries of pleasure. He'd give her until the wedding night. 'But he wanted to hide the boy from me. Perhaps a test, perhaps not.'

'Why? Who is the boy?' Ivar nodded towards where Kjartan stood, held in Sela's arms, his blond head on her shoulder and one of the wooden horses in his mouth. Vikar's heart expanded. He wondered if he would ever get tired of looking at him.

'My son.' Vikar pronounced the words with pride. 'Kjartan is my son.'

'Your…son?' Ivar's hands dropped the rope as he regarded Kjartan with astonishment. 'Now that I look, I can see the resemblance—just. Were you once that good-looking? I fear he favours the mother.'

'Ever the flatterer, Ivar.'

'I know you are a fast worker, Vikar, but this begs the question—how did you conjure the boy up? He looks to be ready to begin his training as a warrior.'

'He will be four in a few months' time. He is Sela's and my son. She neglected to tell me of his existence. He was conceived in wedlock, and I have accepted him as my own.'

'Neglected to tell you?' Ivar knocked his hand against the side of his head. 'How does a woman neglect something like that? Does she know what he stands to inherit, even before you won here? It makes no sense.'

'She did not offer any explanation.'

Vikar regarded the sweep of Sela's neck. He knew what Ivar said was correct. Most women would have wanted the best for their son, and yet she had sought to keep his true identity a secret until…she sought to use it to keep them from marrying. Had she hated being married to him that much?

'Do you think Thorkell knows? He and Bose were close.'

'Thorkell would have told me, if he had guessed. I suspect that Bose has kept the secret for his own purpose, and, right now, I am uncertain if it is the purpose that Sela had in mind. There are dark happenings here.'

Sela gave him a nod.

'I trust that my son and I may retire and wash away the dirt from the journey. That you will not require us further.'

'Is that an offer to join you in the bath, Sela?' Vikar dropped his voice. 'If you wish to entice me, perhaps you should try using a more seductive voice.'

Her cheeks flushed scarlet, but she said nothing as she turned on her heel and walked away. Vikar watched her skirts swirl about her ankles.

'There is a tale to this one, old friend.' Ivar clapped him on his back. 'Come and relate it as we share a cup of ale.'

'It is my affair, Ivar. It always was.'

Ivar rolled his eyes skyward. 'The skald will want to sing about it. It is the sort of tale that excites the ladies.'

'No.'

The rocks crunched under Vikar's feet as he began to walk up the slope. He found it impossible to rid himself of the feeling that it was all too easy, that he was still playing a game against an unknown opponent. His fingers curled around the hilt of his sword.

For now he would watch, wait and pretend that everything was normal. But now, rather than fighting just for his men and for himself, he knew he was fighting for his son, his birthright, and, most of all, for Sela.

'The skald has other things to do. He needs to compose a poem for my marriage.'

'Your marriage?'

'I marry Sela, Bose the Dark's daughter on Freyja's feast day.'

'You are marrying your former wife?' Ivar did not bother to hide his astonishment. 'Sela the Stubborn, you called her. And that was one of the kinder titles you gave her.'

Vikar winced as Ivar threw his former words back at him. He had wronged Sela, but she had also wronged him.

'It serves my purposes.'

'But—'

'I will inspect the hall, Ivar.' Vikar cut through the flow of words. 'The wedding takes place according to Viken law. Nothing must go wrong. I will have no man question mine or my son's right to be jaarl of the north lands. I am through with revenge.'

'*Mor*, I don't like all these men here.' Kjartan hid his face in Sela's shoulder as they walked up the slope towards the hall. 'Make them go. They frighten me.'

'They will not hurt you, Kjartan.' Sela put him down and caught his face between her hands, looking him in the eyes. She had to believe that Vikar would look after Kjartan, if nothing else. 'They are your father's men.'

'Truly?'

'Truly.'

Kjartan tilted his head and appeared to consider her words.

'My father's men,' he said slowly as if the realisation had just dawned on him. His eyes lit up.

'Yes.' The word was choked out of her throat. Kjartan had not even left and she was already losing him. All Vikar had to do was exist. Soon all he would speak about was Vikar and she knew she would hang on every scrap of information about him.

'Do you think he has my horse?'

'Give him some time, Kjartan.' Sela laughed. 'Shall we go into the hall and get you some clean clothes?'

'If we have to, but I'd rather see the horses and the dogs.' She smiled down at her son. He was predictable.

'Go on, then. But you will need to bathe before the evening meal.'

Kjartan made a face, but then he took off at a run.

Sela watched him for a while, hoping that he might return, but the yard remained empty except for a few curious stares from Vikar's men and a single cat that lay in the last patch of sunlight.

Sela glanced up at the raven gables. There was no hope for it, she had tarried long enough. She would have to go in and face what awaited her.

Several of the women who were working in the kitchen dropped their ladles and gawped at her. Several of the faces were openly hostile while others were guarded. Sela gave a nod as an awkward silence hung in the room. She should have guessed that this might happen. The women had no idea of how they were supposed to behave.

'You have returned, my lady.' Thorgerd, the woman who had served as her maid ever since Sela returned from Kaupang, hurried over to her, clasping her to her ample bosom. 'I have been praying to the gods that you would. You have no idea what is out in the forest.'

'Yes, I do,' Sela replied as she disentangled herself from her maid's grasp.

'Is it as bad as they say?'

Sela kept her chin high. 'I survived and that will have to be enough.'

Thorgerd gave a nod. Sela was relieved that she didn't question her further. Later, when she had begun to make sense of it, she would confide in her maid, but for now her feelings for Vikar were too mixed up. How could she explain them?

'Is all well with the women?' Sela asked. 'Do all live?'

'We have been well treated.' Thorgerd gave a small, eloquent shrug. 'Better than we could have hoped for. We have managed to adapt, some better than others. Ina has found yet another new lover… All he had to do was whisper she had very sexy eyes and she melted.'

Sela looked at her women as Thorgerd imparted the latest gossip and news. It appeared much as it had been when she'd left.

She held out her hand. 'You know I had to find Kjartan.'

'No one has said anything against you, my lady.' Thorgerd dipped her head. 'I wouldn't let them. No one blames you for anything. We know how you love your son. What you went through to have him and how you defied your father.'

'I wanted you to know.'

'Thank you, my lady.'

Sela turned to go. 'I will take a bath and then change into my own things. I think I will be allowed my old sleeping quarters for a while.'

'Is it true what they are whispering—Vikar has accepted Kjartan as his son?' Thorgerd asked, motioning for the other women to return to their work.

'Yes, it is true.' Sela paused and waited to see how the women would absorb the news.

'It is well that you finally told him. A boy needs a father,' Thorgerd commented. 'What happens next?'

'We shall be remarrying on Freyja's day.' She forced her lips to turn up into a smile. She wanted her wedding to be much more than an empty union. 'That is the correct day for weddings after all.'

'Remarrying?' The maid's eyes widened. Her hand clutched Sela's arm. 'You are remarrying the new jaarl—Vikar Hrutson? Your former husband? This is a day for celebrating.'

'Some may celebrate more than others.'

'It is good that you finally put your differences aside. I, for one, never thought you should have left. You should have stayed. You see he does have feelings for you. It could all work out.'

Sela looked at her maid, remembering how Thorgerd had been the one friend she could speak with after she had returned from Kaupang, how she had poured her heart out. Thorgerd was one of the few people who knew about Kjartan's parentage. There was no point in denying that she had feelings for Vikar.

'Do not read runes where there are none.'

'Nevertheless, he is *marrying* you and you will be in his bed.'

'Please…' Sela held up her hand, aware that her whole being glowed at the thought of sharing a bed with Vikar. 'It is far from simple.'

'He's a man. You are a desirable woman. Trust your instinct, my lady.' Thorgerd patted her hair. 'I always do.'

'And why are you marrying Sela?' Ivar asked as Vikar and he played a game of *tafl,* 'You always said that you were never going to marry again, that marriage was for simple-minded fools.'

Vikar paused in the moving of his pieces on the board. Ivar had the bad habit of reminding him of his words—words that he knew now were the result of hurt pride more than anything else. 'I have my reasons. I told you the story.'

'Spare me. You only told me part of the tale, the one you wanted me to hear.' Ivar regarded him steadily. 'Who are you seeking to punish? Sela? Or yourself?'

'I have no idea what you are speaking about. You delight in riddles.' Vikar gave a laugh.

Ivar moved another piece. 'I believe you know what I am speaking about. You have spent your life trying to right your father's mistakes while running from your own.'

'What do you mean?'

'When Sela left Kaupang, it was well known that you asked to go on the first available *felag*. You could have gone after her.'

'One of these days, I will forget that you are my friend, Ivar.'

'One of these days you will stop lying to yourself. You are marrying Sela because she is a challenge to you.'

'Is that so?' Vikar leant forward. 'I didn't realise you knew me so well.'

'And another thing, all the women I have seen you with bear a resemblance to Sela.'

Vikar glared at Ivar, knowing his friend spoke the truth. All the women he had had in the years since Sela's departure had something that had reminded him of Sela—her hair or maybe her hands. But all had left him dissatisfied.

The only one he had wanted was…Sela. He had realised that the night they had spent together at the waterfall. He had thrown her away once, but now, despite what she had done to him, he wanted her in his life. He had to find a reason why she had behaved that way. It was not out of spite, he was sure of that.

'I have no wish to discuss this further.'

Ivar moved his piece. 'I believe your king is mine, Vikar. Had I known that you would be this easy to beat, I would have used your former wife as a distraction long before now.'

Bose was using Sela for his own ends, but Vikar knew that the game was about more than power. It was a battle for his very soul, the centre of his being. Sela.

Chapter Sixteen

'Are you going to open it and take out your bridal clothes or are you going spend more time staring at it?' Thorgerd asked as Sela knelt by the intricately carved trunk.

She had passed her hand over it, and had once turned the key, but, thus far, Sela had been unable to lift the lid.

'There is a little time before the purification ceremony. The clothes will all be there, safe from the moths.' Sela's smile died on her lips as she looked at her friend's expression.

'Why have you been avoiding it? Your bridal dress should have been pressed days ago. Flowers gathered for your crown.'

'I had to see to other things. Halls do not run themselves. I wanted the tapestries to be hung and then there was the food, and the songs.'

'An excuse, Sela.'

Sela put her hand on the trunk. When she had last turned the key after Kaupang, she thought never to re-open it. And now, now she was frightened as to what she would find. What memories she would unleash. 'I will open it and then you will see that you are talking nonsense.'

Sela turned the key and threw back the lid. The white dress, lay as she had folded it. Carefully preserved. The young woman who had worn these things had had many dreams, only to have her hopes and illusions ground to dust. Could she face that happening again? Could she go back to that sort of marriage? 'You see, all I needed was time.'

'Kjartan is looking forward to the marriage. Vikar has promised him his father's sword after the ceremony,' Thorgerd said. 'He is so excited by the promise of training. Soon he will spend all his time on the practice field. You will be able to watch him.'

'After the ceremony, Vikar and Kjartan will go to Kaupang. I will see nothing.'

Her maid's brow wrinkled. 'But why have the men been doing all the work to the defences—the work your father and Hafdan neglected—if he does not plan to stay and to rule?'

'Because he wants to show who is in control. His real home is in Kaupang at the court with Asa.'

'Are you sure of that?'

'How could it be anywhere else?' Sela regarded the tapestry behind the trunk as a fist clenched around her heart. Over the past few days, she had been impressed with the way Vikar and his men had worked to shore up the neglected defences, how Vikar had sought out Kjartan and how capable he appeared. However, he did not come near her, barely acknowledging her presence. She found she missed the easy camaraderie they had shared on the journey to find her father and Kjartan. She wanted to believe that there could be a happy ending…somehow. But now, looking at these bridal clothes, she knew she could not face the same sort of loveless life she'd had before. She was losing everything. But had she ever really had anything? 'It is a political marriage, Thorgerd. Vikar wants to ensure peace in the north.'

Thorgerd pursed her lips and picked up the bridal crown. 'This was your mother's, wasn't it? It will look lovely in your hair with candles.'

'I thought to wear something different, more fitting to my status.' Sela picked up the crown and a pair of silver arm-rings slipped out. Her heart turned over. They had been Vikar's private morning gift to her and she had been unable to return them. Slowly she replaced them in the trunk, and put the crown on top. She knew then that she could not do it. She could not have another loveless marriage with Vikar. She could not return to the bride she once was.

The lid shut with a click.

Sela stood up and brushed the dirt off her gown as a pain gripped her stomach. A sudden searing pain. She closed her eyes, knowing that the gods had not answered her earlier prayer. Kjartan would have no brother or sister. Vikar had to know that there was no reason for them to marry.

'Sela, you look like death.' Thorgerd put an arm about her. 'The purification ceremony needs to begin.'

'The purification ceremony will have to wait. There are things I have to do.'

'But there will be a wedding…'

'I don't know.' Sela put her hands to her head. 'I need to right old wrongs.'

'Daughter, where do you go in such a hurry? And dressed in your oldest clothes?' Her father caught her arm as she started to go through the main hall. 'All is in readiness for the feast.'

'I had not expected to see you out of bed.'

'My daughter's marriage is important to me. It will do much to restore this family's prestige.'

Prestige. Position. Power. Sela pressed her lips together. Was that all her father cared about? All he had ever cared about? 'You approve of Vikar Hrutson now? Four years ago you hated him.'

Her father shrugged. 'Sometimes the gods need a helping hand, and sometimes they move in a mysterious fashion. Vikar is the right man for you.'

'You haven't always thought so,' Sela said fixing her father with her eye. 'You were the one who put the love token in my bed. It had nothing to do with Vikar or Asa, and everything to do with your desire to control. And now you hope to cling onto power through this marriage. It won't work that way, *Far*. Vikar is his own man. He always has been.'

Her father's eyes slid away from her.

'Yes,' he said finally, his head bowed. 'I did. Vikar had defied me once too often. You had refused to listen to reason. I wanted what was best for you. I would have done it differently if I had known about Kjartan. It is one of the moments in my life that I am least proud of. I used my daughter like a counter on a *tafl* board, but I do care about you. Can you forgive me?'

Sela's insides trembled. Even a few days ago, she would have found it difficult, but now she knew the truth and knew that whoever had put the love token in the bed did not matter. It was her reaction to the discovery that mattered. She was a grown woman. She could have behaved differently. Her father did not control her life. She could have chosen a different path. 'There is nothing to forgive. The blame is mine. It is time I stopped lying to myself.'

'What do you mean, Sela?'

'I used it as an excuse, *Far*.' Sela gathered her father's hands within hers. 'We both know that. I was looking for a way out, because my pride came before everything. You must not blame yourself. I took the chance you offered, because I could not bear the mistakes I had made.'

'You have become a far stronger person than I.' Her father looked at her with new respect in his eyes. He leant forward and brushed his lips against her forehead. Sela started. He had never been a man given to affection. The last time he had touched her in such a way was when he had promised to accept Kjartan as a member of his family. 'I am proud of you, Daughter. Proud that you found the right man for you…finally.'

'And did you have something to do with Vikar's arrival?'

'Someone had to make sure that Kjartan's inheritance was secure.' Her father's words resounded off the walls. 'You showed no inclination to secure it. So I had to take steps.'

'Were you in contact with Thorkell?'

'Thorkell and I have had communications. He might have exiled me, but there were ways.'

'Were you the one who alerted Thorkell when Hafdan left?'

'Why would I do something like that?' her father asked quietly.

'Because it would be your way.'

'As you know so much about me, you answer your own question.' Her father turned to go. There was a dignity in his movements though he was a shadow of his former self. Despite all his faults, he remained her father. 'And, Sela, I did say that you needed a strong man when I am gone. I want you to be safe.'

Safe. That was different to being happy. But she knew she had to give Vikar the choice. She had to do it. She could not face going back to the old marriage.

Sela ran up and caught her father's arm. 'Thank you.'

'For what?'

'For giving me the courage to face my future.'

'I haven't given you anything, Sela. You make your own way in this world.' He tried to scowl, but Sela could see the love in his eyes. 'I need to know that you will be looked after, that Kjartan's inheritance will be protected.'

'You will be here for a long time.'

Her father shook his head. 'My race is almost run, Sela. There comes a time when you are too tired to go on. I have done what I had to do for Kjartan's sake. Family matters far more when you are old than when you are young.'

'But it is love that matters most. I cannot settle for security.'

'What did you say? Come back here, Sela. Do not do anything foolish.'

'I am about to do something that is right.' Sela picked

up her skirts and ran. If she hurried, there would be time. She had to give Vikar the choice. He had to know that there was no longer any reason why they had to marry. It was better now. She did not want any lies or tricks between them. She had to explain. 'I can't marry Vikar, not in this fashion.'

'Where are you going?'

'To give Vikar his freedom.'

'But Kjartan…'

'Will be taken care of.'

'Do you love Vikar?'

Sela stared at her father. 'Yes. And I cannot face a one-sided marriage.'

'As you wish, Daughter.'

'I do, *Far*, I do.'

The grave mounds were silent, silhouetted against the sky and fjord. Memories of his previous wedding assaulted Vikar from all sides. This time he was no young jaarl with little land, making a marriage for political convenience. This time, he held the power and he was marrying because he wanted to. He wanted Sela. He knew that, but he wanted her on his terms. And yet Bose's whispered words haunted him—was Sela even now slipping away from him? Returning to how she was back in Kaupang? Would he find the hall a loveless, empty place? He wanted everything, and he would have nothing without Sela.

'I always hate this bit of the ceremony,' Ivar said. 'The retrieving of the sword from a burial mound.'

'It is necessary.'

'Even for a remarriage?' Ivar pulled his ear. 'Then it

is a good a reason for not marrying again. I shall tell Thorkell that when I refuse his next offer of a bride.'

'Thorkell appears determined to marry us off.' Vikar gave a short laugh. 'All winter he kept dropping hints about marrying.'

'He wants the jaarls of Viken to have sons, and be settled to women of his choosing.'

'I doubt he would have chosen Sela for me, but he will have to be content with my choice.'

'If it subdues his northern borders, he will be very content.' Ivar gave a laugh. 'He is as wily as Bose the Dark sometimes. I should not wonder if he thought about it when he insisted you go north. Perhaps he even had an inkling about Kjartan.'

'Sela swears her father told no one about Kjartan's parentage.' Vikar pursed his lips. It had crossed his mind about Thorkell's intentions, but he also believed Sela. She had kept Kjartan's parentage a secret…for her own reasons.

'Very little escapes our king. He learnt from a master, remember.'

'But all of that is for later. First I have this ceremony to go through. My wife will be mine. She will not run from me this time. The ceremony will be on my terms.'

'Ah, your reasoning begins to come clear.' Ivar tapped his nose. 'Come with me, and Erik the Black can go over your family history with you, make sure the recitation is correct.'

'My history doesn't matter,' Vikar said. 'It is my future with my wife and child. But Sela still holds her secrets tightly to her chest. She has not explained why Bose was willing to accept Kjartan when he knew he was my son.'

'And have you told your secret?'

'What secret is that?'

Ivar put his hand on Vikar's shoulder. 'That you love her, that you want to spend the rest of your life with her.'

'Deeds, not words, Ivar.'

'Sometimes, women need words.' Ivar thumped his chest. 'They need to hear what is in there, or so my wife used to say to me.'

'And did you say the words to your wife?'

'Not nearly often enough before she died.'

Vikar shook his head. 'I can't, until I know all her secrets.'

'Then I predict your marriage will not be a success.'

'That is your opinion.'

Ivar gave a low whistle as he looked over Vikar's shoulder towards the hall. 'Your bride-to-be has arrived. It does not look as if she is going through with the purification ceremony.'

Vikar saw Sela headed towards him with a determined look on her face. Her fair hair streamed behind her and she had not taken time to put on a cloak. The breeze moulded her gown to her figure. Vikar's blood leapt. His fingers itched to unwrap the layers and reach the woman that he knew lay underneath. Ruthlessly he suppressed it. Sela was breaking all convention by coming out here to find him. It could only mean one thing. She had come to say goodbye, and he knew that he could no more bind her to him than he could keep the waves on the shore.

'Why are you here, Sela?' he asked before Sela had reached the mound. 'It is customary for a groom to only see his bride at the ceremony.'

'I need to speak to you, Vikar. Alone. Now.' She hesitated. 'Please.'

'Your wish is my command.' Ivar made a bow. 'Take your chance, Vikar.'

Vikar gave his head a shake. Not here. Not now. Later, after they were married, then he would make things different. Now all she needed to see was that the marriage would happen.

'What is so wrong that you need to speak to me? Has one of my men terrorized your maid? Or has the meat failed to roast? What disaster has happened?'

'No disaster.'

'Then tell me why you are here, Sela.'

Sela searched his face, looking for a softening of his features, some sign that he was happy to see her, but found none.

He must never guess how much she had wanted to carry his child. How she had hoped the child would prove a way to truly put their past behind them. She twisted her apron-dress around her hands as the speech she had practised on her way to the burial mounds vanished from her brain. How could she say goodbye when her heart clung to the hope that someday he might return to her? But how could she face a marriage like the one they'd had, the one that had nearly destroyed her, and would surely do so this time?

'What new intrigue do you wish to discuss with me? What is so important that it cannot wait until after the ceremony?' Vikar asked. His voice was light, but his eyes were remote. 'Kjartan is waiting up in the hall. He is excited about the marriage. I have promised him my father's sword.'

'We don't need to marry for Kjartan to have your father's sword. We don't need to marry for any reason. Kjartan's inheritance is secure.' She said the words quickly before she lost her nerve. She prayed fervently to any god that might be listening that he would accept the explanation. That she wouldn't have to explain about her feelings for him. 'Let me go, Vikar. I beg you.'

'What new development has happened? The hall is at peace, Sela. I am through with your tricks. What excuse are you giving this time for abandoning me? For abandoning our son?'

'I am not pregnant.' Sela fought to keep her voice steady. 'There is no need for a ceremony. Take Kjartan and go from here. It is the only reason you wanted to marry me. You have your son and none will try to claim his inheritance through me, through what passed between us.'

A muscle jumped in his cheek. The faint breeze ruffled his hair, but his features appeared hewn from stone.

'Sela, you are not giving me a reason. Let me understand.'

'And if I asked you on the life-debt…' Sela made one last try. She struggled against the great gaping hole in her middle.

'This marriage goes ahead, Sela, even if I have to carry you kicking and screaming to the altar.' He grasped her arms, pulled her against his body. 'Are you going to pretend indifference?'

'What we shared is past, Vikar. You said that yourself.' She licked her parched lips. The temptation was great, but all that would happen is that she'd go back to a loveless marriage and eventually it would all start again. 'We are no longer the same people we once were. You saw how it was before. The passion we shared vanished. Our marriage was a hollow sham.'

Vikar stared at her. 'Our passion vanished?'

'Yes.' She bit out the word and knew she was lying, lying to save her heart.

'Actions speak louder than words, I always find.'

Her lips tingled, and she started to say something, but his mouth swooped down, took the breath from her lips. She clung to him and then it was over. He put her away from him and his eyes had taken on a cynical look.

'What is your next excuse going to be? When are you going to admit the truth?'

She put her hand to her aching lips, hating the fact that she wanted the bruising kiss to continue.

'Is that a demonstration of what is to come?'

'If you like.' Vikar shrugged.

'I do not.' Sela scrubbed at her lips.

'Are you denying the passion between us? It existed before and it still burns now.'

'Passion fades, Vikar.' Sela hesitated. 'I need more than that. I can't go back to what we had. I cannot face Kaupang again. I refuse to have the sort of marriage we had.'

'I never asked you to.'

Never asked you to. The words rang in her ears. The confirmation of her fears. She turned and started to go. She had lost everything. The only thing left were her few remaining shards of dignity. A single tear trickled down her cheek, but she kept her back straight. She had lost. Her whole world had ended. She took a stumbling step away from him. She would survive, but it would only be existing.

'Stay, Sela. Stay with me.' Vikar called out and she heard the anguish in his voice. 'I need you, Sela. I need you now more than I did when we fought the wolf. Stay with me. Please, I beg you.'

'You need me?' Her heart was thumping so loudly that she was certain she had misheard. She had to have misheard. Vikar would never say that to anyone. 'Why? You have Kjartan, your men, this hall.'

'I need you, Sela, Bose the Dark's daughter. I am nothing without you and that's why I want to marry you.' His hands caught her shoulders and turned her around. The face she had thought remote was contorted with emotion, vulnerable in a way she had never seen it before. 'I tried to show you how much I wanted to be a part of your life, but you would not see. My words are plain, but they are from my heart. Don't abandon me, Sela. Let me come with you, and be with you.'

Sela grew still. This Viking warrior was asking her? 'Are you asking me to marry you? To have a real marriage, a partnership?'

'No, I am begging you, Sela. Be my wife in truth. I need you.' Vikar went down on his knees in front of her, buried his face in her gown. 'Stay with me for ever at my side and in my bed. My entire world was destroyed when you left.'

'But Asa...' Sela looked at his hair, afraid at how desperate her being was to believing his declaration. This time, she had to be certain. 'I had no part of your world then.'

Vikar's arms dropped away and he stood up, facing her, but making no move to draw her into his arms. Sela heard her heart pounding in her ears. She had risked everything.

'Asa was a way to keep you at a distance.' He hesitated and then his jaw firmed and his gaze held hers. 'I was afraid of my feelings for you, afraid of their power over me. I was frightened and I chose the wrong path. She is a beautiful statue with no heart. I have never been intimate with her. You must believe that.'

'I believe you,' Sela breathed. Her fingers reached up and touched his cheek. His whole world? She found she had to believe him. 'I was wrong to go and not to fight for you.'

'We were both young, Sela. It is not an excuse, but now having found each other again, will you make us part?' He put his forehead next to hers. 'Asa may be my queen, but you are the queen of my heart. Always.'

'But you let me go,' Sela said in wonderment. 'You knew where I had gone. You did not follow. You made no real attempt.'

'It is one of the episodes in my life I most regret. My pride got in the way.'

'Your pride?'

'When my father died, I vowed never to let my emotions rule me as his had done. Then I married you, and discovered that all I wanted to do was be with you, but I wanted you on my terms. I wanted to be the only one in your heart. When you abandoned me, I told myself that it did not matter.' He threaded his fingers through hers. 'It was wrong of me. I have learnt there is enough love in my heart for both you and Kjartan. Hopefully, even now, in time, you will find a tiny space in your heart for me.'

She looked at him, humble and vulnerable. She knew what it had cost him to say those words. And how happy they made her.

'What is in the past is past,' she said quietly. 'I owe you a life-debt, Vikar, but more than that I love you. I would give you my heart but you already possess it.'

'I love you, Sela. Have my children. Stay at my side. Love me.' His words were firm, but his eyes pleaded with her.

'I want to. I will. I do. For always,' she answered without hesitation and lifted her face to his.

'There is something I want to know,' Vikar said against her hair after a long while.

'Ask and I will answer if I can.' Sela raised her hand to his cheek. 'I want no more shadows between us.'

'There are three new graves in your family's burial mound. I know of your brother and his wife dying. Who is the third? Whose child?'

'Their child,' Sela said slowly. She took a deep breath and was glad of Vikar's arm about her waist. The time was right to tell him, to explain why her father had accepted Kjartan and had allowed her to keep him hidden. 'They died from a fever when I was in labour with Kjartan.'

His eyes narrowed. 'Did you have the fever?'

'I gave birth burning up with fever, yes. Kjartan had it as well.' Sela closed her eyes. She had never considered that he would notice something like the graves. 'It is the true reason that my father agreed to accept him. My father had just lost his son, and his grandson.'

'Your story begins to make sense.' He put his arm about her waist, drew her close. 'But why did you think I wouldn't accept him?'

'Kjartan was a weak baby, Vikar,' Sela said. 'We both nearly died. They brought in ice blocks. My father…

nearly refused, but I wanted Kjartan to die a Viken. I don't think he considered we would live. It was an act of mercy on his part. You may say what you like about my father, but I know he loves me. He wanted the best for me. And I wanted the best for my son. I fought for his life and I was determined he would have the best of everything. I misjudged you, Vikar Hrutson. It was wrong of me.'

She waited. Would Vikar understand?

His fingers gently raised her chin so she was gazing into his eyes, eyes that were not filled with hate or anger but love and understanding—for her.

'It pains me that you went through this without me. I want to spend the rest of my life taking care of you and thanking the gods that I have such a lovely and generous woman for a wife.' Vikar's voice caught. 'I have loved you almost since we first met. I love our son because he belongs to you and me. Now can we get married and begin our lives again? Together.'

She saw the love in his eyes. For their son. For her. For ever.

'Yes,' she said. 'Always.'

'Good,' he said and nodded towards the hall. 'We have an audience. Do you want to tell our son or shall I?'

Sela looked up and saw her father leaning on a stick with his hand on Kjartan's shoulders. Kjartan wore a worried look. She held open both her arms, and he darted into them. Vikar's arms closed about both of them. 'Let's tell him together.'

Their shared laughter floated up into the sky, and Sela knew that this, this was how life was meant to be.

Author's Note

Researching marriage and divorce during the Viking era is difficult. The major written sources for the period are the various surviving sagas. And while weddings, marriage and divorce often feature in the tales, little of actual substance is there.

For example, there is no exact blow-by-blow description of a wedding. Several sagas do mention retrieving swords, purification ceremonies and a ghost to recite family history, but nothing appears to be exact. How much reflects what was happening during the Viking period and how much reflects twelfth-century Icelandic society when the tales were first written down is a matter for much conjecture.

The sagas were an oral history before they were written down, but they were also entertainment. Thus some parts are clearly historical, but others aren't. And the separation can be difficult. Also, the sagas do tend to reflect Christian, rather than pagan Viking, values. The women who divorce in the sagas are often branded as troublemakers. And some of the reasons for divorcing seem spurious.

That women as well as men were given the right to divorce, without having to have a guardian involved, was noted by Ibrahim Yaqub in the tenth century. Yaqub, a traveller from Spain, noted 'their women have the right to divorce; a wife divorces when she wishes'. Later Scandinavian codes of law also provide some evidence that Viking women could divorce with relative ease.

Books that I found useful include:

Jesch, Judith, *Women in the Viking Age* (1991 The Boydell Press, Woodbridge Suffolk)

O'Brien, Harriet, *Queen Emma and the Vikings: The Woman Who Shaped the Events of 1066* (2005 Bloomsbury, London)

Magnusson, Magnus KBE, *The Vikings* (2003 Tempus Publishing Stroud, Gloucestershire)

Magnusson, Magnus and Palsson, Hermann, (trans.) *Laxdaela Saga* (1969 Penguin Books London)

Palsson, Hermann and Edwards, Paul, (trans.) *Seven Viking Romances* (1985 Penguin Books London)

Roesdahl, Else, *The Vikings* (revised edition), translated by Susan Margeson and Kirsten Williams (1998 Penguin Books London)

Woods, Michael, *In Search of the Dark Ages* (2nd edition) (2005 BBC Books London)

On sale 4th July 2008

GUARDED HEART
by *Jennifer Blake*

They are the most dangerous men in New Orleans, skilled
swordsmen who play by no rules but their own – heroes to
some, wicked to many, irresistible to the women they love…

When alluring widow Ariadne Faucher requests private
lessons from rakish sword master Gavin Blackford, he cannot
help but be fascinated by this statuesque beauty, cloaked
as she is in mystery…

Ariadne proves a quick study, her resolve fuelled by a passionate
vendetta, and their lessons crackle with undeniable electricity.
But has her all-consuming vengeance rendered her heart
impervious…even to such a virtuoso as Gavin?

The Beckoning Dream

When her brother Rob was arrested, Mistress Catherine
Wood accompanied a stranger – pretending to be his wife!
– to Holland on a spying mission. With roguish charm her
'husband' made no bones about wanting Catherine in his bed,
while she was surprised how hard it was to hold him at bay as
they travelled into danger together…

The Lost Princess

Having never met her future husband, Marina Bordoni,
Lady of Novera, reluctantly set off to her wedding – only to
be kidnapped and held to ransom! Rescued by an arrogant
stranger, Marina began a mad trail across Italy. Flung closer
to a man than ever before, Marina shocked herself by
relishing every danger…and her rescuer!

Available 6th June 2008

Collect all 10 superb books in the collection!

The *Regency*

Lords & Ladies

COLLECTION

More Glittering Regency Love Affairs

Volume 24 – 1st August 2008
The Reluctant Marchioness by Anne Ashley
Nell by Elizabeth Bailey

Volume 25 – 5th September 2008
Kitty by Elizabeth Bailey
Major Chancellor's Mission by Paula Marshall

Volume 26 – 3rd October 2008
Lord Hadleigh's Rebellion by Paula Marshall
The Sweet Cheat by Meg Alexander

Volume 27 – 7th November 2008
Lady Sarah's Son by Gayle Wilson
Wedding Night Revenge by Mary Brendan

Volume 28 – 5th December 2008
Rake's Reward by Joanna Maitland
The Unknown Wife by Mary Brendan

Volume 29 – 2nd January 2009
Miss Verey's Proposal by Nicola Cornick
The Rebellious Débutante by Meg Alexander

Volume 30 – 6th February 2009
Dear Deceiver by Mary Nichols
The Matchmaker's Marriage by Meg Alexander

FREE!

2 Books
and a surprise gift!

We would like to take this opportunity to thank you for reading this Mills & Boon® book by offering you the chance to take TWO more specially selected titles from the Historical series absolutely FREE! We're also making this offer to introduce you to the benefits of the Mills & Boon® Reader Service™—

- ★ FREE home delivery
- ★ FREE gifts and competitions
- ★ FREE monthly Newsletter
- ★ Exclusive Reader Service offers
- ★ Books available before they're in the shops

Accepting these FREE books and gift places you under no obligation to buy, you may cancel at any time, even after receiving your free shipment. Simply complete your details below and return the entire page to the address below. You don't even need a stamp!

YES! Please send me 2 free Historical books and a surprise gift. I understand that unless you hear from me, I will receive 4 superb new titles every month for just £3.69 each, postage and packing free. I am under no obligation to purchase any books and may cancel my subscription at any time. The free books and gift will be mine to keep in any case.

H8ZEF

Ms/Mrs/Miss/Mr .... Initials ....

Surname ....

BLOCK CAPITALS PLEASE

Address ....

....

.... Postcode ....

Send this whole page to:
UK: FREEPOST CN81, Croydon, CR9 3WZ